P9-AZW-414

LION HEART

Also by A. C. Gaughen

Scarlet
Lady Thief

LION HEART

A SCARLET NOVEL

A. C. GAUGHEN

BLOOMSBURY
NEW YORK LONDON NEW DELHI SYDNEY

First published in the United States of America in May 2015
by Bloomsbury Children's Books
www.bloomsbury.com

Bloomsbury is a registered trademark of Bloomsbury Publishing Plc

For information about permission to reproduce selections from this book, write to Permissions, Bloomsbury Children's Books, 1385 Broadway, New York, New York 10018
Bloomsbury books may be purchased for business or promotional use. For information on bulk purchases please contact Macmillan Corporate and Premium Sales Department at specialmarkets@macmillan.com

Library of Congress Cataloging-in-Publication Data
Gaughen, A. C.
Lion heart : a Scarlet novel / by A. C. Gaughen.
pages cm
Sequel to: Lady thief.
Summary: After escaping Prince John's clutches and longing to return to Rob in Nottingham, Scarlet learns that King Richard's life is in jeopardy and accepts Eleanor of Aquitaine's demand that Scarlet spy for her and help bring Richard home safe.
ISBN 978-0-8027-3616-1 (hardcover) • ISBN 978-0-8027-3617-8 (e-book)
1. Robin Hood (Legendary character)—Juvenile fiction. [1. Robin Hood (Legendary character)—Fiction. 2. Courts and courtiers—Fiction. 3. Love—Fiction. 4. Adventure and adventurers—Fiction. 5. Middle Ages—Fiction. 6. Great Britain—History—Richard I, 1189–1199—Fiction.] I. Title.
PZ7.G23176Lio 2015 [Fic]—dc23 2014027501

Book design by Donna Mark
Typeset by Newgen Knowledge Works (P) Ltd., Chennai, India
Printed and bound in the U.S.A. by Thomson-Shore Inc., Dexter, Michigan
2 4 6 8 10 9 7 5 3 1

All papers used by Bloomsbury Publishing, Inc., are natural, recyclable products made from wood grown in well-managed forests. The manufacturing processes conform to the environmental regulations of the country of origin.

For my brother Kevin—
As your little sister, I may have gotten a lot of your roar,
but you have always had the strongest lion heart.
I love you.

CHAPTER ONE

There were no light. I had gotten used to it, in a way. I always rather thought that I were a creature of the dark—moving in it felt like my home, and that hadn't changed. I weren't the sort that went mad in the dark.

Sometimes—like when the last time you saw daylight you watched your friend die, staining the snow with his blood—it weren't so bad to be haunted.

The strange thing were how much I missed the light. I'd gotten a taste of it, in Rob's kiss and touch, in the fickle, brutal shine of hope, and I wanted it back. I didn't want to be a thing of darkness anymore.

I ran my hands on the wall, feeling first with my fingers until I found the flat bit of rock I'd pried free from the wall. It weren't a knife, but it gave me the same kind of calm to have it in my hand. I squeezed my half hand round it, pain aching through the stiff, scarred stumps that were left of my two fingers.

The noise were the first thing to announce the visitors. A heavy iron *clang* that ran over the stones, rushing its way to me. And then the footfalls, too many for just David, my favorite guard. At least two people—beyond that it were hard to tell.

I sat up straighter, staring at the cell door.

The light came then, the tiny flicker that spread like fingers crawling over the wall to get to me. Holding a breath, I tucked the stone shard back against the wall.

When the torch appeared, it were almost blinding. I blinked against the brightness as David came, holding the flame, and behind him, in heavy boots and a thin cloak, came Prince John.

He stopped in front of the door to my cell, looking me over. "Marian," he said. "You should greet your prince. Haven't I taught you any manners yet?"

I stared back at him.

"I'll take that as a no," he sneered.

I didn't move.

"Very well, then. Give me your necklace."

"What necklace?" I asked.

"The one my mother gave you. The one you somehow smuggled in here with you, because it's not with any of your belongings. And without it, she'll never believe you're dead."

I gripped the rock tight. *Dead.* "Why don't you come in here and find it yourself?"

"Don't be stupid," he growled. David moved a little, enough to make his armor give off shivery metal noise.

"She'll never believe I'm dead. Because you'll never kill me, we both know that."

He smiled at me. "Do we," he said.

"You won't risk Mummy hating you forever. Isn't that why you keep moving me around? You don't want her to find me."

"It's only a matter of time," he said, shrugging.

"Until what?" I asked.

"Until she—and the rest of England, including your foolish Hood—forgets about you entirely." He smiled at me, and his teeth gleamed wet and yellow in the light. "You are *nothing,* Marian. Do you know why I keep you here? Why you will stay here until I am king, until people say the name of Robin Hood and ask who that is? Because you will be *forgotten.* You have ceased to matter."

"I think I'll matter quite a bit to you when my father returns and pounds you into the dirt for hurting me. You remember him, don't you? The King of England?"

His face twisted. "The necklace, Marian!"

Slow, I shook my head.

"Get another guard," he ordered David.

David hesitated for a breath, meeting my eyes, but he walked down the hall and rapped on the door. Thomas came in, the only other guard who had been with us the whole months he'd kept me traveling round. David unlocked the door as Prince John ordered Thomas to restrain me.

Thomas stepped in and grabbed my wrists, pulling me up and pushing me hard against the wall. He held my wrists in one hand and wrapped his other round my throat as David stepped in.

"Easy," he growled at Thomas. "Don't forget, sir, that she is still a noblewoman."

Thomas's eyes flicked to David, and he let go of my throat and just held my wrists above my head. I took a breath, and his eyes wandered down to my chest as it rose.

"Forgive me, my lady," David murmured, patting down the filthy, tattered dress I'd been in since days after my capture, since Prince John decided Eleanor, my grandmother, could exert too much influence and I should be hidden from her.

David saw the chain fair quick, drawing it up rather than touch any bits he shouldn't. He bowed and handed it to Prince John, who looked at the glitter of the moonstone.

"The only thing you'll accomplish is more pain for yourself when the Lionheart returns and seeks vengeance for his daughter, *Uncle,*" I snarled at him.

Thomas's hold grew lighter at the mention of my father.

"Yes, your father has done *so* much to show he loves you, hasn't he?" Prince John mocked.

I frowned.

"But you're right. My brother has quite the temper," he told me, still smiling, weighing the stone in his hand. "I wonder what I should do about that."

"Run," I told him, glaring over Thomas's shoulder.

He smiled in his dark way and toyed with the chain of the necklace. "You keep assuming that I won't dare kill you, Marian. You think I am so frightened of my mother's disapproval and my brother's wrath that it will stay my hand. But she has changed her mind before, and kings will come and go. You may have noble blood, but you are a common thing. You see the world as fixed and finite, and it is not. It is liquid and ever moving, and one act can change everything."

My blood rushed to ice in my veins, and I didn't say anything.

"Your father has been captured, Marian," he told me, his words slithering out from his evil smile. "Held ransom by the Holy Roman Emperor. He will never set foot in England again—so just imagine what I would do to you now."

Thomas's hands squeezed harder.

Prince John chuckled. "Guards, come along. I need to speak with you both about her *arrangements*."

Thomas held me until David and the prince were out of the cell, and then he locked the door behind me.

I sat back down on the ground, breathing hard.

—~—

It weren't long when Thomas and David came back, now without the prince. I tucked the rock into my sleeve, standing to meet them.

"Where are we going?" I asked. If they were planning to kill me, it would be best to do it here. Caged and in close quarters, I'd be less likely to get away. And I weren't big enough that they'd worry about the weight of carrying me out. I glanced at their weapons. They both had their knives drawn, but not their swords.

"We're just moving you," David said, nodding to me, trying to calm me like I were an animal. "I believe the prince was only trying to scare you, my lady."

"Stop calling her 'my lady,'" Thomas snapped. "She's a traitor to the Crown."

David bristled. "She's a princess," he returned. "Something you ought to remember, sir."

"Open the gate," Thomas ordered. He were shifting his weight, foot to foot. Restless. Ready.

David frowned, noticing it as well. "What did you and the prince discuss, Thomas?"

"When?" he said, but he were a bad liar.

"When I left to call for the prince's horse," David said.

"Open the gate," I told David soft.

"I asked you a question, sir," David told Thomas, raising his knife and resting his hand on his sword hilt.

Thomas turned to David. "Don't get in the way," he warned him, shaking his head slow.

"Of what?" David asked, lowering his stance. He were ready for the fight that were coming, but Thomas were the brute of the two of them. In the narrow space of the hall, I didn't want to watch David die.

"Open the gate, David, please!" I called, coming closer.

This distracted Thomas for a moment, and David raised his foot and kicked him hard. Thomas reeled back and stopped, charging at David with a roar.

There weren't nowhere for them to fight. Thomas heaved David up against the stone wall, and when David swiped at him with the knife, Thomas jumped back.

"You know what we have to do!" Thomas shouted, drawing his sword. "We are the prince's knights; we must obey his orders!"

David shook his head, holding fast to his knife. "Those are not my orders."

"He knew you wouldn't agree to kill her!"

"Then why did you?" David demanded. "I will put you down if I must, Thomas. For all the time we have served together, do not make me do it."

"You think a few months of following this girl around makes us brothers?" he snarled.

"The oath we swore as knights makes us brothers."

"The oath we swore demands we obey him!" Thomas said, lunging forward.

David jumped into his lunge, grabbing Thomas's hand and slamming the sword and Thomas's wrist against the iron door. David tried to stab Thomas, but Thomas grabbed David's wrist and they held, trembling with the force of fighting against each other's strength.

"I never swore an oath to the prince," David growled. "I swore an oath to the queen mother."

I slammed the rock shard as hard as I could against Thomas's captive hand, still holding the sword. The rock caught and tore, blood rushing out.

Thomas yelled and dropped the sword. His hold lost strength, and David's hand pushed forward, stabbing him in the side where his armor didn't cover.

Thomas tried to reach for his own knife, but David punched him across the face. Thomas hit the stone wall and slid down it. He didn't get up, though I saw his chest move with breath as the red spread out beneath him.

"Come along, my lady," David said, fumbling with his keys to get the door open.

"You're one of my grandmother's knights?" I asked him.

He looked up at me, nodding. The key clicked and the door opened, but I didn't move.

"She knew where I were the whole time?" I asked.

He shook his head. "No. She told me contacting her would be too dangerous; we couldn't risk Prince John questioning my loyalty. But she told me to protect you at any cost."

I shivered, nodding and coming out of the cell. He took off his heavy cloak and wrapped it round me. I pulled it tight. "Can you take me to her?"

He nodded. "Yes, my lady."

I stopped. "I'm sorry you had to do that, David."

His mouth were tight. He didn't lie and say it were fine, that he were glad to do it. He gave me a sharp nod, I reckon more so I knew he heard me than anything else.

"Thank you," I told him.

He sighed. "We should go."

I nodded, crouching and taking Thomas's sword from his still body, and capturing his knife besides. I stood, and David led me down the hall to a larger chamber that guarded the hallway. There were a door there, and I could just see the dark night out beyond it.

"Stay back," he murmured to me. "The castle is well guarded. I don't know how much they know of what was meant to happen."

"Let me help," I told him. "You can't fight them alone."

His mouth settled into a grim line. "You aren't strong enough for that, my lady. And there are too many of them."

"They may not know that it were meant to be you and Thomas," I told him.

He looked at me. "We can't risk it if they do."

I sighed. "Where are we?" I asked him.

"Bramber Castle," he told me. "Sussex. We're only a few hours' ride to London."

I opened the door, looking out. There were two horses, and affixed behind one of them were a cart filled with hay and a white cloth, the perfect size to hold a person. I shivered.

"What did you think that were for?" I asked him.

He shook his head. "That wasn't out there before. Thomas must have ordered it hooked up to the horses." He looked at me.

"But why would he want my body?" I asked.

"Maybe Prince John wanted . . . proof," he said slow.

I nodded, shutting the door. "Of course he would. Which also limits the time we have until Prince John discovers what's been done."

"Not necessarily," David said. "He wouldn't have wanted to risk being seen in public with your body. Thomas must have had another location to meet him. I can forge Thomas's hand well enough and send Prince John a letter."

"But the guards here still need to believe it," I told him. I looked down the hallway to where the cell were at the end. "But I may have an idea for that."

—w—

David looked at me and crossed himself.

"What?" I asked.

"My lady, I find this quite chilling."

I touched my face. I'd rubbed mud from the cell on my skin, letting it dry gray and white, before smearing Thomas's blood on me, spattering it on my face. To anyone who saw, I would look truly dead.

I looked at my hands, paler than usual and chalky looking, with blood on them. A dead man's blood. "Yes," I told him. "Well, that is the idea."

He nodded, and with a sigh, he put his arm around my back and crouched to sweep under my knees. He picked me up and carried me to the end of the hall. "Remember," he told me. "Try to move—and breathe—as little as possible."

I nodded, shutting my eyes and letting my head fall limp in his arms, craning back at an awkward angle.

The door creaked open, and I felt the chill of the night air around me. It were late spring now, months since the winter when I'd first been imprisoned, but the nights still held a chill, like the sun couldn't quite keep its hold on the world.

My hand slipped from my stomach, stretching out at an awkward angle, but I didn't dare move. I didn't know who were in the courtyard with us.

"Move the sheet," David ordered someone. I heard rustling, and David lowered my body onto the hay. It were sharp and hostile, poking into skin that weren't supposed to be able to feel it. I felt a harder weight beneath me—David had put Thomas's sword and knife in the cart before me. I couldn't move enough to grab them, but knowing they were there were a comfort.

"Christ," another voice murmured. "She's a child. Who was she?"

"You're not paid for your interest, sir," David said sharply. "This letter must be taken to the prince immediately. Have your messenger see it directly into his hands, do you understand?"

The cloth came down over my face, pitching me deeper into darkness, and I opened my eyes a hair, cautious. I couldn't see anything, which should mean they couldn't see me.

"Yes, sir."

"Tell them to open the gate," he ordered.

"Yes, sir."

Moments later, the cart started to move slow, only to stop again after a short distance. I felt a low shaking and wondered if they were raising the portcullis.

"Where's the other fellow?" someone asked.

"We had some difficulty with the prisoner," David said. "See that your priest gives him a proper burial."

There were some low noises I couldn't make out.

The shaking stopped with a metal grunt, and the cart began to move again.

After a few moments, I heard the portcullis shudder closed behind us. As we rode out, I knew we were near the ocean. I could feel it in my bones, and I could smell the salt in the air, laced with peat smoke, like I had fallen into the ocean blue of Rob's eyes. It were as if Robin were there, behind me, beside me, just out of my sight, but when I turned to look at him, there were only darkness.

—~—

I nodded off at one point, and woke as we were slowing down. I tugged the sheet down careful so I could see out a tiny sliver.

We were in the woods, on a path wide enough to hold the cart. I couldn't see anyone else. "David?" I called.

"Stopping for the night, my lady. Are you comfortable there or would you prefer the ground?" he asked.

I tugged the sheet down so I could breathe easy. It weren't a matter of being comfortable; in three months I'd barely moved, and I were weaker than I could ever remember being. I didn't much want to move.

Shivering a little with cold, I wrapped my hand around the sword. Having the means to defend myself at last, more than anything, helped me sleep.

—~—

When I woke again, the cart were moving, swaying in a way that were sleepy and gentle and made opening my eyes again difficult.

It were just past dawn, the sky still rich with blushing like the young thing it were. I loosed my fingers from the sword, stretching them from the grip I'd had through the night.

I looked around, wanting to sit up. We were on the road with people round us, though, and I didn't dare, nudging the sheet up over my face again.

There hadn't been overmuch in the way of food for the past few months, but I were growing hungry in true, and as the cart rolled on, I kept checking to see when we might be clear enough for me to speak. After more than an hour, we passed a fork in the road that left us traveling alone.

"David?" I called, tugging the sheet down. "David?"

I sat up, stretching my arms and back.

"David?" I called again, and a scream answered me instead.

I grabbed the sword and twisted round to see a man *not* David falling off the saddle. Chucking off the sheath, I jumped from the side of the cart, landing in the dirt with my worn, tattered boots, lunging for him.

"Christ on a cobnut!" he yelped, ducking behind the horse. "Lady thief, stop this madness!"

"Allan?" I cried, stopping. "What in God's name is going on?"

He peered round the horse. "Good Lord, you're even scary when you're dead."

"I'm not dead!" I shouted.

"Well, I didn't know that before!" Allan shouted back.

"What did you do, Allan? Where's David?"

"I only knocked him out," Allan said. "He'll be just fine."

"What are you doing here?" I asked him. "I've been out of prison for bare hours. How did you find me so quick?"

His shoulders lifted. "I've been ordered by our fair sheriff to find you," he told me. "And I found you. And I thought—I thought I'd found you too late," he said, and for a moment he didn't look his teasing, foolish self. He looked weary and sad. Then he stepped forward and hugged me, straight off my feet.

"*Oof,*" I grunted. "Allan—Allan, put me down."

"Yes, lady thief. I just—" He stopped, looking up. "God is great and powerful and loves to mock mortals like—"

He never finished the sentence as David slammed into his body, bearing him to the ground. He raised a knife over Allan's neck.

"No!" I yelled. "David, stop!"

David froze, looking at me, and Allan whimpered. "My lady, this man—"

"There has been a terrible misunderstanding," I told him. "Please get up."

David jumped off him, and Allan struggled to his feet as I caught sight of a gash on David's head. "Allan!" I cried. "Did you do this?"

"The goddamn coward hit me with a *rock,*" David grunted, touching the wound.

Allan shrugged. "I don't have a very strong punch."

David glared at him, crossing his arms. He looked around. "My lady, we should get you off this road if you hope to remain dead."

"You're *trying* to be dead?" Allan asked, frowning. "I don't understand."

"Better dead than murdered," I told him. "We need to get to the queen mother. Can you help us get to London?" I asked.

Allan puffed a little. "Of course I can. But I rather think we could move a little faster if you're alive. If he looks a little less like a knight."

"Fine," I told him. "Then I need to wash. Have you lot seen a river or well or anything?" I asked.

"A river about a mile back," David said.

I nodded. "Can you two find clothes and food, and I'll meet you?"

"I won't leave you alone, my lady," David said. "He can go where he wishes, but I'll come with you."

I were still weak, and God knew there were more dangers for us to face, so I didn't fight him. He came with me and waited a ways from the river while I stepped into the ice cold, rubbing blood and dirt from my skin. It snaked away from my body in muddy swirls in the clear water.

And then it were gone, and the river were clear, like such filth had never truly been.

CHAPTER TWO

Allan did well. He got fresh clothes to dress me as a boy and traded the cart for two more horses. He'd procured food somehow, and David and I swallowed oranges and roasted cauliflower, salted pork, and fresh bread.

Allan watched me. "Are you sure we shouldn't be going to Nottingham, my lady?" he asked.

I shook my head. "I have to see the queen first, Allan. Then—" At the thought of Rob, his eyes wrapping me up and tugging me in, a thrill shot through my heart so hard it hurt. I pressed my hand there, and Allan nodded sharp.

"Then I'll get you to the queen," he promised.

"We should go," David said. "We'll make London after nightfall as it is."

I nodded. "All right. Let's go."

~

It weren't long past midnight when we came upon the city; we'd heard bells on our way, chasing our horses with their low, dark sound, but the hours riding felt like years. It ached everywhere until every move felt like a blow. Seeing the queen—telling her what I'd heard—were the only thing that made me grip the saddle tighter.

Even when we made the city, I knew we had a while to go. Westminster Palace were farther along the Thames, away from the dirt and grime of London proper, and we had to make our way through London first.

I shut my eyes for a moment and near fell off my horse, clutching the saddle with shaking arms.

"We'll be at the palace soon, my lady," David promised me.

I drew a breath. Palace. *Royals.* "Christ—I didn't even think—Prince John will be there," I realized.

He shook his head. "No, my lady. The prince said he was riding north."

A sigh chased out of me, and it seemed to take more of my strength with it. I nodded.

We slowed at the sight of Newgate, the tall city wall that had been made into a prison under Henry's rule. It were fast becoming legend I'd been a thief, but I'd never ended up there myself.

"Who goes there?" called a man from the guardroom.

"We're knights in the queen's service," David called. "And this boy is under her protection. We're headed to Westminster."

"You best go round the city," he called.

David frowned. "That's not possible. Why would we avoid the city?"

"There have been riots," the guard said. "Closer to the White Tower and the river."

"Not here, then," David said.

"No."

"Then let us pass. We don't have time to spare," he said.

"Eh," the man grunted. "It's your necks."

I looked at David as the gate were raised slow.

"A knight," Allan muttered. "As if I would ever be a *knight.* I'm far too handsome to be a knight."

"Shut. Up," David ground out. "If your mouth endangers my lady, I will extract it."

"Always so *angry.*" Allan sighed.

They let us pass through and lowered the gate behind us.

The road were dark and empty, but every hair on my neck stood on end.

"Not far now, my lady," David told me.

"Let's hope it's not the worst of the ride," I returned.

We made our way toward the Strand, the road that led out to Westminster Palace. We'd bare made the road when a noise started to rise behind us.

We turned round, and I could see the glow of orange light seeping through the streets.

I frowned at David, and he looked grim. "Stay close to me, my lady."

"Something's happening," I told him.

"Then we should *hurry,*" he insisted.

I nodded, spurring my horse.

Our horses started to gallop down the lane, and the crowd finally showed themselves from between the buildings. I looked back as they pushed into the lane. We were far enough ahead, and faster besides, that I didn't need to worry.

Looking forward, I tightened my thighs on the horse, and they shook in response. My whole body trembled and shivered, too tired and weak by half. But after months in a prison, locked in a box and brought to my knees, I were free, and I weren't letting my own weakness stop me.

The road turned, and I thundered round the bend. It weren't long until I saw the tall turrets of Westminster Palace in front of us. I stared at the flags, trying to see well enough to make sure the prince's flag weren't up there.

My head snapped forward when I heard David roar, "*My lady!*"

He and Allan were stopped; there were a wall of guards with swords drawn, guarding the palace from the rioters. I pulled sharp on the reins, looking behind me to the growing noise of the crowd.

"Let us through!" David bellowed. "The queen mother is expecting us!"

"Desist or you will be run through!" a guard yelled back. "No one shall come near the palace tonight!"

I hesitated. It would be an easy thing to throw off my hat and raise my chin and tell them I were a princess, Richard's daughter, Eleanor's granddaughter. They would take me behind their swords and they would defend me.

But then Prince John would hear I lived, and he would change his plans, bend his mother's ear, and make sure I were thought a liar for my words.

Before he found another way to see me dead.

"Follow me, my lady!" Allan shouted, pointing back at the road.

"Are you mad!" David roared.

"Ride fast to try and break through and go sharp right," Allan said. "We have to get away from the rioters!"

I nodded, trembling in the saddle. I spurred my horse hard, David out in front of me and Allan somewhere behind.

We turned round the bend, and the rioters were closer than I thought. They'd separated for David, but now they were turned, looking at him, and not moving for me.

My horse reared and tried to stop at the same moment, twisting to the ground with an unearthly scream. He threw me off as he went down, and my legs landed bare shy of the horse's back. People swept back from the horse, stepping on my body as I struggled to move away, off the road.

My sword were gone—I couldn't even see where it went.

I got to my knees, and a body slammed into mine, sprawling me backward again.

Panicking now, I got to my knees again, desperate to stand, fearing the force of the crowd. I got one foot under me, and someone pulled me up.

"Hush, I have you," a voice said in my ear.

My blood rushed over with dizzy relief. "Allan!" I cried.

"Hold on to me, lady thief. We need to get you out of here," he told me.

I nodded, holding tight to his arm. I'd lost a boot, and the other one were tatters. I felt every rock in the road as we pushed against the tide of people, trying to find a way off.

We made it back to the heart of London, and Allan tugged me down an alleyway that weren't half as crowded. He nodded me ahead, farther away from the mob.

"My lady!" David shouted, grabbing me as we pushed down into an alley that were open and dark.

"Lady?" someone growled, grabbing me round my waist.

I yelped as one arm held me tight and the other started patting and grabbing my clothes, looking for money or jewels or God only knew what else. Three other men set on David and Allan as the man pulled me off my feet.

I drew my legs up and let them drop, slamming my heel into the man's kneecap. He howled and dropped me, and I whipped round to shove my elbow against his face.

He roared out a curse, covering his eye and wheeling back.

One man were bleeding on the ground and David dispatched a second. Allan slung a punch over the third with a little whimper. The man stumbled, and I jumped over him, running down the alley. Allan ran ahead with his long loping legs, leading the way. I followed behind him, and David followed behind me. I were the middle. The weak point—the one that needed defending. I'd always been one of the guards, not the guarded.

It weren't far, now that we were away from the crush. Allan took us down closer to the river, to a tavern that bore the name Rose and Thorn, and I near collapsed against the door, heaving for breath. "It's shut," I told Allan.

He looked wounded, knocking twice, pausing, and knocking twice more on the door.

We waited several long moments.

The door opened a crack, and whoever were behind it saw Allan and opened it.

He nodded us in. I went first, and a young man led me into the tavern room. Windows that would look onto the street were boarded over, and there weren't no fire in the hearth. There were a few candles on a table near the casks, and two other people at a table. They looked up at me.

One were a boy, and the other were a grizzled old man.

The one who led me in pointed to a bench. "Sit."

I blinked at the sound of the voice. "You're a girl," I realized.

She looked at me like I were mad. "So are you."

She turned away from me, going to the back, and I sat at the bench, feeling strange and put out of my own body.

David came and sat at the bench of another table, his back to the wall. It were a soldier's choice. He could move from there, cover me, and fend off attackers, while still sitting closest to the door to defend an exit.

Allan didn't sit. He paced, jumping to help the girl in men's clothing with cups for us and a plate of bread. "My thanks, Kate," he said.

She frowned at him as she passed us ale and the bread. I took a piece of the bread and handed the rest to David, and he took some and passed it to the others at the table. "You shouldn't have brought her here," Kate said to Allan.

This made the others look at me, and the bread went to ash in my mouth.

"Not here, Kate," Allan warned.

"They can be trusted," Kate snapped. "As much as I can, at least."

Allan frowned.

My surprise must have shown. "I know who you are," Kate told me, crossing her arms. "I've heard you're a bastard royal," she said to me. "And if King Richard's dead, you can bet your head will start causing an awful lot of problems."

"He's not dead," I told them. "That's what the rioting is about?"

Kate nodded. "We heard he was killed in the Holy Land. And Prince John set off to murder the king's nephew to replace him as the heir."

I shook my head. "The king's been captured. Ransomed."

"By who?"

"I don't know," I told them. "But the man who told me had no reason to lie."

Kate frowned. "Every man has a reason to lie."

"Not when he were planning to murder me a moment later."

This settled over the others, and the man and boy looked at each other.

"How did you find us?" David asked, looking at Allan. "You never said."

"I told her," Allan grumbled. "You were too busy knocking my block off."

"*Me!*" David returned, but Allan weren't paying him mind.

"We've all—we were told you were dead," he said, looking at me.

I put the bread down. "We?" I repeated low.

"It wasn't more than a week after you left Nottingham that our noble sheriff got a letter, telling him you'd been executed." My chest squeezed. "He never believed it. Not once. But he sent me south to find the truth of the matter, and for all the people I know, I couldn't find you. Rob said that if you were dead you'd be easy to find, but I never had the same faith. Until a few days ago, when I followed the prince to Bramber," he said, looking up and crossing himself dramatic.

"And Rob—" I didn't know what I wanted to ask. But the feel of his name on my mouth were painful.

"Doesn't know, yet. I couldn't write to him till I were sure. But he writes to you," he told me. I frowned, confused, and he went to a satchel I hadn't noticed, opening it and pulling out a small stack of papers, looped together with a ribbon. He came and handed them to me, and I reached out to touch them.

But my hands were filthy, bloody and dirty and cut, and I pulled back.

I looked up at Allan, and to my horror, saw pity bright on his face.

"Come on," Kate said. "You lot can't go anywhere tonight. I'll show you where you can wash up and sleep."

"Thank you," David said.

"Thank you," I repeated.

She glared once at Allan and nodded her head back toward the kitchen. She led us out to a tiny little outdoor bit with a basin of water in it. "Beds are upstairs. If you want to wash, I'll show him up," she said to me.

I nodded, and she tossed me a cloth from the kitchen.

David glanced round, nodding once. "Would you rather I stay close, my lady?" he asked.

I shook my head.

Shutting the door behind them when they were gone, I pulled off the pants that I'd made quick work destroying, and I left the loose shirt on, pushing up my sleeves and using the cloth to clean off my skin and make a slow record of my wounds.

My shoulder were scraped and ragged from where I fell on it, with matching wounds on my hip. The soft inner bit of my other arm were cut where I'd been stepped on, but not bad. My hair were a matted mess, and I were thinner than I'd realized—I could feel my bones under my hands, sharp and raised under the thin layer of skin.

When I were done, I opened the door again, and Kate were there. "Here," she said, handing me a pile of clothes. "Clean. It's no lady's dress."

I took it. "Thank you," I said.

She nodded once, looking me over before leading me back through the room and up a narrow stair. She showed me a little bedroom and I went over to it, staring at the bed.

She hung in the doorway, but after I didn't move for long minutes, she started to turn. "Very well," she said.

"Thank you," I called. She stopped. "Thank you. It's been—thank you."

She looked at me, coming back to the doorway. "Where were you all this time?" she asked.

My shoulders lifted. "I don't know. Different castles. Different prisons. He moved me often, and at night. I never knew."

"Prince John," she said, and her voice were low and dark.

I nodded. "You're well informed, for an innkeep."

She shook her head. "Inn's my father's," she told me. "I'm a trader."

"A woman trader?" I asked.

She gave me a slow, side-slung smile. "Not an entirely legal trader."

This made me smile too. "You're a pirate."

"I've been called worse." Her mouth tightened, and she looked down, like she were considering something. "I loot ships to feed people," she said. "And I train the orphans to be sailors. England is falling apart, you know. With or without Richard alive."

I stared at her.

"It isn't just Nottingham. I wasn't sure if anyone had ever told you that."

My head dropped.

"Good night," she said, shutting the door to the room.

Changing into a clean shirt were all I could bear to do before falling asleep.

CHAPTER
THREE

I slept like the dead. When I woke, it were to full, body-aching pain, but it were also to the sun. It came in through the window to lie over me like a blanket, and I didn't move for a long while, looking at the light, feeling the heat of it on my skin. I trailed my fingers through it, wondering if I could just touch it, just hold on to it, maybe I could change everything else.

Shutting my eyes, I remembered it so clear—the feeling of waking up with Rob, his heartbeat under my cheek, making me feel that we weren't so separate, that if we stayed like this long enough we'd melt into each other. Like somehow we could become unbreakable.

Standing from the bed, I put on the rest of the clothes that Kate had given me—boy's pants and a thick tunic. Outside my door I found a clean pair of soft old boots, and I put those on too.

Downstairs, David and Allan were swallowing bread and bacon and hard eggs like men possessed. Kate were watching them, fair disgusted.

David saw me first. He stood from the table, and Allan swallowed a bite and did the same. David bowed his head to me, looking surprising less like a knight without his royal uniform. "Good morning, my lady."

"Lady thief," Allan said, mocking him a little. David scowled.

"Please don't do that," I told them both.

Allan sat back down, but David looked uncomfortable. "My lady, you're a princess. I can't—"

"And yesterday I were a prisoner," I told him. "Please sit."

"Yes, my lady," he said.

"Yes, my lady," Kate mimicked under her breath. I frowned at her, and she lifted her shoulders in innocence.

"How did the palace fare last night?" I asked, scared of the words.

Allan waved this off. "Very well. They never so much as got within the gates, and all the nobles had already fled."

"They had?" I asked.

Allan nodded, pushing the bowl of hard eggs to me. I took one and a piece of bread. "The lot of them got out when the word about Richard first came; that's why everyone thought he was dead."

"So Eleanor isn't at the palace?" I asked.

He shook his head. "She's with most of the court at Windsor, last I heard."

I frowned. "Could Prince John be there?"

"I don't know, my lady. Why do you want to see the queen mother?"

I glanced at Kate. "When Prince John thought I were about to die, he told me that Richard had been captured and held for ransom—but he said that Richard would never set foot in England again."

"That makes no sense," Allan said. "The queen mother would happily raise any sum to retrieve her son, and she certainly has the will to do it."

I nodded, raising my eyebrows.

"Unless he has some sort of plot in place to make sure that the ransom isn't paid," Allan realized.

"Or that Richard doesn't live to see it," I told him.

"Christ on a cross post," Allan murmured.

"The queen mother will want to hear of this as soon as we can get to her," David agreed. "And I shall relish reporting her son's behavior to her besides."

"Very well," Allan said. "Eleanor first."

"You shouldn't go to Windsor," Kate said, looking at me. "The whole royal court is there. Even if Prince John isn't, there will be someone loyal to him. You'll never get to the queen without being seen. And the longer you can stay dead the better, especially with this information."

I frowned, but I couldn't disagree.

"For what it's worth, I'll look to the sea. If he's taking men or orders across the water, someone will have heard about it," she said.

"What about my lord Winchester?" Allan asked.

Confused, I looked to him. "What about him?"

"Winchester Castle is little more than a day's ride from here. We could send word to the queen mother to meet us there; his men would never betray you, would they?"

The Earl of Winchester had been the truest friend to Rob, and by virtue of that, to me. "No," I said. "Never. Do you have some you trust to get a message to Eleanor?" I asked.

Kate nodded. "I do."

"I'm coming with you," Allan told me, his face serious for once. "I promised Robin that I would find you. I'll see you back to him before I leave your side."

My breath caught at the idea of seeing Rob again. How easy it would be to leave here, to slip from David and ride north until my body broke, until I found myself in front of Nottingham Castle.

I cleared my throat, wishing it cleared my head, and nodded. "Very well. And thank you, I suppose."

"Thank you, I suppose," Allan repeated, one eyebrow lifting up. "Well, from you, my lady, I'll take it as the sweetest endearment."

"I'm sorry," I said. "Thank you."

"You don't need to apologize, my lady," David insisted, meeting Allan's eyes in challenge. Allan smirked at him.

"When can we leave the city?" I asked.

Allan and Kate looked to each other. "Before dark would be best," Kate said. "Or tomorrow, but I think it's better to leave before that."

I nodded. "Where can we get horses?"

Allan just smiled.

—∾—

We stole the horses. Sort of. They were horses that the mob had stolen from the palace the night before, and it were a simple thing for Allan to start a brawl until those that stole them were all a bit busy.

And yet, if my blood were to be believed, I were at least in part the rightful owner of those horses.

Which were fair stranger than stealing them, in truth.

Kate gave me a cloak, and her father gave us a sack of food for our travels. We rode at a much slower pace than David and I had the night before. The roads were full of people now, traveling to and from London. It weren't a happy sight—people were worn and broken, tattered and tired. I felt foolish to be on a horse.

And yet I were worn and broken too. Every bump in the road were agony to my bones, and beyond any pain, I were just weary. Weary and so aware that the only place I wanted to be were in Nottingham, and this road were taking me in the wrong direction.

We passed by Windsor, and I kept my cloak up and my head down. Not like any of the nobles were on the road with us—God knows there would have been a bigger fuss if so—but still.

When we went through Runnymede, a gorgeous piece of royal forest that the road slashed across, all bright green hills and sun dappling through gray clouds, a troop of knights came galloping through. People dashed to get out of their way, and I led my horse off the road, sliding off his back as they passed. Their cloaks snapped out behind them, and I saw the royal banner on their clothes.

They might have been Eleanor's knights. But they might have been Prince John's too.

So I kept my head down.

—~—

We got to Silchester just before nightfall. It were a large town but not large enough to be called a city; it stood at the crossroads that led all over England, and they were very particular about closing their gates at nightfall to keep out vagabonds and unwanted travelers. We managed to shuffle into the town with a large group as they began to lower the portcullis.

It weren't until the gate were full shut that I saw the royal knights, and my heart seized in a panic.

"Stay close, my lady," David said.

I nodded, and Allan nodded once at me.

There were two knights, and they were directing people to the well in the center of town. There were a man there, standing on a small box and holding a parchment with seals flapping off it. I frowned.

"The King of England, Richard the Lionheart, has been captured. For the release of our noble king, the Holy Roman Emperor has demanded a sum of 65,000 pounds of silver."

I gasped, and I weren't the only one. The amount were ungodly high.

"To pay for this, the queen mother has instituted a tax on the people of England; one quarter of your income and the value of your holdings is now due to the Crown of England."

I could bare hear him. People started to cry, to shout and wail. The knights banged on their shields until people began to quiet. "Good God," I breathed.

"Your overlord will collect this tax from you," he shouted. "And they will in turn pay that money to the Crown."

He stepped off the platform and people's voices began to rise, protesting and yelling and crying.

Two knights began to shuffle him out, around the people, paying no mind to the violence that were about to start. "Where are the nobles?" I asked Allan.

His shoulders lifted. "Not here."

Someone threw something at one of the knights that were still standing by the well, and he rocked backward—it were a clod of dirt, and other than leaving a smear on his armor, it didn't do any damage.

The knight beside him drew his sword and stepped into the crowd. The people parted, and a hush spread, making it loud and awful when someone screamed.

I pushed forward fast and hard, but the people were a solid mass, and I couldn't get far before David grabbed me, hauling me back.

"Let me go!" I yelled at him. "Let me—"

David clapped his hand over my mouth. "You're *dead*," he told me. "Do not let yourself be blinded by the suffering of one person, my lady. You must think of the suffering of England itself."

He swung me around so I couldn't see, but people gasped as the screams changed to deep, awful sobs. I clawed at his hand on my mouth until he trapped my hands as well.

"Stop, my lady!" he growled.

"Please!" someone yelled, and I turned. There were a priest there, and he were ushering people to the church. "Please, let us turn to God!" he cried.

People moved. People started going into the church, quiet and frightened now, and I saw what had happened.

There were a young man lying in the dirt, blood pouring out of his throat still. A woman knelt over him, sobbing and rocking back and forth, and the knights just stood there, watching.

David's arms loosened a little. "There's nothing we can do. The boy is dead," he said quiet.

Allan looked about. "We should go to the church," he said.

"I could have helped him," I told David.

Allan shook his head.

"You think I shouldn't act for one boy?" I demanded. "You think that England is some higher thing? *One life* is England. *Every life* is England." Shaking my head, I spat at his feet. "You didn't choose England. You chose my life over his."

"He was already dead—" Allan started, looking at the church as if staying out too long would hurt us.

"Yes," David said. "I chose your life over his."

I covered my face. "The people can't survive this," I told him. "They can't pay a tax that high, not when they're still starving from the last one."

David met my eyes heavy. "And if they can't, King Richard won't survive either. And what will England be then?"

I shook my head. "Even if they pay the tax, royal knights can't do this. They can't just kill people in the name of the Crown."

Allan looked frightened. "The Crown doesn't stand for justice in England, my lady Princess?" he asked. "You've shocked me to my core."

They nudged me toward the church, and I went, staring at the boy.

I hadn't saved him. I couldn't save him. And I didn't know what were left for me if that were true.

CHAPTER FOUR

We stayed in the church with the people of Silchester all night long. The knights left when things were calm again, and the people sat together in the pews, crying, raging, sharing their stories of how they couldn't possibly pay.

I wondered if this were what it had been like in Nottingham after I left, when John Little's body lay bleeding in the courtyard. Were everyone shocked into stillness and silence, or were they wailing, unwilling to move from that spot?

David helped the priest to lift away some of the benches and make room for people to sleep, carrying whatever materials he could. Allan found some sort of instrument with strings and he were playing it with charm.

I sat in the corner, listening. I didn't have anything to offer them. I didn't know how to steal this tax for them. I didn't know how to help.

If you embrace who you are, you might find a great many tools at your disposal. They had been some of Eleanor's last words to me, and they haunted me.

If I were some strange version of a princess, would I have been able to stand up there and tell the knights to stop? Would they have listened?

It wouldn't undo the tax, though, nor the fact that England needed Richard, if only to protect Her from Prince John. I wouldn't change anything.

Besides—I were dead. I had to stay dead.

—w—

We left at first light, slipping from the town. A hush had come over them all, this sad kind of accepting. There weren't no other choice; that had been made clear to them fast and swift. The boy's blood were still in the dirt by the well, making it rich and black.

I wondered if John Little's blood were still in the courtyard at Nottingham, staining the stones where Prince John had killed him to get to me.

There were more people on the road. Maybe they thought if they left their homes, if they traveled somewhere else, they could avoid the tax. Maybe they had somewhere safe to go, but it all felt desperate and sad.

We made Winchester late in the day, and city guards were turning people away at the road before they even got to the city gates. "No visitors!" they shouted. "No visitors!"

David nodded once to us, going over to one of the nonshouting guards. I saw him speak with him, point at me, and speak with him again. The guard shook his head, and then shook his head again. David's face got grim looking, and he came back to us.

"I told him the earl was expecting you," he said. "They won't let us in."

My stomach dropped.

"But he said there was someone they could send with a message, but he got angry when I wouldn't give your name. What can we tell him, my lady, that won't betray you?"

"Huntingdon," I told him quick, the title that should have been Rob's rolling fast off my tongue. "That's the only word he'll need to hear."

Allan glanced at me, but David nodded, not questioning. David told the guard and the guard went off to the castle.

We moved off the road, going to a tree and sitting in its shade. The spring day weren't overwarm, but the sun made me feel weaker.

"This is because of the tax, isn't it?" I said.

Allan nodded. "Winchester has the reputation as the very best of overlords, my lady. He won't let his people suffer for this tax. I'm certain many people want to be counted amongst his vassals right now."

"Ourselves included, it would seem," David said. "How are you feeling, my lady? You should be able to rest for a few days here."

"I'm fine," I said quick, but Allan looked at me.

"You're ill?" he asked.

I scowled. "No."

"She was imprisoned," David grunted. "For three months. That takes something out of the body, sir."

"Weren't you her jailer?" Allan asked.

David met his stare. "Yes. And I took the best care of her that I could."

I patted his arm. "I'm very well, David."

"So what does that entail?" Allan pressed on. "He let you eat occasionally? Didn't beat you quite as badly as he was meant to? You must tell me more so I have new fodder for a grand song about your brave and valiant acts, Sir Knight."

David stood.

"He killed another man to save my life," I said, looking at Allan. "And I won't let you mock him for that."

Allan sighed, lying down in the grass. "Fine. I'm too pretty for all this serious business."

"I can make you a little uglier, if you wish," David said.

Allan lifted his head. "So you agree—I'm pretty," he said, smiling.

"Christ," David muttered, putting his head in his hands.

—

It took a while for the guard to return with a letter in his hand. I opened it.

My lady M—
This guard will take you to my private hunting lodge outside the city. You will not be safe within the walls. I will join you as soon as I'm able.
—W

I handed it to David as the guard tapped two others and came back over to us. He bowed. "We are fetching horses, my lady. My lord instructed us to take you to his lodge. Forgive our earlier mistake."

"Hasten your efforts so the lady might forget the slight," David snapped. I frowned at him, and David gave me a tiny hint of a smile.

The horses appeared in short order, and we mounted ours as the guards readied themselves. They led us down the road and into the forest near the walled city, to a guarded but modest manor house.

We'd bare set foot within the manor wall when the doors opened again and Winchester appeared, the same tall, handsome young lord I remembered. He saw me and stopped, drawing a deep breath.

Shaking his head, he came to me and bowed. "My lady Princess," he said quiet. He kissed my good hand. "I never thought to see you alive again."

I squeezed his hand on mine. "It's good to see you, Winchester. My lord, this is Sir David, and you may remember Allan a Dale."

Winchester nodded to both of them. "Welcome. Forgive the location, but we are currently entertaining Prince John's knights in the castle, and I assumed by your subterfuge regarding your name that you did not wish to be known. You must come inside, rest, and tell me how it is you came to be here."

"Yes," I told him. "But first, I want you to know that I asked Eleanor to meet me here. There is important information she needs to hear—not the least of which is that I'm still alive."

His eyebrows lifted. "Eleanor? And her ladies?"

I frowned. "Yes."

He near smiled. "Oh. That's excellent. Fine. Of course, I would love to receive the queen. I'll make sure she is diverted here so the city is not aware of her presence." He dropped his head in a bow. "Come. Let's go inside. I'm sure you and your men are hungry."

"Yes," Allan said, grinning.

"Shameless," I heard David grunt.

"There's no glory in shame," Allan said back.

"So," Winchester said, sitting at a rather intimidating table after bringing us food and drink and seating me beside him. "Please tell me how you came to be here, my lady."

"Prince John tried to kill me," I told him.

Winchester's eyes flicked to Allan. "I had heard he had accomplished that deed long ago."

"He held me in prisons. Away from Eleanor, I believe."

Winchester tapped the table. "I was helping her," he told me. "Eleanor. She didn't believe John had killed you, and she tasked me with finding you. I think I came rather close too. Were you ever at Arundel or Brackley castles?" he asked.

"Yes," David said. "Both."

Winchester frowned. "And how would you know that?"

"Eleanor put a knight in Prince John's employ to protect me," I told him. "David were—David was one of my captors, but he saved my life." I stumbled over the right words.

Winchester nodded at him. "Your service, sir, is most deeply appreciated."

David looked down.

"I saved her life too," Allan said. "From a horde in London! She would have been trampled to death if it weren't for me."

"Yes," I said, nodding. "Thank you, Allan."

He smiled, satisfied.

Winchester looked at me. "Does Locksley know yet?"

I shook my head. "No. I can't get word to him, not if Prince John still thinks I'm dead." Maybe I would be able to find my way to Nottingham after I told Eleanor; maybe Rob could hide me in the castle until my father returned, and I wouldn't endanger the people with my presence.

Maybe.

"Perhaps I can get word."

I took in a breath. It spun out before me, Winchester whispering the words to Rob. I could see his face, trying to keep the secret in, relieved and desperate—for only a moment before he stormed out of the castle to find me, wherever I were. If he knew I were alive, he'd burn down Hell itself to get to me. He'd leave the people alone with Prince John as their overlord to find me.

The breath rushed out of me. Unless it were me, telling him in the flesh, the only thing that would come from Rob knowing were the kind of danger that would leave him dead. And I couldn't go to him until King Richard were safe, and my being alive again wouldn't purchase someone else's death. "Let me think about it," I told him.

His brows knit together, but he nodded. "Why would Prince John dare to kill you? And why now, after hiding you for so long?" Winchester asked.

I looked up at him for a moment. "I think he means to kill Richard. Or try to, anyway. He told me that Richard would never return to England."

Winchester leaned back, his jaw tight. "That damn coward," he grunted. "While I believe it, that is a very steep charge, Marian. Do you know how?"

I shook my head.

"You're right," he said. "He'd never risk harming you if he thought he'd have to face Richard."

"Which makes me wonder if he's been planning this since the day he took my fingers," I said to him, my words soft.

Winchester glanced at me, and then toward the hand I kept hidden under the table, and made a *hmm* noise.

I looked away. "You're refusing people at the gates?" I asked.

He sighed, nodding. "For now. Too many people are coming through, and the city can't hold them. I have enough money and food to keep my people safe, and until I figure out how to do more, that's all I can promise them."

"We were in Silchester when the news came," I told him. "The knights killed a boy for throwing something at them."

His shoulders dropped. "I will see what I can do to help them," he said solemn.

"I didn't mean for you to take responsibility," I told him, shaking my head.

"And yet I must. Nobles are frightened, Lady Marian. They aren't defending their people, much less taking care of them. They are afraid of mobs and riots, of starvation and poverty. They are neglecting their duty. But I will not forget what that duty is. Even if I must do the work of others."

"Perhaps that is true," I told him. "But you didn't kill that boy. I didn't kill that boy. I will find out who made that man believe he had any right to do it." I shook my head. "Have you . . ." I drew a breath, trying to find the words. "When did you last—when did you see him?"

He swallowed. "A few weeks ago."

I just looked at him.

"He . . . he would greatly benefit from hearing you're alive," he told me.

His careful words stabbed me. "He's not doing well," I said.

"He's not bad," Allan said, and I looked to him. "He's just not nearly the same man he is when you're with him, lady thief."

Winchester wouldn't look at me.

I tried to swallow, but the thought stuck in my throat.

"My lord," said a quiet voice, and Winchester turned to one of his guards. He gestured him forward, and the man murmured something to Winchester, who sighed. He nodded.

"Lady Marian, please excuse me. There's a dispute in the town I should go settle."

I nodded.

"Eat and drink; I don't know when the queen mother will arrive, but you should probably rest," he said, and his eyes moved over me in the same way David's did. I pulled the cloak tighter around me. Honestly. I were alive, and after three months in prison, I were grateful for that.

—w—

His servants led me to a room, while David and Allan went to the knights' barracks—to Allan's horror—but before they went Allan pulled the small stack of letters he'd shown me the night before from his satchel. He handed it to me, meeting my eyes and nodding once, and I took it, holding it against me.

I sat in the room, staring at the pile. There were five letters. I'd counted them twice, laid them all out without breaking their seals. They were numbered, but it were strange—they weren't in any order I knew. The first were 27, then 52, then 76, then 91, and 132. Each one bore my name. The first one had my name in tight scrawl, like it were hasty, desperate, but 76 started to get wider, looser, softer. Easier.

I traced the letters with my fingers, but I didn't open them. Now that we were here, now that Eleanor were coming, maybe I could go back to Nottingham.

But no matter where I went, if Prince John knew I lived, he would find me. He would hunt me down, and he would make the people I loved pay for my being alive before he took my life at last. He'd branded me a traitor, and there were little I could do to stop him.

Maybe he wouldn't kill me. Maybe he'd throw me back in a prison, a place of darkness, until the world forgot I'd been there at all.

How long would it take Rob to forget me?

There weren't no answers that would satisfy me. But I knew that if I opened one of Rob's letters, saw his writing and pictured him penning the things to me, I'd go. I'd go straight away to Nottingham, and I'd risk watching him die in front of me at Prince John's gleeful hand.

Stacking and tying them careful, I put them away and lay on the bed.

CHAPTER
FIVE

Eleanor didn't arrive until the next morning. When she came, it were in a carriage, with a small cadre of knights behind her. I frowned to see it from a window of the manor—she were the queen mother. She needed more protection than a handful of knights, no matter how loyal they were.

I came away from the window, waiting for her in a private chamber. I paced as moment after moment ticked by. Longer. Longer. Longer. I stared at the window, wondering if there were any risk of this being a trap. I'd only seen her carriage, after all, not her person. The message could have gone astray. Someone else could have read it and known what it meant. The person behind the door could be Prince John himself.

I didn't have any weapons. Why had I not considered that before now?

The door latch lifted, and it opened slow. I held a breath, looking at it.

Eleanor's pale face were flushed with color, her eyes bright and filled with water as she stood before me. The water fell, crystal drops running over her skin as she swept forward, pulling me hard into her arms. She were shaking, and I hugged her back without a thought.

"My God," she whispered in my ear. "My God."

Her hands touched my hair, touched my face, pulled me back from her a little to stroke my cheeks and then hug me again.

"You're *alive,*" she breathed.

I nodded tight into her neck.

"I will not fail you again, my girl. I will protect you, I promise." She nodded hard against me, like she agreed with her own self. "I'll make you a lady-in-waiting. Or perhaps—perhaps you should leave. John thinks you're dead, doesn't he?"

"Yes, but—"

Her eyes narrowed. "He will know of my displeasure, Marian, but I confess that keeping you from his sight may be the smartest choice for now."

I pulled away. "Your displeasure."

"Yes."

"So . . . what?" I asked. "You will scold him? He near killed me! A man died in the attempt, and all you are is *displeased*?"

"What do you want of me, Marian? His temper got the best of him."

"No—he *planned* this. He tried to murder me in cold blood, Eleanor. He stole my necklace, and he wouldn't watch while they did it. He wanted to be far enough away that he could deny it."

She shook her head, proud and resolute. "He wouldn't dare."

"But he did. So, why, Eleanor?" I demanded. "Why would he kill me now, when he wouldn't have dared before? Your disapproval hasn't changed. He knows that. But there's one person he fears more than you. There's one person he knew he'd have to answer to, and damn soon."

Her mouth turned down, her white face stony and cold. "That isn't true."

"He's planning to kill Richard, Eleanor," I told her.

"Why would you say such a thing?" she demanded. "He would never—"

"Hurt his own flesh?" I growled. "His own *blood*?"

She glanced over me. "He doesn't have it in him to kill Richard, Marian."

"Well he's planning to. Or planning to thwart the ransom somehow, I'm not sure. Only that he tried to kill me because he believes Richard will never set foot in England again."

"You don't know that!" she snapped at me.

"He said so!" I snapped back. I looked at her, straight in her eyes, blue like the coldest ocean water. "Do you really not believe that Prince John would covet his brother's throne?" I asked her. "That he could easily murder his own nephew to surpass him in the succession?"

"He needs armies! Men, and Englishmen will not follow him. The nobles can be bought, but armies are a different thing, my girl." She shook her head.

"Armies he can buy as well," I told her. "In France, to start with. Think, Eleanor—to capture a crusader on a mission that has been sanctioned by the Pope is to risk excommunication from the Church—why would the Holy Roman Emperor ever risk that? What would induce Prince John to such a crime? He doesn't want the Crown of England for himself, or he would have invaded instead of sending a ransom demand. Prince John could have set all of this up, Eleanor. Everything."

"John doesn't have that kind of money," she said. "He's a fifth son, even if he is a prince."

"He has the will," I told her. "He has the kind of manipulative mind to put such a thing in motion. You know he does."

"You will not tell me what I know," she said. She turned away from me, and paused for a breath before she left the room, shaking her head.

I watched her go, shocked.

I came out of the chamber, and David, Allan, Winchester, and two women were staring after where the queen had gone. One of the women were Lady Norfolk, an older woman who had been the queen's lady a long while. The other were an awful young girl, a pretty thing who even after the queen stormed off were staring up at Winchester.

She turned her head to me and she smiled bright, dipping into a curtsy.

Winchester beamed, stepping forward. "My lady Marian, may I introduce Lady Margaret, daughter of the Earl of Leicester."

"My lady Princess," she said, reverent.

I nodded my head to her. "So Eleanor is telling people I'm her granddaughter?" I asked.

She straightened, glancing at Winchester, and I wondered if that meant he told her. "A select few, my lady."

"Please," Allan huffed. "She has half the minstrels in England singing of it. It's the most purposefully worst-kept secret in Europe."

"I've heard so very much about you," Margaret said, looking at me still.

"Oh," I said. "You have?"

"Yes," Winchester said quick. "I told you the queen has been searching for you."

Lady Norfolk looked fair disapproving, which were a bit of a feat since I'd only ever seen one utterly blank expression from her. Allan chuckled.

"The queen won't hear of it," I told them. "She doesn't believe Prince John would hurt Richard."

"He tried to *kill* you," David said. "How is that different?"

Lady Norfolk raised her chin in a look that were a pale mimic of Eleanor. "She's a mother," Lady Norfolk said flat. "Not one of you understands what that means."

I sighed, thinking of the letters in my room. Nottingham were starting to seem farther away than ever. "If she won't help us, we have to stop Prince John on our own," I told them.

"But you don't know how the prince intends to act," Winchester reminded me careful. "How can we stop something if we don't know what's going to happen?"

I crossed my arms. "Eleanor said something interesting—Prince John doesn't have a tremendous amount of money. Is that true?"

"Of course not!" Allan crowed. "He's John Lackland!"

Winchester lifted his shoulder. "He's lord of a few holdings—Nottingham included, as you'll remember—mostly properties that have reverted to the Crown and that he doesn't entirely hold in his own right. He exists by his brother's beneficence," Winchester said. "He'll collect money from those, which is more than many have, but no, he doesn't have access to the royal coffers or the fortune of Aquitaine."

"So Eleanor's right. He needs an army if he hopes to take the crown. Even in the most peaceful ways, he'd still need men to protect his claim to the throne."

"He needs money," David said.

I nodded.

"But . . ." Margaret started to say something, but her eyes darted round the room and she stopped, putting her head down.

"What?" I asked her.

"Well—the money. The queen came south to start collecting the funds for the tax, but the prince went north. Within a month, he'll have thousands of pounds of silver at his fingertips," she said. "As will the queen."

"That's not good," muttered Allan.

"But it doesn't make sense to steal it as he goes," I said, shaking my head. "He needs to raise 65,000 pounds—Eleanor won't let a ship leave without the full amount on it." I stopped, looking at Allan. "A ship. Of course—that would be the smartest move, to fill a ship and send it to the wrong place. Steal the ransom and use it to buy an army, not the king's freedom."

"And what does that change?" Eleanor said, returning slow from the hallway she left by. "Nothing. We still have the daunting task of raising this tax. We must bring the English people to the brink and then find a way to stop them falling over. If he means to steal the tax after it's raised, that's one thing. But we still need to raise it. And we still need to protect you," she said, looking at me.

"So you believe me?" I asked.

"No," she said, shaking her head. "No. I believe John will act with pride and honor. But I recognize the temptation. I pushed his brothers to rebel against their father, after all. The night before you are crowned is the last full night of sleep you ever get—everyone who has even a loose claim will take their chance to end your reign and with it, your life. The key is not to give them an opportunity, and the only thing that I will agree upon is that this is an opportunity. But I won't lose either of my sons to it."

I swallowed. For now, it were enough. I nodded, once.

"But I also won't lose my granddaughter. So I will send you to Ireland."

"*Eleanor—*" I started.

She held up a hand. "No. You cannot go to France, because whether or not you're right, John has friends in France. It's the first place he'd turn to for armies for a rebellion. And you wouldn't be able to hide there. I can't get you safely to any of my daughters, so I'll send you to Ireland. It's close, and you can be safe there until this mess blows over."

"Eleanor, no," I snapped. "I'm not fleeing the country!"

Her hand fell to fold into her other. "Really. He will kill you, Marian." Her throat worked, and she looked up, blinking fast. "Do you know how many of my children I have already buried?" she asked me, her voice a harsh whisper. "I have yet to bury a grandchild. Do not ask me to do this. Go willingly, or I will find a way to make you."

I glanced at David, her chosen arm. He looked between us, unsure. Would he be loyal to me or Eleanor, given the chance?

She looked to Margaret. "Margaret, fetch my letters," she told her. Margaret dipped and ran off to obey her, and Eleanor's white throat worked, sharp wrinkles filling and falling. "I have letters from your father. A pardon for your crimes, and a letter of creation. Technically the creation was for Gisbourne, but it falls to you in his death."

I blinked at her. "Creation?"

"Of title," she said. "The king has the ability to bestow and revoke titles. It was the only way he could make you inherit an earldom as a woman."

"I know what a creation is, Eleanor. Richard—my father—pardoned me?" I asked.

She nodded. "I wrote to him the moment you were imprisoned. I had it for months, but John wouldn't admit you were alive. And if you're not alive, you can't be released." She came closer to me, skating her hands over my arms. "I told you. He has always looked after your welfare, even when you didn't know your true lineage. He has always thought of you, Marian. Your father is an excellent man."

I looked into her eyes. "I'm sorry, Eleanor, but I cannot leave. I can't just . . . go."

"Think of your sheriff," she told me. "If you stay, your Robin will find you. He will stand for you against my son. And he will fall, like your friend fell. He will bleed for you, and he will die."

I pulled away from her.

He will die.

Rob's face, frozen like John Little's, with shock and sudden knowing, like he could see Death creeping toward him over my shoulder.

He will die.

Blood running out of Rob like a swollen spring river gone red.

He will die.

Rob's blood staining the snow, staining the stones in the courtyard, staining my eyes.

"Lady Scar," Allan said, stepping toward me with a frown.

I scuttled back. "I'll go. I'll go," I breathed.

"My lady," Allan said, his shoulders dropping. "It's the very wrong direction."

"But she's right," I told him, feeling water fill my eyes. "She's right. And I won't watch him die."

Eleanor nodded, coming nearer to me and blocking out my view of Allan. She clasped my shoulders and brought me closer, leaning her forehead against mine, and I shut my eyes, feeling the water slip down my cheeks.

CHAPTER
SIX

"She's playing you like the strings of a damn harp!" Allan snapped at me, taking my things out of the satchel as I tried to fill it up.

"Stop that!" I yelled at him, slapping his hands.

"Ireland?" he said. "I'm *from* Ireland! Why do you think I came here?" he said. "Nothing good in Ireland." He frowned. "Except the ale. The ale is fine."

"Do you wish me to detain him, my lady?" asked David, watching with a scowl and crossed arms.

"No, David, thank you," I told him. "Allan, really," I said, snatching a dress back.

"And what are you going to do with that?" he asked. "A dress. A fancy present from Eleanor to buy your silence!"

"You wish to speak to me of dramatics?" I asked, pushing him back from my things. He were right—they were almost all gifts Eleanor had given me in the last day. I'd never owned much of anything in my life. "People will die if I stay here!"

"What makes you think they won't if you go?" Allan demanded.

I looked to David, and he lifted an eyebrow.

"If Prince John doesn't know I'm alive, he won't go after Rob. He'll leave Nottingham alone. He has no reason to bother."

"Oh, you're quite right. He's had so many excellent *reasons* in the past," Allan said, flouncing about with a cloak. "I'll starve the people because they're quite bothersome. I'll murder Gisbourne because he's ceased to be useful. And in fact—I shall cut off your fingers because you annoyed me and I don't know how to talk about my feelings," he mocked.

David stood. "You will not make a joke of my lady's pain," he said.

I pulled the cloak from Allan, and David stepped between us, staring Allan down. Allan met his challenging eye contact with a devilish smile, not breaking away.

David gave him a good solid push back, and Allan went, still smiling at David.

David shook his head.

"I won't go with you," Allan told me.

I scowled. "No one asked you to come."

He looked offended in a rather dire way. "Who will entertain you?"

David snorted, and Allan frowned at him.

I pulled up another dress, and tucked it into the satchel. Beneath it were the stack of letters, and the sight of them sliced into my belly like a knife.

Allan didn't have to be quick to snatch these from me. I were staring at them, and he picked them up, turning them over. "You haven't opened a one," he said.

"No," I said, my mouth going dry.

"So that's it, then," he said soft. "You don't want him anymore. The greatest love story I've ever had the chance to tell, and you're throwing him away." His head tilted. "In fact, why don't we just do that," he said, going to the window.

"Allan!" I yelled, diving for him as he pushed the shutter open. "Allan, don't!"

I grabbed one arm, jerking it back and slamming my knee into his bits. He wailed, falling back and curling dramatic onto the floor with a howl.

David were right behind me, crossing his arms and watching Allan writhe on the floor instead of assisting.

I took the letters, pressing them into the satchel and buckling the leather shut. I turned to Allan as he started to rise, weakly leaning on the wall. "You think this is easy? That I'm being cruel?" I snapped. "Maybe I am! But I'd rather love him for the rest of my life than love him now and lose him soon after."

Even as the words left my mouth, they didn't feel true. Rob's and my love had always been made in the cracks, the jagged little edges that came from the ruin of something else. It were a place that weren't supposed to be filled with love, but that's how it had always been. Our love filled the broken bits and made us whole again. There weren't no perfect time to love him, not ever, and it had always been with the threat of death and hurt hovering round us. And we'd love each other anyway. Sure, and true.

"You're giving up, my lady," he told me.

"You don't understand," I told him. I hefted the bag up, and David shook his head.

"Leave it there, my lady. I'll pack the horses," David told me. "You go on."

"Good-bye, Allan," I told him.

He shook his head. "It's not good-bye, lady thief. I'll never believe that."

I sighed. "David, I'm going to say my good-byes to the others."

David nodded, and I went out of the room. I were in a skirt now, and I kicked at it as I walked down the hallway. I felt along my back; Eleanor had even purchased two knives for me, and I slid one out of my bodice. I turned it in my good hand. My stumps ached, but the fingers I had left were still sturdy for gripping things. I held the knife in my bad hand, squeezing it tight.

I could hold it. It were awkward, and painful, but I could hold it.

"You're a lady now," Eleanor said, and I raised my head to see her down the hall. "You don't need knives, you know."

Flipping it up, I caught it with my good hand. "Even a lady needs something sharp at her disposal," I told her.

"That's what words are for." She lifted a shoulder. "Or knights, perhaps."

"You're not traveling with many," I said.

"No," she said. "Most are still covering the countryside, making announcements, assisting their lords. They are returning to me as fast as they can, but for now, we have enough." She sighed. "I always like having more men about, but I'll make do."

I nodded.

She waved me into her chambers, and Margaret were there, beaming at me in her strange way, and she handed Eleanor a cloth. Eleanor took it, unwrapping the cloth, showing my moonstone.

"This was when I believed him," she whispered to me. "That you were dead."

I swallowed.

"Here," she said, holding up the chain, and I bowed my head. She slipped it around my neck, and the weight settled down, finding the dip between my breasts. She looked at it and nodded. "Where it belongs."

"Thank you, Eleanor," I told her. I jerked forward, hugging her.

"There have been many sins between us, my girl," she said, petting my back. "But family protects one another. I will always keep you safe."

I pulled back. It were a finite promise, but I knew she meant it. "Bring my father back," I told her. "I very much want to meet him."

She smiled at this. "I cannot wait for that bright day, my girl." She pressed her hand to my cheek. "Now, David will escort you to Bristol. There should be a ship within a day or two—by the end of the week at the very least—headed for Ireland. You can both buy passage and send word to me when you are met by Theobald Butler—he is far more loyal to me than he is to John, and he will protect you." She handed me a letter. "This will explain everything to him." She gave me two more papers, both with ribbons and seals flapping off. "These are your pardon and your creation," she said.

Holding them against myself, I drew a breath. "Tell me that this is the right thing to do, Eleanor," I whispered to her.

She raised her chin. "It is the only thing to do if you want to protect those you love," she told me.

I sighed.

"Ladies," Winchester said, coming to the open door and bowing to us.

"Winchester," I said, smiling. "Thank you. For everything you've done for me."

He didn't smile. "You're welcome. Of course."

"Walk her down to the courtyard, won't you?" Eleanor asked Winchester. "We still have some packing to do. Margaret—stop simpering."

Margaret flushed and turned back to her task.

"Where will you go next?" I asked her.

"Toward Cornwall," she said. "Perhaps up toward Devizes Castle first, and then down to Cornwall. That way we can travel all along the south coast." Her mouth tilted up. "And I'll have an excuse to stop in Bristol and ensure that you're off all right."

"Good-bye, Eleanor," I told her.

She nodded once, her mouth pressed tight shut. She waved me off and turned away, and Winchester offered me his arm.

He were silent down the hall, down the stair, down another long hall. We were about to make the courtyard, when I asked, "What is it, Winchester?"

He shook his head. "It is not my place, my lady."

"You've been an excellent friend to me, Winchester. Please."

"This is wrong," he said soft. "Locksley thinks you're dead. You're lying to him—you're asking me to lie to him." He shook his head. "More than that. You're torturing the man. A man who has seen too much torture in his life by half."

"She's not wrong," I whispered to him. "You know he wouldn't think of the danger. You know what he would risk for me. And I won't ask him to do it."

"That doesn't make this right," he told me.

We walked into the courtyard. It were clouded and dark, the sky heavy with rain like unshed tears.

"I can't make you choose differently," he said. "But I wish you would."

I shook my head. I mounted my horse, and David bowed to Winchester, who just looked at me with stone in his eyes.

David mounted, and I spurred my horse, looking to the roads. One went north, to Nottingham, to Rob, to the light and his love and the feel of his heartbeat melting into mine. He would choose the north road, if it were him. He would move heaven and earth to return to me.

The other went west to Bristol. I stared at the north road, but I took the one west.

I wouldn't fix a broken thing only to see it shatter before my eyes a moment later.

—~—

I weren't close to good health yet, and we could only ride so far and so fast; it would take us three days or more to reach Bristol. We stopped at an inn that night, and David told them we were man and wife. He slept on the floor while I lay awake on the bed, staring out the window, thinking of Rob. It felt like leaving England and putting that much space between us were saying good-bye to Rob, to all the love I'd ever had for him, and I had only three days and however long it took to get a ship to figure a way to do it.

—~—

The next morning, we saddled the horses, and the stable boy brought out a third horse with him. "Boy," David said, pointing. "That's not our horse."

"Of course it isn't," Allan said, coming out from the inn with a wide stretch and a yawn. "It's mine."

"Christ Almighty." David sighed. "I thought we got rid of you."

"You don't wish that for a moment," Allan said, mounting his horse. "Besides, did you really think to go to Ireland without one of her favorite native sons?"

"Clearly a foolish hope," David muttered, mounting as well.

I swung up onto the horse, feeling my body ache as my muscles settled into place. "Play nice, boys."

"*I* am devoted to your every request, lady thief," Allan told me. "I cannot speak for the errant."

"A word, my lady," David said. "All I need is a word from your mouth and I will physically prevent him from following us." He met Allan's eyes. "Or walking."

"A fool for beauty, that's what I am. An utter fool. Never saw a pretty lass that couldn't spin my head three ways till Sunday. God himself crafts the lines of a pretty face, I always say, and so how could you say no? You're looking at God. God's work, even—it's like looking at *Christ*," Allan prattled on.

"Am I supposed to be the lass?" I asked him. "Because I still don't recall asking you to come."

"There's still time to send you home," David added.

"You haven't listened to a word I've said. Patriotic duty? Sworn to protect my king's fair daughter, nay, his country? A man cannot say no to such things. It goes against my honor. The fiber of my being!" Allan proclaimed.

Rolling my eyes, I reminded him, "You're Irish, Allan. Richard isn't your king, and England isn't your country. And I haven't seen much of this honor you claim."

He looked mortally wounded. "Have I ever acted dishonorably to you, fair thief?"

"It doesn't count if you suspect she'd cut your hands off," David grunted.

"It counts," Allan and I said at once.

"What about men?" I asked him. "Are you saying men are not crafted by God?"

It might have been the sun, but I could have sworn he colored up a bit. And as someone who hid her blushes fair often, I figured I knew better than most. "Men are the crudest castoffs of God's work, I must say," Allan said.

David chuckled.

Allan frowned. "Are we there yet?"

I glared at him. "Does it look like we're there yet?"

He looked round us, to the cow pastures beyond the dirt road we were riding down. Our horses were in a quick canter, and Allan were frowning along.

"Do you never ride?" David asked. "Even the lady is more accomplished than you."

"I grew up riding," I explained. "Even if I didn't do it much for years after."

"I ride very gracefully," Allan said with a sniff. "You two just enjoy it more." He leaned toward me on his horse. "We could leave him here, fair thief," he confided in a none-too-quiet whisper. "If you can forgo your penchant for big, strong men."

"*He* is required protection by the queen. And it has nothing to do with my penchants, Allan—I just tend to be in the same business as big, strong men, only they need to be twice as tall and twice as heavy to do what I can in half the time," I snapped. "And if you're coming along, I hope you'll serve as much of a purpose as he does. Do you have any contacts in Bristol?"

"I have friends everywhere, my lady."

"Well, then perhaps you'll keep your ear to the ground and your mouth blessedly shut?" I said.

David chuckled.

Allan pouted. "You know that's mostly through an extended network of people with ears to the ground, don't you? I don't like putting my ear to the ground." He pouted further, brushing dust from his bright red cape. "In fact, I don't much care for being dirty."

"Allan, stop, for the love of God," I asked him. "Just stop speaking for a while."

David chuckled again at this, and I glared at him. He shrugged in return. "I didn't comment when you called me required protection, did I?" he asked.

I sighed, but Allan weren't speaking for the moment, so I rather thought I'd try to enjoy it.

I were surprised by how much I did enjoy it. I missed being outside, I missed being away from the city. The trees were in sap, and the smell were enough to get drunk on, to let my mind swirl back to Sherwood and Nottingham and kisses in the dark woods, the rough swipe of bark against my back, and the hot swipe of Rob's hands on my front.

I shut my eyes. *Forget him, forget him, forget him.*

It didn't seem near that easy.

CHAPTER SEVEN

The three of us made Bristol three full days after leaving Eleanor. The port city seemed prospering and heaving, with Wales in sight across the narrow channel. It bristled the hair on my neck, having an enemy so close and my escape so near.

Escape.

It were quick work for Allan to find the next ship to Ireland that were leaving in three days' time, and we went to an inn to stay for the in-between. Riding through the country hadn't meant a lot of gentle nights, and all three of us were happy for a hot bath, even if it were expensive. I went first, and donned a set of men's clothes over my hot, damp skin.

Tucking my growing hair up under a hat, I went down to the tavern without the boys. I just wanted time to myself, and they were growing happier with each other, even if I couldn't much call their friendship fond.

I had every intention of sitting and eating, happy and warm in the tavern, but we were back at the ocean, and I could smell it, and Rob seemed just beyond me, mocking my thought of leaving him behind. I left the tavern and went for the water, trying to find him again. Trying to be with him in these salty half moments, trying to call up some piece of him that I could take with me.

I found the port and followed the water's edge out along the city till it fell into big rocks with places to hide. Picking my way out over slippery black boulders in the gleam of the moon, I finally found one that weren't too wet and had a place I could tuck into besides.

The heat were gone from my skin, but the damp were still there, and it made the night seem colder again by half. I shut my eyes and breathed it in and wished him to me.

His hand touched my face, and water welled up in my eyes but I didn't open them, holding onto his shadow self as long as I could.

"*Come back to me, Scar. I don't understand why you won't come to me.*"

"To protect you," I whispered. "Because I love you."

"*It's not you that will hurt me. It's Prince John. He'll kill us all, Scar, just because he wants to.*"

"Not if I'm not there. Not if I don't provoke him."

"*Do you really believe that?*"

"Not if I kill him first," I told Rob, overhot and fierce.

"*Then what the hell are you doing in Bristol?*" he asked.

I shook my head. "I'll kill him," I promised Rob. "Just stay here with me a while longer."

"*I'll never leave you,*" he told me, and I felt his arms on me. "*As long as you love me, I'll be here, hidden somewhere in your heart.*"

The water slipped out, and I tried to imagine his arms tighter on me, holding me tight enough to be real, wondering if those words were meant to comfort me or haunt me. "I'll never stop loving you, Rob. Never."

"*Then I'll always be here,*" he said, brushing a kiss into my hair.

—∞—

I fell asleep like that, with the rock of the ocean waves, the cold of the night and fresh bite of the wind taking me away from myself. Wrapping me up with Robin like I could keep him there. When I woke up, I thought it were to a seagull cackling good morning, but it were someone laughing.

Turning slow to not be seen, I looked around. There were two women in the water, rucking in nets in the shallows.

"I'll buy a pound of butter," one said.

"Just a pound?" the other said. "I'll buy the whole cow and have cream and butter and milk for years."

"That's awful work," the first said. "All that cranking and squeezing and churning."

"Then I'll hire someone for it. A good little lass that could use the coin."

The first clucked. "Heavens, I wouldn't never have a little young thing running around my husband. No good, that one."

They both laughed at this. "Well, if our husbands were any good, we wouldn't have our butter cow, would we?"

They laughed again. "How much do you think it will be?"

"A chest for each of us, at least. Nothing but fancy dresses and servants and—"

"As long as it buys us warm socks and a hot fire, I'll be right grateful," she said, and I heard them splashing in the water. "Awful cold still."

"You're a simple woman. I've always liked that about you."

The first made a grunting noise. "As long as those men don't get strung up—then we'll be in a bit of a fix for those warm fires, won't we?"

"They won't. They'll all look out for one another; they always do."

Another grunt.

"Besides, it ain't as if the queen is all that heavily guarded."

My limbs were stiff with cold. My feet weren't sure on the wet rocks. There were bare enough light in the sky to see by. But I didn't wait a breath before running for the inn.

David, Allan, and I were armed to the teeth and on our horses in moments, and my horse tore ahead in a fast gallop with David behind me and Allan behind him, racing down the road from Bristol to Bridgewater Castle, where Eleanor might have been.

There were a spot that were perfect for it. There had been a portion of the road that went through a thick forest with grand trees, and I'd even had the stupid thought that it reminded me of our ambush spots in Nottingham.

We broke into the dark of the forest and were blind for a moment, but I didn't slow down. I heard the clash of weapons up ahead, and my heart seized as I knew, sudden and sure, that there were at least one more thing than Rob that I could lose, and she were an old white-haired lady that I never wanted to love.

I saw the knights in full fight, and a man in plain clothing reaching into the carriage and obviously scrabbling with something. More than half of him were outside the carriage, and without thinking much, I leapt off my horse and slammed into him, gripping his waist to tear him from the carriage.

It were enough, and my weight pulled his off and we fell, landing hard in the dirt, side by side. He groaned and started to get off me, and another man grabbed me up from the ground.

I stabbed him in the gut before he could do the same to me, and he let me go. The man in the dirt were starting to rise and I kicked his head. He went still, and a flashing arc of a sword came down on me. I hit it away with my knife, but the man cuffed my head with his free hand, swinging the sword round again.

Cutting a quick stripe on his hand made him drop the sword, and I stepped on his foot and slammed my elbow to his head. He dropped, and I took a deep stride to get back to the carriage, and whatever new assailant were there.

A man were trying to pull Eleanor out of the carriage, and she were hitting him with her stick but didn't have enough space to get a good swing off. He backhanded her, and she made a soft cry, a weak hurt noise.

I'd never heard Eleanor make any kind of sound like that.

I should have thought of those women I heard talking. Wives. Family. Children.

But I didn't. I jumped forward, hooking my arm round his shoulders, and I slit his throat. He fell back quick, spraying me with blood.

Eleanor met my eyes, and hers were wide and bluer than ever. She nodded once, and I shut the door.

"Margaret," she told me, pointing to the open door on the other side of the carriage.

I growled out a curse. I hopped up on the chests in the back and looked out.

There were blue cloth in the woods, and I followed the flash of bright. Margaret were fighting hard, but her small hands weren't doing much as the man covered her mouth and tried his best to uncover the rest of her. Her gown were torn and she were sobbing under his hand.

She were making enough noise to cover my approach, and I came fast as I could without him turning. I kicked my boot up between his legs and he howled, dropping her. She screamed and pulled away from him, and he grabbed her arm.

"Don't you touch her!" I screamed at him, fisting my half hand as best I could and slamming it into his face.

The pain of the punch rushed up my arm. It were the good kind of pain, the simple kind that made sense.

I hit him again.

You can't quite take a punch, Scar, John told me once.

I hit him again.

You're no good for punching, Rob told me.

What they never said were that they were the ones meant to be punching.

They were meant to be beside me, punching while I planned, strong-arming while I cut.

A team. A band. Complete.

Arms came round me, but they weren't my bandmates. They were from Lady Margaret, and she were a sobbing, shaking little thing, and I couldn't lift my hand.

I looked down. The man were breathing—just, but it were there, in the bubbles of blood round his mouth.

Sagging against a tree, I hugged her tight.

We didn't go on to Bristol. We went to Glastonbury, one of the oldest abbeys in England. Maybe the world; it were the oldest place I'd ever heard of. The whole party were rushed into the big stone walls fast, and I abandoned my horse to stay with Eleanor in the carriage. Margaret were sniffling and couldn't much stop shaking, and Lady Norfolk were trembling but grim-faced as ever. Margaret had let go of most of me, but she still clutched my hand like it were a holy relic.

I'd gotten blood on her. My hand were still bleeding, dripping into the carriage, and God only knew where else I were bleeding from. I watched my fist drip. It were easier than seeing a splinter of fear in Eleanor's blue eyes. It were easier than seeing this girl treat me like a savior.

We were all hushed and quiet as we were given rooms, and food, and a bath. Eleanor bathed first, and we all attended her. Or tried. The first thing I touched, I stained with blood, and Lady Norfolk pushed me back.

So I watched. Sitting in the stone sill of a window, I breathed, and I watched over them. The bleeding on my hand slowed, and no one spoke as they brushed Eleanor's hair—so much longer than I thought it were, since I'd only ever seen her styled and pinned up—and put her safe into fresh clothes even as the purple on her face bloomed outward like it were reaching for me.

"You," Lady Norfolk indicated, pointing to the bath.

I shook my head.

"My lady Princess," she insisted.

"I'm not a princess," I told her, my voice cracking on the word. "And I've the most blood and dirt. The water will be ruined after I'm in it. Go."

She gave me a sharp nod and took her place in the bath, then Margaret. I saw scratches on her body that stung her in the water, and I found myself baring my teeth.

Ruin. Ruin were all around me, and I couldn't stop it none. I brought it to me like I were calling it down from the sky.

Finally it were my turn, and Lady Norfolk and Lady Margaret helped peel the clothes off me. I were tired and broken, and I felt beyond shame, so I let them do it. They poured a bucket of hotter water into the bath, and when I sat in it, a hundred pains and aches stung to life.

They set to me, Margaret on one side and Lady Norfolk on the other, scrubbing me clean, taking the muck from the wounds well enough to make water run out my eyes. A shadow came over my face and I saw Eleanor, grim and solemn, kneel down behind me.

She rubbed something into my hair that smelled like Nottingham in springtime and scrubbed her hands through my hair. She rinsed it through with water, gentle and slow.

A brush touched my temple, grazing over the skin before it slid back into my hair. Water dripped down my face faster.

Margaret scooted closer, wiping my face with her cold fingers. I shut my eyes and a sob were racked out of me, and Eleanor kept brushing my hair as Margaret leaned forward and put her cheek to mine, letting me cry.

I had taken her attacker, and she took my tears. It were an uncommon kindness, and I didn't know what to do other than hold on to her and take their gift.

CHAPTER EIGHT

We didn't have any of the ceremony befitting the Queen of England. The monks all came to pray over Eleanor, and Eleanor herself went to all of her knights and kissed their hands in gratitude for what they'd done for her. She kissed Allan and David too. She had lost one of her men and made arrangements for him.

She sent messengers out to tell of the incident, and at my insistence, to call for more knights and a separate party to see the silver she had back to London. It would take a few days, but I refused to let her leave until she had more men attending her, and she had only to glance at the wrapped body of her fallen knight to agree with me.

David and Allan stood by me, silent and true. When Eleanor returned to her rooms and asked to take food there, I nodded to them.

"I'll stay with the queen tonight," I told them. "Will you lot be able to hold your own with the knights?"

David frowned. "My lady, I *am* a knight."

Allan slapped his chest. "We'll be fine, my lady. I know what you mean."

"I think she meant that I will have to spend half my time looking out for *you*," David grumbled, and I smiled at him.

Allan moved, making some promise of a song if an instrument could be found, and David took a breath and let it out, looking at me. I saw his hand move, like he would have liked to touch me, and then thought better of it. "I'm sorry I failed you, my lady."

I looked up. "Failed me?"

His eyes were on my hands, and they glanced over my face, where there were a bright bruise ringed with scrapes and cuts. "You were hurt. I should have protected you. I treated you like a man, like a warrior, and I shouldn't have—"

"We both protected the queen. That's the important part."

He shook his head. "You're a princess. You're meant to be protected."

"Not above the queen. And besides, I can protect myself, David."

He frowned deeper at this. "I'm very sorry you have to, my lady."

I didn't know what to answer. I didn't have to fight—I loved fighting. No—love—that word weren't right. Not now, not since love meant something hot and boundless fixed in Robin's gaze. I *understood* fighting. I remembered the dark days in London when I were a girl, the long trek down there, when my sister and I waited for people to save us. They never came. Later, in Nottingham, I remembered the fear that had rushed through me, seeing Gisbourne again, wondering if he could hurt me and the people I loved as easily as he had when I were littler. And I remembered the power, the hope, of teaching Missy Morgan how to hold a knife like I might save her some of the fear I'd been through.

I could never be happy waiting for David to save me. I had been frightened before, and now I couldn't stand to give into that fear, to let it take me and rule me and keep me. And so I did what I had to do.

By the time words formed in my mouth, he were gone. I went back to Eleanor's rooms, and my stomach twisted at the sight of the food. I ate a little bread, but it felt ashy and dry in my mouth.

"Ladies," Eleanor said. I didn't even notice her gesture, but it seemed a clear command enough that the two women rose without a word and left the room.

I were sitting on a padded bench, in a dress—the ladies hadn't had much on hand in the way of men's clothing when we bathed—and facing the fire. Eleanor stood and sat beside me, but the opposite way, so our legs were pressed together but I were looking into flame and she were looking at the cold night of the English countryside.

"My girl," she murmured. "You were fearsome today."

I shut my eyes. "Yes."

"I have been through battles, Marian." I turned to her a bit, the profile of her white stone face bright. "I rode in the Second Crusade—did you know that?"

"I thought it were a story."

"Was," she corrected. She shook her head. "No. I rode. No one touched me, and I swung my sword and carved a path through men. Through flesh." Her eyes shut. "It was gruesome, to say the least. The blood—I still carry that blood on me, some days."

I looked at my hands, and they were bandaged, clean, and if anything, a little pink from scrubbing and pain. I'd washed off the blood of men's lives.

"I wasn't very good at it. It made it easy to never do it again. I was making a statement, trying to inspire our men. And I did—oh, I did. And I learned more about what sends men to war. What keeps them alive when they're there."

I knew she looked at me then, but I looked to the fire instead of her.

"They're fighting for something. I've made a life of convincing them they're fighting for me, but that's rather beside the point. A fighting man will die without something to fight for."

"And a woman?" I asked her.

She drew a slow breath. "Everyone needs something—someone—to fight for, Marian."

I turned my eyes to her slow, and she met mine with a sad smile like she knew what I were about to say. "I'm not going to Ireland," I told her soft.

She smoothed my hair back over my shoulder, nodding with a heavy sigh.

"There is no safety to be had," I told her. "Death has walked this far with me as a shadow just behind me, and all I've ever had, chained in a dungeon or hiding in the forest, is my ability to fight. To never give up. To never let this awful world win. You told me to protect the things I love, Eleanor, and I will do that the only way I know how. In Nottingham, with Rob, with a knife in my hand. I will try to stay out of Prince John's notice as long as I can manage, but he will find out I'm alive. And when he does, I will do everything I can to stop him."

She nodded. "Then there are things you can do. You're a noblewoman, now—not an earl in your own right, but you control an earldom. You're one of the highest ladies in the land, and not so far below John himself. You must show the nobles that—and make them see that John's retaliation can strike them as well."

I frowned. "Eleanor, if I represent an earldom, I have dependents, don't I? Vassals. People who are being asked to pay the tax. Who is collecting it from them? Was this land taken from someone else? Do they know?"

She glanced out the window. "It was taken from the Crown's own coffers, my dear. It was one of the lands John oversaw."

My eyes widened. "My father gave me Prince John's toys to play with, and he didn't think that would stir up trouble?"

"Nottingham," she said, looking back at me. "He gave you Nottingham. You're the Lady of Huntingdon now."

A shiver ran over me. "Rob's title," I whispered.

She nodded.

My eyes shut and I shook my head. Rob had never betrayed that title; he had grown up as the heir to Huntingdon, and he'd returned from the Crusades to find his father dead and his title stolen from him, but he had ever acted as the earl. Protecting his people the way he were meant to. For me to have that title now—well, God had a very strange sense of humor. "You would have let me get to Ireland before I ever thought to read that paper."

"Yes," she said, unapologetically. "It complicates things."

"Only if I leave," I told her.

She gripped my hand. "This path—I cannot keep you safe, Marian."

"I've never been safe," I told her. "No sense in starting now."

—∾—

The next morning, I went walking about the grounds, at an utter loss with what to do with myself. I wanted to leave and ride hard for Nottingham, but I were injured and weak, and I didn't want to leave until Eleanor were safe. So I meant to sleep and ended up walking, and I saw Margaret's bright gown in the graveyard amidst all the gray stone and quiet.

I came up to her. She were sitting in front of a grave with a crumbling stone of a marker. "Friend of yours?" I asked.

She glanced up at me. She weren't quite as young as I thought; maybe around my own age, just—sweeter. Newer, in some way. "Do you know who is buried here?" she asked.

It were fair clear I didn't, since I just asked, so I sat beside her and waited for her to tell me.

"King Arthur and Guinevere," she told me.

I frowned at the grave marker. "Shouldn't it be more grand?"

She nodded. "Yes. It should. But they've been dead a very long time."

"I wouldn't have been buried with her," I told her. "Guinevere was disloyal. With his best friend—the worst sort of disloyal. She buried him as sure as a knife, and took the whole of his kingdom down with her."

She smiled. "Wouldn't we be Guinevere in that story?"

I started to tell her I'd never be disloyal, but I wondered if that's what it meant to marry another man, to run to another country, when my heart were firm in Rob's chest. "No," I told her.

She shook her head. "It's wonderful," she said. "Arthur—he loved her. He loved everything about her. And even when she hurt him and was cruel to him, he still loved her. It seems a precious thing, for someone to know the very worst part of you and love you anyway."

I frowned.

"You don't think?" she asked.

"It's hard to argue when you say it so prettily," I told her.

She smiled.

"And it seems strange that you'd have a care for the worst in people. You don't seem to have much in the way of darkness," I told her.

Her smile went watery. "That's good, I suppose—you don't want everyone to see your darkness, do you?"

I frowned deeper.

"That man—yesterday—" she said, halting. "He would have taken me. Moments more, he would have done it. And I wonder if my—someone would still have me if that happened."

I looked at her. Were she betrothed? "Marriage is just about money," I told her. "If you still had that, you'd be well enough. Unless you have a particular man."

She bit her lip, glancing back at the abbey like someone might hear. "Saer loves me. And I love him."

"Oh." *Rob.* "Well, loving someone makes you forgive just about everything," I told her. My chest felt tight and out of breath. "Besides, willing and unwilling are two very different forms of being disloyal."

She shivered. "I'd never been so frightened in my life," she whispered. "And my first worry was that somehow this whole thing made me less in his eyes." She shook her head.

"Will you tell him?" I asked.

She nodded quick. "I can't imagine keeping it from him."

My thoughts ran back to the last night I saw Gisbourne alive, and how he'd tried to hurt me the same as that man tried to hurt Margaret, and how I knew then I could never tell Rob. I wondered if that meant I loved Rob less than she loved this Saer.

"I can't imagine keeping anything from him. You know."

"I don't think I do." I sighed, still remembering Rob that night, how he'd touched me and my fear had rushed away and I still hadn't told him.

"Well, you know Saer so well," she said, glancing around again.

"I do?"

She nodded, and her words tumbled out in a rush like a secret she'd been waiting to tell me. "He speaks so highly of you. He even gave me a knife when he heard I'd travel with the queen, in case of something just like this, even though I don't know how to use it. I don't even carry it with me. But he did that because he said you used one so well."

"And I know him? He hasn't just heard something about me?"

She laughed. "My lady, do you not know my lord Winchester's Christian name?"

"*Winchester*?" I repeated. "Saer—Winchester is your Saer?"

She flushed, but smiled and nodded.

"Oh. Yes, of course, you know I know him."

"But that wasn't the first time you met him, was it? He said you're beloved of his dear friend."

Rob.

"Robin Hood," she told me, with a grand smile, like she knew my secret. "Or Locksley, as he insists on calling him. So much less romantic!"

I stood, hampered a bit by the dress. "I don't want to talk of . . . him," I said. I wished it didn't sound like a plea on my lips.

"I'm sorry!" she cried. "I didn't mean—I just—I never get to speak about him. My father hasn't agreed to the match, and we're not supposed to be seen together. I can't tell anyone, and I thought—" She stopped, and I knew I'd silenced her.

"I would like to hear of Winchester," I told her. "He's been an incredibly kind friend to me, and I have nothing but loyalty for him. But the other—Robin Hood—I don't want to speak of him." It were easier to say Robin Hood. That didn't bring to mind Rob's face, his eyes, his hands on my skin.

She lifted a shoulder. "I have enough to say about Saer to fill several days."

My brows pushed together at this comment, but she didn't notice. She simply took my hand and started to walk, chattering on about every detail of their lovely, traditional, perfect courtship. There were kisses and gifts and secret walks that were the closest they got to scandal.

There weren't no death, no torture and nightmares and bruises and cuts. There weren't nights when they were so close together and kept apart by a husband that would have sooner seen me dead than loved me.

"You were married, weren't you?" she asked me, tugging on my arm. She knew I weren't paying enough mind to her.

It weren't really a good question to ask if she wanted me to talk more. "Yes," I said.

"When were you engaged?"

I frowned. "A lifetime ago." Then my frowning got worse. "You said I was married, not that I am."

Red rose in her cheeks. "Yes. I know—I know your husband died."

I remembered it clear, the sight of Gisbourne's big body twisting slow in the wind. I'd felt free. And a darker emotion, when I'd realized why he died—just so the prince could use me to hurt Robin, use me to take the position of sheriff away from Rob.

Gisbourne had hurt me from the first, when I were a defiant little girl and he'd cut the scar in my cheek and marked me forever. He'd hunted me down as a thief, and he hurt me as my husband. And yet before he died, he'd told me, *your unassailable loyalty and unshakable belief should have been for me*. Like I should have cared for him, when all he ever wanted were to hurt me. But caring for him weren't something he could take from me against my will.

"Saer—Winchester—he told me about him. About Lord Leaford."

"Told you," I repeated, my blood running cold. "What did he tell you?"

She glanced around, nervous. "I don't know. He just told me. About Nottingham, and seeing the two of you there. And—" She started and stopped.

"And?" I demanded, stepping forward.

She stepped back, scared and open now. She were blinking fast but her eyes had tears in them. "He told me Leaford was cruel to you," she whispered.

Cruel. I remembered that night, that awful night, when Gisbourne tried to force me, the cold promise of his hands pulling at my skirt and the fear. The fear worst of all, that he could steal it out of me when no one else could.

Her arm touched mine and I jerked away. "He had no right to tell you of anything I suffered at Gisbourne's hands."

"It was deplorable!" Margaret continued on. "Why shouldn't he speak of a man without honor? Why shouldn't he decry that? And Winchester—he didn't even know you were a princess. Did your husband?"

"What does it matter?" I yelled at her, high and empty in the quiet of the graveyard. "A princess? Does that make it worse, because when a man took a blacksmith's daughter he had a royal ring on his hand? You don't know these things and I'm glad that you don't, but all men are like that, Margaret. All of them. They are rotten and dying inside and some cover it up better than others." My mind filled with thoughts of the fishwives that were crying in cold houses now, their husbands' blood still on my hands. "Maybe we all are. Maybe we are all rotten and dark inside."

She shook her head. "You think you're the first to call me silly?" she asked soft. "Or foolish, or naive, or sheltered. Protected, perhaps. I have two older brothers. I've heard all of it before. That they stand for me against the bad things in this world. That they swallow it so I will not know its taste. And maybe that's so. Maybe I'm lucky in that regard. But I have spent a lifetime watching people scoop up the pain for other people. And sometimes it's genuine, and kind, and noble. But sometimes I see them do it because they are terrified of what they might be without that pain to glorify them, Lady Marian."

I felt her eyes on me, but I didn't look at her.

"Sometimes it's harder to be bright when you feel the darkness inside you. Sometimes the very hardest thing is to let the pain go."

I shook my head, and walked past her.

CHAPTER NINE

I went back to my room and made sure my things were gathered. I wanted to leave as soon as Eleanor's new knights arrived. In a dress, in stone walls, with the blood of a man who were just trying to feed a family on my hands—I didn't know myself. I needed to ride. I needed to move.

Eleanor were there, waiting for me.

"Is everything all right?" I asked.

"No," she told me. "Your speech is abysmal, your manners are worse, and we have roughly two days to change all that so that you can charm the nobility."

I crossed my arms. "How does any of that matter?"

Eleanor's brows lifted, drawing her chin up with them. "Marian, John never won the nobles. They don't like him. Some of them fear him well enough, but nothing warmer. Their memories of Richard are distant and dimming. If you can win them over, you will win your war before anything is ever fought. And since I believe you intend to head for Nottingham the moment one of the aforementioned lords appear, I will do what I can."

I didn't move forward.

"Forget it all, if you like. Richard certainly does when it pleases him. But you will know what I have to teach."

Drawing a breath, I moved into the room.

It were an abbey, and there weren't anything in the room but a bed and a kneeler, so I sat beside her on the bed.

"Good," she said. "Now, you have a natural ability that John never had. You care about people. You listen to them. He's spent so much of his life wondering why no one pays him more mind that he forgets to listen to others."

"You want me to listen."

"Yes. Which includes not interrupting me, my girl. In my life, I've discovered people want two things—to feel important, and to feel useful. Take my knights for example. They would give their lives for mine, and they do it because they feel they have the ability to do so, and because they know their sacrifice would save my life. Important, and useful."

"That isn't always true," I told her, frowning. "People want all sorts of things. Love. Forgiveness. Hope."

"But all things come straight down to appreciation and purpose, Marian. We want our love acknowledged, returned, and we want it to make some kind of difference. We want it to change something. We want the exact same from forgiveness and hope."

I closed my mouth.

"Make people feel important," she told me. "And give them a way to serve a purpose. The purpose may not be to you—I'm hardly speaking of sending someone to fetch you a cloak—but a real purpose. What is your purpose, my dear?"

My shoulders lifted. "I don't know."

She touched my chin. "You do. Why can't you go to Ireland? You put it so beautifully yesterday."

"Because all I know how to do is fight to protect the things I love," I told her, confused. "But I don't understand."

"That is a purpose many, many people can see themselves reflected in. If you make room for others to serve that purpose in their own way, you will be able to win the nobles and the people alike."

I shook my head. "I don't understand, Eleanor. All along, Prince John has hurt me because of my connection to Rob, and the way the people love him. That won't protect me."

"Oh, my girl," she said soft. "You don't see how the people love *you*, do you?"

Shaking my head again, I admitted, "It's not me, Eleanor. It's always been Rob. He's captured their hearts from the first, and the shine just rubs off."

She smiled like she knew something I didn't, and nodded. "Very well, I'll allow you your wild misconceptions for now. But the common people are by far the harder feat—listening to them, knowing what they want and helping them get it—those are difficult things. Nobles are easier. And once you win them, John won't be able to hurt you, because you're not only a woman, a person they are trained to protect, but you represent their own power. If a prince can lash out at you, he can harm any earl, any lord without warning. And they will protect their own just as you will."

"They are hardly trained to protect women," I said with a snarl. Prince John enjoyed hurting me, and de Clare, the heir to the Earldom of Hertford, took his own sick pleasure in my pain.

"Small men will always hurt things that are weaker than them," Eleanor told me. "But they betray themselves in so doing. Richard would never hurt someone like that because he doesn't have to."

Weaker things. I would never be counted as such.

I pushed my shoulders back. "If this will stop small men, very well. Teach me what I need to know."

—∾—

Three days after we arrived, we received our first answer to Eleanor's call. It were a small company of knights, headed up by the Earl of Essex.

He walked into the cloisters where Eleanor sat and I stood behind her, washed in the sun. He were a tall man dressed in blue, a color that reminded me of Rob. He were young and dark-haired, a quick sharpness in his step that spoke of a fast, sure-footed fighter.

He knelt before Eleanor, letting his cape sweep over his shoulder to pool on the ground.

"My lady Queen. Lady Norfolk, Lady Margaret," he greeted. A courtier—that were the only way he'd know their honors so well. His eyes flicked to me, and my chin raised.

"May I introduce Lady Huntingdon," Eleanor said, gesturing her hand at me.

He looked sharp to Eleanor.

"Huntingdon," he repeated. "I thought those were Prince John's lands."

"My Richard thought to see his daughter better taken care of," Eleanor said.

My blood rushed faster. I knew she'd do this—she told me that invoking Richard's name would help my cause, that we needed nobles at our side before the news of my life and creation reached John—but still. Hearing my father's name spoke as such so plain, so clear, it brought iron to my bones.

His eyes dashed to me again, and it weren't with warmth. It were a look of danger, but he bowed his head. "My lady Huntingdon," he greeted.

"My lord Essex," I returned, bowing my head.

"My lady Queen, I have brought you a company of knights to answer your call. Your lack of protection was a disgrace to us all, and I will see you safely conveyed," he pledged her. He dashed his head down.

"Thank you," she said. She touched her bruised cheek, and he lifted his head to watch her, a sad, vulnerable smile on her face. "It is such a welcome relief."

"Does the vagabond that did that to you still live?" he asked, his voice a low half growl.

I looked at the ground, but Eleanor's cool fingers slid around my arm. "No," she said. "My granddaughter saved my very life."

She took my half hand in hers, and I saw his eyes go to it.

"You're Marian Fitzwalter," he said, standing.

I pulled my hand away from Eleanor. "I was." Though true in a strict sense, I'd never once called myself "Marian Gisbourne," and I weren't about to speak the words now.

He frowned. "I have heard much of your . . . deeds, my lady," he said.

Eleanor did not seem surprised. "She and my son's wife, Isabel, seemed to have much in common at Nottingham. They both have a tremendous concern for the common people." She paused. "I'm surprised that didn't come up in your many walks together at the palace."

"She's a *thief*," he said, glaring at me.

"She's the daughter of a king," Eleanor snapped back. "And the lady of an earldom. She may have played at being common, but she has always been royal."

I didn't note the effect this had on Essex. Her words struck at me—were that true? All this time, Scarlet had felt like my true self, and Marian felt like a dress that never quite fit. What if it were the other way around? What if Scarlet were the falsity all along?

"Marian," Eleanor said, tugging at my hand. "Are you feeling quite well?"

Nodding quick, I squeezed her hand. "Yes, Eleanor."

She held on to my hand but looked at Essex. "She has been recovering," she explained. "Most recently from saving all of our lives in that dreadful episode, but before that from Prince John's unlawful detainment of her."

"Unlawful?" he asked, raising his eyebrow.

"The king pardoned her actions, but John would not release her. I am quite displeased with him," she said grave.

Essex frowned.

"Perhaps you would escort her for a short walk, your Grace. It so helps her strength, and yet I don't like the idea of her walking alone in such a weakened state."

I scowled. "Eleanor, I surely—"

"Very well," Essex said, glaring now at me.

Eleanor nudged me, and Margaret smiled gentle at me as I walked around them, clamping my mouth shut tight to take his offered arm.

"Lead the way, my lady," he said.

I drew a breath and led him.

—∾—

We didn't speak for a long while. We left the cloisters through the arched walkways, and went out to the church garden that neighbored the graveyard. The sun ducked behind a cloud, and I envied its ability to do it.

I looked at his hard stone face and sighed. "Why did you agree to walk with me?" I asked.

"My queen asks, and I do her bidding," he told me.

"Yet you take the princess's word over hers and form a low opinion of me," I said.

He glanced at me. "She said you spoke like a wild thing."

I swallowed. "I don't always."

"She said you were cruel to her."

My brows drew tight. "Never with intention, my lord. She and I often disagreed, but she was also one of the few women who ever had an opinion. I liked that about her." I wanted to tell him that she mocked me, that she were cruel to me and never the other way round, but I hardly thought that would sway him. "Besides, I always rather thought she and I have an enemy in common."

"Enemy, my lady?" he said, leaning his head to me with interest.

"Do you know how I came to lose my fingers?" I asked him. "Did she ever tell you that?"

"Just that you didn't have them," he told me.

"Prince John cut them off me," I told him soft. "He asked my husband to hold me still, and he cut them off with a knife. Because I displeased him."

He looked straight ahead, a muscle bunching up in his jaw. "That has nothing to do with Isabel," he said, defending her.

"Perhaps not," I said. "I am not in her highness's confidence, and I would never ask you to betray such to me. But I've known cruel men. They are cruel to anyone who cannot fight them back. And I cannot imagine Isabel has never witnessed that, even if he wouldn't dare hurt her."

Essex looked at me, his eyes heavy, dark, and guarded, and I wondered if Prince John *had* ever hurt Isabel.

He looked ahead, and his throat worked. "I was not under the impression you were someone who could not fight back."

I lifted my shoulder. "He took my fingers. He tried to murder me," I said, and Essex's face jerked to look at me. I looked at him. "I can fight back. But more importantly, my lord, what I can never do is give up."

"He tried to kill you. A lady of the court. A *royal*."

I nodded. "And I'm sure he will try to make a liar of me—he's clever, and he planned this, while I never had such luxury. But yes."

"He knew of the pardon?"

I shook my head. "I don't know. Perhaps."

"But he knew of your relationship? He knew he is your uncle."

"Yes."

"It's a wonder he didn't fear Richard's reprisal. I cannot imagine the king will take well to that."

I looked at him. "It *is* a wonder," I said back, slow and meaningful.

He drew a breath, looking ahead again. He let it out slow. "Do you know of any plans to that end?"

"Not yet," I said. "Not so concretely."

"You cannot win against Prince John if you do not win Isabel," he told me.

I frowned. Were she that powerful? "Why?" I asked.

"Because if you don't win her, you cannot win me. No matter what danger it might save her from, I won't betray her friendship."

My brows lifted.

"And without me, you won't hold against him."

I nodded. "Well, I thank you for your honesty, sir."

He glanced round, his eyes catching to the north. I followed his gaze and saw a cloud of dust rising on the horizon. "Another noble has answered her call," Essex said. "Allow me to lead you back."

I nodded.

CHAPTER
TEN

Two others arrived. They were Hugh Bigod, the son of the slightly more elderly Earl of Suffolk, and, looking particularly frantic to ensure the safety of Eleanor's ladies, Winchester. I watched as Eleanor greeted him and his eyes fell to Margaret the whole while. Margaret looked at him in the same warm way, but it were shy and unsure now. Since that man put his hands on her.

A storm rolled in on Winchester's heels, and as much as I wanted to leave, I weren't in a state to risk being ill by riding all night in the rain. Eleanor bid me to stay for dinner, and I obeyed.

Eleanor dismissed much of the pomp and circumstance that her guests should have observed. She called for a modest dinner with the abbot and her attendants and guests.

"How do your counties fare, Winchester?" Bigod asked him.

"Better than most, my lord. They have survived the tax without incident, but times are very difficult. We've opened the castle stores to help those who can't find enough food," Winchester said. He glanced at Margaret, and she smiled at him, proud of his efforts.

"You must guard yourself against abuse," the abbot warned. "In these dark times it is easy for someone to take advantage of such generosity."

Winchester shook his head. "Surely you'll agree with me, Abbot, but as long as I have the ability to share such largesse, it is my duty to offer it to my tenants. Let them take advantage if they will; it is worth the chance to help those truly in need."

The abbot nodded, but continued, "We must not, however, contribute to the delinquency of man. To tempt a weak-willed man is to abet his crimes."

"With respect, there is no crime when it is about food, Abbot. Not in my mind—or my shires."

"You would not persecute a thief for stealing bread?" Essex asked. "Or certainly not you—but your guards and knights and sheriffs in your stead?"

Winchester leaned back in his chair a little, looking at me. "No. It has been made apparent to me that if one of my tenants feels he must steal, I have failed him. Not that he is a criminal, a danger to us all, or an outlaw. He steals because there is an injustice in the system."

"Sometimes," I argued. "But some people just like to see things broken and destroyed."

He nodded slow. "And I will see those men stopped, my lady Princess." His eyes fell to my hand, and I snatched it off the table like he'd burned me.

"You said better than most," Margaret asked, her voice quiet and shy. "Is England faring poorly?"

"Yes," Essex said. "Port towns and those with heavy trade are surviving, but crops did not fare well this year. People are close to starving, and with this tax—well, many cities have had riots."

I nodded. "I saw the riots in London. Worse, I saw how the people failed to resist in Silchester."

Bigod looked worried. "My lady, you were unharmed?" he asked.

"She barely escaped London with her life," Eleanor said. "And in Silchester, she helped the people."

I shook my head at her. "I was no hero there, Eleanor. I dare say my knight and"—how to describe Allan?—"my companion were more help than I was."

"There are more riots?" Bigod asked.

Essex nodded. "Yes. Our people seem to have gone rather mad," he said.

"They aren't mad," I said. "They're starving. They're confused. And the nobles will not help them; Winchester's behavior seems strange and out of place, and it is—but that is what the noble class is pledged to do. Nobles must protect their people and use their power, wealth, and influence to do so."

"And unfortunately, much of this pain cannot be avoided if we are to bring Richard home," Eleanor said.

"We will," I told her.

"How should we proceed?" Winchester asked, drinking his wine. "With so many able lords at your disposal?"

I glanced at him. "I'll head north at first light for Nottingham," I said.

Winchester nodded once, understanding. "My lady, would you allow me to escort the silver you've already collected down to London?" he asked. "I will take half my men and see it locked safely in the treasury."

"Has the court returned to Westminster Palace?" I asked.

Eleanor nodded. "The riots have stopped, and Windsor isn't nearly as fashionable."

"Bigod and I can stay with you, my lady Queen, and repeat the task as you amass more contributions," Essex offered. "With our companies, of course."

"Very well," Eleanor said. "And Winchester, you will return and report back to me."

"As you wish, my lady Queen," Winchester said, dipping his head to her. When he raised it back up, he looked at Margaret.

It made me burn for Rob.

"Perhaps you shouldn't travel alone, Lady Marian," Margaret said soft.

I looked to her.

She were looking at her lap. "If the queen isn't safe, for certain it won't be safe for you to travel, and not with the prince . . ." She trailed off, looking round. Bigod didn't know the prince had tried to kill me.

"I have two men who will protect me better than a company of knights can," I assured her. "Speed and the ability to keep our heads down will serve me well enough."

"What route will you take?" Eleanor asked. "And I wish to be informed the moment you arrive in Nottingham."

"Most likely west to Oxford, up through Northampton and Leicester. I imagine we'll stay out of cities as best we can."

She glanced round the table, but she nodded thoughtful to me.

—≈—

After dinner were finished, Eleanor brought everyone to sit by a fire in the abbot's quarters. On the way there, Margaret tugged me back.

She drew a breath. "I don't want you to leave your grandmother because of what I said. Forgive me if I was more frank than is appropriate. I had hoped we could be friends, and more than that—I wish you would ride with us. I don't—I don't want to go—"

Her chest were heaving hard and she wouldn't look at me, and my heart snapped. I tugged her to the side, pulling her to me and putting my arms around her, awkward one moment and fierce the next. "That's what the new knights are for. You'll be well protected on the road, especially with Winchester's knights looking out for you. I was fair shocked he will leave you to go to London at all. You'll be lucky to go anywhere alone again," I teased her.

She shook in my arms. "I didn't tell him," she whispered. "I haven't had a moment alone, and the words—I don't know how to say such words."

My heart sank. I should have known that, that she needed to talk to him in private. I could arrange such a thing, and I hadn't thought to. "Come," I said. "I will find a way for you to be alone with him."

She shook her head. "No. Not now—he's right, he needs to take the silver to London. But he'll come back, and I'll tell him then."

I nodded. I pulled back from her, and she sniffed. I pulled my knife out, and put it in her hand, pushing her fingers to hold it right. "Keep the knife Winchester gave you in the carriage. Hold it like this. Remember, any man will be surprised that you fight back at all, so just jab this wherever you can and scream yourself hoarse. All right?"

She nodded, handing my knife back to me. "I will."

I tucked it back into its hiding spot.

"You don't know—I can never thank you—" she started, her face crumpling again.

"Hush," I said, smoothing her tears away. "You can't cry, or Winchester will wonder what's wrong."

She nodded, drawing a ragged breath. "Are you going to return to him?" she asked. "Robin Hood?"

My blood thrilled, and I had to nod. "I will always return to him. I can deny it all I like," I told her in a whisper, "but when someone holds your heart, it's impossible to stay away."

She gave me a weak smile. "I know this as well."

I smiled back, wrapping her arm round mine. I drew her forward to join the others, and when we walked into the room, I found Winchester's eyes on the door, restless and worried.

They met hers, and she nodded once, and he nodded back.

I wondered if this were what Rob and I looked like—this secret, quiet language. Love clear enough for everyone to see.

Essex and Bigod were looking overhard at the fire, and I reckoned they saw what I saw. Eleanor beamed.

"Margaret, you look frozen. There's a seat close to the fire by Winchester," Eleanor said. "You must take it."

Winchester dropped his head and gestured for her to take it. She sat, and he sat beside her, and Eleanor smiled.

"Meddlesome woman," I murmured to Eleanor as I sat beside her.

"Meddling is my very favorite thing, Marian," she murmured back.

Early the next morning, I changed into men's clothing and made quick for the stables, asking the hands to ready my horse and leaving my pack bags with them. I went to the barracks, hearing drunken laughter loud inside. For a moment, if I shut my eyes, it were like I were walking into Tuck's, and Rob would be beyond the door, Much would be bothering Tuck, and John would be alive.

Opening the door, I quick remembered it weren't Tuck's. The small group of men chasing spirits to the early morn went quiet, and a few of the more dutiful ones jumped up to attention. The others followed slower.

"Are Allan and David in here?" I asked one of them.

"They left," he said.

"Left?" I demanded.

His shoulders lifted. "Forgive me, my lady. They keep to themselves most times."

I frowned. "Which way?"

He pointed, and I thanked him and left. I went out to the yard, toward the gate.

Rounding the edge of the building, I heard a grunt and Allan rushed past me, tripping and falling flat on his back. "Goddammit, David!" he roared, touching his mouth, which were trickling blood.

"You—" David stalked toward him and they both caught sight of me. David went still and pale, and Allan groaned as he got himself off the ground.

"Gentlemen," I drawled, crossing my arms.

"He started it," David snapped out quick.

"I've no doubt. Are you two drunk?"

They shook their heads. I couldn't smell the reek of alcohol on them, so I reckoned it were true.

"Care to tell me what this is about?"

Allan looked to David, and David looked back at him. It were Allan that shook his head. "No, fair thief."

"Are you two able to ride?"

David's face were growing red now, and I wondered if Allan had landed a punch of his own. "Yes, my lady," they both said.

"Good. We leave as soon as you gather your horses and belongings."

"Yes, my lady," they said again.

Shaking my head at this new lunacy, I went back to the stables as they went into the barracks to fetch their things.

CHAPTER ELEVEN

We went up to Bath, and from there tried to stay off the main roads to make Oxford within two days of leaving Glastonbury. We would have stayed out of cities altogether, but we needed more food, and we were less likely to cause a stir in a large city than a tiny town.

Oxford were a huge city. It were close to London in size and activity, but it weren't on a major waterway, just a river to carry goods in and out. We made the city by midday, and entering the city were strange—there weren't many people about, and those we saw turned their eyes from us quick.

"What the hell is going on?" David asked.

Allan looked to me. "My lady, I've several contacts here, if you'll allow me?"

I nodded to him. "Go find out."

He turned his horse down a narrow street inside the city gates.

David and I continued on, riding toward the huge spires of the cathedral at the center of the city. Not far from the grand building, we heard shouts. Awful shouts, terrible cries of pain, punctuating a dark silence.

I spurred my horse, and found a large group of people that parted for the big beast coming up behind them. I slowed my horse as I broke into the circle. There were at least thirty people on their knees, staring at the ground with huddled bodies and tied hands, and in front of them, a man with a back of vicious red, bleeding stripes screamed as the whip struck down on his back again.

I leapt off my horse. "What is this?" I bellowed. "Who are you? What are you doing to these people?"

The victim collapsed against the whipping post as his torturer turned to me. Without words, the older man snapped his whip at me.

It cracked on the bit of my shoulder that ran into my neck, and I clamped down against the pain, twisting back as David jumped in front of me with his sword drawn. "Drop your weapon!" he roared.

"How dare you two interfere with my justice?" the man snarled.

"This looks nothing like justice," I returned. The cut at my neck burned and I felt damp trickle on my skin. "I demand to know your name."

"I am Lord Robert D'Oyly," he snarled. "Master of Oxford Castle and the constable of this shire."

"And why are you treating your people like this?" I stared around at the large, silent crowd, with eyes that wouldn't meet mine, and wondered how the people could be so still as their loved ones were hurt. There were no other knights, no guards, just the people outnumbering this man and unwilling to act.

"They refuse to pay the tax. They will be punished for failing to serve the Crown!" He turned back to the quivering man in front of him, and raised his whip again.

"Stop!" I roared, running in front of him and pushing him back.

He dropped the whip and drew his sword fast, arcing it down at me. I dropped to one knee and drew my knives, crossing them to prevent his sword from crashing into my head. I pushed him off and jumped up, twisting and striking out with one knife and the next until he jumped back. David went behind me and untied the man.

D'Oyly swung again and I twisted as David helped the man up.

Boy. He were a boy, fifteen at the most. This tyrant had been beating a boy.

I bare knew my next moves. I swung my knives fast, furious, throwing him off balance and stepping in close beside him to drive my elbow under the blade of his shoulder, and he dropped his sword. I recoiled and drove my elbow into his face, and he dropped.

A noise grew louder, over the pounding of my heart. I heard the rattling metallic stomp of armored men. I backed away from him as knights came into the city center, and the people looked terrified. Well and truly terrified.

Walking through the knights were a man without armor, his hands clasped behind his back. His cruel, sharp face twisted into a familiar smile, redness flooding into his cheeks.

My heart froze.

"Lady Leaford," Prince John snarled, his face mottled red with anger. "How nice to see you still alive. I had heard the very worst things about your fate."

I stood still, my knives in my hands.

"And you," he said, looking at David. "You look familiar."

"It's Lady Huntingdon now, Prince John," I told him, trying to draw his attention back to me.

That worked. His glare were sharp and heated. "You're mistaken. Huntingdon is mine," he growled.

"Not anymore," I told him. "Not according to King Richard. Who also saw fit to pardon me for that . . . misunderstanding between us."

I saw his mouth tremble, his rage bare contained. "When you tried to kill me, you mean."

"I think you know more about trying to kill people than I do," I said, turning my knife in my hand. "When I try, I don't fail."

"You're interfering with my justice again, Marian. You have a rather nasty habit of doing that." He lifted his shoulders. "Come along. We shall chat in private."

"She's not going anywhere," David snapped, a few feet away, watching D'Oyly, who had recovered his feet, and the knights too. Watching my back, as it were.

The prince chuckled. "I only wish, my lady, that you would let my vassal continue his task."

I glanced at D'Oyly, wiping his mouth. "His task," I repeated.

"Yes," Prince John said cheerful. "These people won't pay their taxes. They need to be reminded what fate lies before them if they fail to pay." He looked at me, and I could see his thoughts coiling behind his eyes like a snake. "Unless you feel that they should not have to pay. That they should not help bring my brother home to his throne."

"How do you know that they can pay?" I demanded. "If they can't pay, it's a failure of their lord, not the people."

D'Oyly shrank back.

"I'm trying to inspire them, my lady. Isn't that what you're so good at?" he sneered. "Inspiring people to act? Even when it leads to their deaths."

Hate pounded through my heart and it made me feel overstrong.

I could kill him. I could kill him right here.

I stepped forward and halted.

But how many others would die, would be hurt, in my wake?

I looked at the people—men, women, children bare old enough to have had their first kiss—waiting to be whipped. These people didn't need my vengeance. They needed my protection.

"I won't let you hurt any of them."

He laughed, and his eyes glittered. "Fine, Lady Leaford, I'll offer you a bargain. If you are so willing to stand for the people, then you can kneel for them as well."

Everything went silent. A knight shifted and his armor creaked with it.

"Kneel at the post, Marian, and be the martyr you seem to believe you are. Take their lashes and I won't hurt them."

The people kneeling on the ground looked up. The first time they had raised their heads, and they looked to see if I would take their pain away from them.

"You will not touch her," David growled. "She is protected by the queen mother. She is the Lady of Huntingdon!"

Prince John's smile turned into a snarl. "I cannot force it upon you, Marian," he said, with what sounded like deep regret, "but volunteer and it is the only way I will spare their pain."

I dropped my knives. I cast off my hat and let my hair run over my shoulder the bit that it could. People gasped—which were fair odd, since Prince John had been calling me a "she" for a long while—and I pulled off the stiff tunic.

Prince John looked angrier still.

"My lady—" David protested, gripping my arm. "You can't—"

I threw him off. "Look at *them,* David. Of course I can."

"I will take her place!" David yelled, throwing down his sword. "Punish me instead!"

"No," Prince John snapped, glaring at me. "It is her or it is them."

Glaring all the while at Prince John, I went over to the post and knelt. I were facing the people who were meant to be whipped instead, and they were staring at me. Staring, like I were some strange creature.

"D'Oyly," Prince John snapped. It sounded like a command.

I heard someone moving behind me. A hand touched my back and I jumped. It caught my shirt and drew it up to my neck, leaving it to hang loose in front of me, leaving my bits covered in a small act of mercy.

There were low murmurs and noises. I weren't sure if it were from my scars—there were a long, ragged one left by Gisbourne's sword, from my shoulder spanning down half my back. There were others besides that I hadn't seen in years but still felt tight when I twisted this way or that. Scars never left, even when you couldn't see them. Maybe they were just making noise for a woman's naked back. A noblewoman, at that.

Which never felt more like a lie than when I were kneeling in the dirt. I looked down, and saw thicker clumps of dirt, dark and wet. Blood, I imagined. Other people's blood.

"Do it, D'Oyly!" Prince John yelled.

Nothing happened.

"No, my lord Prince."

"I will remove you from your station," I heard Prince John growl, low, meant for D'Oyly alone.

"You don't have the power to do that, my lord Prince," D'Oyly whispered, but he didn't sound near as brave as his words.

"Michaelson!" Prince John roared, and I heard chain mail rattle forward.

"My lord Prince," he said.

"Lash her."

There were a long pause.

"Do it!" Prince John screamed.

"I cannot strike a noblewoman," the knight said.

He called for another man, and I shut my eyes. I couldn't hear the exchange, but I heard Prince John scream, "Give it to me, then!" he roared.

I turned. David launched forward, but one of Prince John's knights held him off and David set about fighting him. Prince John took the whip from where it lay in the dirt, and he came toward me.

I stood.

"Kneel!" he screamed. "Or I will kill all of them!"

"I will sacrifice anything to protect these people from your pain," I told him, fierce and loud. "But if you swing that whip, it's not for the people. It's so you can hurt *me*. I am not where you get to vent your childish anger. I am not weak, and I am not broken, and I will not be hurt by you. I am Lady Huntingdon. I am King Richard's daughter, and I am lionhearted too. Get out of here and leave these people alone."

There were no sound but wind, snapping cloaks and clothing out, pushing my hair off my shoulders. I felt like an avenging angel; I felt like the arm of God.

And I watched as, with hate in his eyes, Prince John left the city of Oxford.

CHAPTER TWELVE

The knights followed Prince John, and Lord D'Oyly asked us to come to his castle. Tired from the road and still bleeding from the lash at my neck, I agreed, and sent David out to fetch Allan.

We'd bare made it into the castle when seven horses galloped up and Essex threw himself off his horse. He saw me and stopped, straightening. "My lady Huntingdon," he said, looking fair relieved. "We must get you out of Oxford."

Lord D'Oyly and I looked at each other, and I frowned at Essex. "My lord, what are you talking about?"

"Prince John is on his way here. He sent word to the queen mother that he was coming down after her attack, and her intelligence has him very close to Oxford. She fears for your safety, my lady."

"Your attention and haste are very much appreciated," I told him, bowing my head. "But unnecessary. Prince John has come and gone, and unfortunately he is very aware I'm alive now."

He straightened with a frown. "You're not harmed?"

Lord D'Oyly gave a ragged sigh. "It's a rather long tale, my lord, if you would like to join us inside."

I turned a little, and Essex said, "You've been cut. The prince did this to you?"

D'Oyly flushed, and I said quick, "Come inside. I'll explain everything."

Oxford Castle were large, and old, but not rich. There were none of the trappings of excess that I'd expected, which I suppose weren't strange—D'Oyly were just a lord, and even if Oxford were rich, it were his only holding.

Unlike me. The Huntingdon holdings spanned all of Nottinghamshire and beyond. Nottingham Castle. Belvoir Castle. Haddon Hall. There were a grand old keep in Locksley called Huntingdon House.

Where Rob had grown up, naturally. I loved him, and I had the one thing that could make his happiness complete—the title he'd been denied so long ago.

Lord D'Oyly led us to a hall, small for such a thing, and called for food. He brought a woman to tend to my wound, and she drew me to a corner, for my modesty or some such thing.

Half of Oxfordshire had just seen my scarred back. I didn't reckon I had much left to defend.

I could hear the murmurs of D'Oyly telling Essex what had happened, and once Essex looked back at me, his sharp, angry stare pointed straight at me.

He turned away a moment later.

When the woman were done with her task, I thanked her and went back to the others. I sat in a chair, and leaning back made all my muscles ache.

"Are you well, my lady?" asked D'Oyly.

"You hurt your vassals," I told him.

His jaw went tight and muscled. "Rarely. But if necessary, if it will protect more people in the end, yes. On the scale that Prince John wanted me to—no."

"And yet you didn't tell him no."

He looked at me. "I didn't realize I could. Until you."

I sighed. "I didn't change anything about the tax, my lord. Or about Prince John's right to collect it from you as your overlord."

His shoulders rolled back a bit, and even sitting, he looked taller. "It changed something for me, my lady."

My mouth fell into a hard line. "Good."

Essex watched me, and looked brief at D'Oyly, and said nothing.

—∾—

By nightfall, David returned, without Allan in tow.

"He's *gone,*" he told me.

"You can't find him. That's not the same thing," I assured him. "It isn't as if he's left the city." I frowned. "Is it? You two fought over something in Glastonbury, yes?"

Color rose on his face. "Nothing relevant, my lady."

I shook my head. He could keep his secrets; I never much enjoyed when people tried to pry mine away.

"Very well," I said. "I want to leave at dawn, so let's go look for him."

David nodded, and it weren't long before I were back in men's clothing, covered over in black wool and leather, slipping out of the castle and into the night.

"I searched every street," David said as we went to the town. "The only reason he wouldn't return is if he's hurt. I can't *find* him—" he growled, stopping short.

I frowned at him. "He would limp home to great display if he were hurt. He'd live on just to let everyone fawn over him." I shook my head. "No, if Allan's not back, he's got a purpose. And we won't find him in a street." I nodded down a dark alley and started off.

David were a moment or two behind me, hissing my name. He caught up quick, walking behind me, casting me deeper into shadow as we moved deeper into the city.

I saw warm light up ahead, and heard music even from far down the lane. We came upon the place, a break in the stone wall with a little worn wooden door. People were jumping and laughing in circles, dancing to the music pouring from a few instruments in the corner.

The door were low enough to see over, and I didn't open it. I tucked my hat lower, looking round, feeling something tight in my chest. There were a ring of children in the center of all the dancers, doing a poor job of playing along and hopping to the right tune. I looked at the musicians—I knew Allan played a few instruments, but I didn't have a lick of an idea what they were.

There were three men and two women—one only half of a woman, bare more than twelve I reckoned—and none of them were Allan, bright and noisy and noticeable.

Just as I nodded to David to move on, the music stopped, one instrument at a time until something with strings played by the youngest one were the last thing playing and she stopped, embarrassed. The dancers all stopped slow, rippling out from one woman standing a few feet from the gate, staring at me.

I turned away, ducking from their attention. The last thing I wanted to do were ruin their fun.

"My—my lady, isn't it?" the woman said before I'd full gone.

Pausing on the street, I didn't turn back.

"I was next," she said soft. Everything else were quiet, so I heard it.

Turning back, I looked at her. Three children in different sizes—and like enough to the young one with the strings that I reckoned she were hers too—crowded near her skirts. Her mouth twisted down like she were 'bout to cry. I remembered her, kneeling in the street, like a thing. Like she weren't a person, a mother, a wife. Like all there were to know about her were crimes that weren't her fault.

"Come," she told me. She came forward, opening the door and holding her hand out. "You must come in. What's making you run these streets?" she asked.

I stepped forward, coming closer slow and halting. "My friend," I said. "I'm looking for my friend."

She took my hand. Hers were rough and worn, a good kind of a hand. A hand that had worked its whole life. "Who's this friend?" she said. She nodded toward the others. "We know everyone in Oxford. We'll find him for you."

She brought me to a bench in the corner of the small courtyard and I sat.

"Allan a Dale," David said for me. "He's a—well, he's many things, but I think minstrel is the most of them. Favors a red hat."

"I know Allan," a boy round my own age piped up. "Saw him not long 'go neither."

She pointed to the door. "Fetch him, would you?"

He nodded and dashed out the door, two of his lanky fellows following behind.

"Now come," my new friend said. "You need your strength. I can't send you off again without a full meal and a good song." She waved her hands like a wizard at the others, and they went to do her bidding.

Her daughter started to play again, alone for a start. Her strings made sweet notes that were made just for this moment, a breath of joy in a lifetime of hardship. The others joined in, and the sound grew full and round.

They brought me a trencher of meat and bread with a hunk of butter and hot, roasted potatoes. I started to eat slow, and she chattered while I did, telling me about her family, six children in all. She introduced them all to me, except for Emily, the one playing, and Roger, one of the boys that had run off to fetch Allan. She told me about their life—her husband were a dyer and she helped him and made a bit more on the side with washing, and Emily could get some work playing here and again. They usually made it by, but the taxes cut too deep. It were too much and they didn't have the money.

"Lordship's not usually so bad," she told me soft. "We were petitioning him for something—more time, less money, something. And that prince came in right when we were doing it. He had his guards catch us all, and the next morning, there we were. The prince didn't even come to watch his handiwork."

"He watched," I told her. "Somewhere. I'm sure he didn't want to be seen, but he couldn't have come near so quick when he saw me if he weren't."

"He hates you," she said.

I nodded. "He does."

"Mum!" yelled Roger, and he kicked the door open and twisted in, one of two boys carrying Allan with his arms strung round their necks. I stood, and David leapt over to them, taking Allan.

Allan's head lolled forward, and he realized it were David holding him, and he leered up at him. He started to salute and David's lip curled. He let Allan fall.

"Christ on a cricket," Allan garbled, rolling slow in the courtyard. He saw me, rolling to sit up. "Lady thief!" he cried. "Heard they—" He laughed drunken. "Tried to whip you into shape!"

David punched him across the face.

Allan dropped like a sack of potatoes.

I crossed my arms. "Was that necessary?"

"I won't tolerate an insult to your person," David told me, straightening his tunic. "But no. That was more for my enjoyment."

"Well, now you have to carry him, you know," I told David.

He raised a grim eyebrow to me. "Worth it."

With a sigh, I thanked everyone for their help, and stood as David hauled Allan over his shoulder.

"Wait—" the woman said to me. I didn't know her name, and having heard the names of each of her children, I weren't sure if I could ask now. Like I should know her already. She drew a breath, looking at me. "Is he coming back?"

Everyone were quiet, looking at me.

"Oxford is his vassal," I told her. "He has a right to be back here."

"You will stay, then?" someone else asked.

My breath hitched. "I can't. I don't have the right to be here."

"But what will happen to us? What's to prevent him from starting back up tomorrow?"

"I don't know," I admitted. "Oxford—he'll be better."

Roger nodded to me. "We'll be better, m'lady. I won't let him hurt anyone anymore. Even if I have to wear a hood and learn the bow to do it."

There were shouts and grunts, all agreeing with the boy.

They'd be killed if they fought back. He were a boy—a young boy, not trained in hardship the way Rob and Much and John and I had been. He still had a heart, and he'd lose it.

But if they did nothing, they'd be whipped, and taxed, and broken.

I shook my head, stepping back from them. "I can't," I told them. "I can't tell you what to do. What choices to make."

Roger's mother put her hands on his shoulders. "You've shown us all we needed to know, my lady. Thank you."

CHAPTER THIRTEEN

The next morning I went to Allan's room and opened the door, finding David already in there, rumpled and mussed, sitting in a chair and staring at Allan. He started to stand when he saw me, and I shook my head.

David eased back with a sigh.

"How is he?"

David's shoulder lifted. "Well enough, I think." He leaned forward and slapped Allan's exposed cheek. "Wake up, you lousy drunk," he growled.

Allan jerked and looked at David with a sleepy smile, then turned and saw me. "Just the lady I wanted to see."

I snorted. "I'm certain." I came forward and sat at the end of his bed, careful not to jostle my back. "I'm hoping it's to tell me that you didn't get stone drunk with no reason and there's some plot in all this."

He sat up full with a groan. "Christ Almighty, Lord, I don't deserve such a pain in my head." He touched his face and then his eye, wincing. "And I think I've been beset by ruffians."

"That was me," David grunted. Allan looked wounded. "You had the audacity to make light of how *he* injured her," David seethed.

Allan's face dropped. "My lady, I didn't—"

I waved my hand. "I'm hardly concerned with drunken prattle, Allan. But I still believe there's a method to your particular idiocy, so tell me now if I'm wrong."

He rubbed the uninjured half of his face. "There's a reason for sure, my lady. I've learned well that men are never so unguarded as when they think there's a drunkard around. I caught a string of gossip, and I followed that thread as far as I could."

David seemed even more angry by this. "So you-you-you *drink* to find information?" he sputtered. "That makes no damn sense—you don't even remember me punching you. How can you remember anything else?"

Allan's eyebrow lifted. "It's a hard line to walk, to be sure, but someone has to do it." He leaned toward David, his eyes narrowing. "And you'd be damn surprised what I remember, sir."

David shook his head, standing and going to the wall, farther from Allan.

"Information, Allan," I reminded. "If you two wouldn't mind keeping your antics till later?"

Allan sighed. "I can't confirm it—I was in the middle of doing just that, but I was quite rudely interrupted. But if it's true, it's bad. It's exceptionally bad."

I waited.

"One of the lords loyal to the prince—he was with him at Nottingham, my lady, and if I remember he wasn't particularly fond of you."

"Who?" I asked.

"De Clare, the heir to the Earldom of Hertford. He and the prince have been thick as thieves since Gisbourne's death, and he started mouthing off when a barmaid wouldn't have him. He said that within the year, he'd be the right hand of the king—of the new king."

I frowned. "That's hardly news, Allan."

Allan looked at me. "I know. Someone praised you—the daughter of the king—at that, and he laughed. He said Richard wouldn't come home and you would be shown your place. Someone challenged this, and he said there are ways to kill a person without ever laying a finger on them. He said all you have to do is murder their heart."

I sat back, my chest tight.

"What the hell does that mean?" David said. "That doesn't even make sense."

"We have to go," I whispered.

David looked to me.

My shoulders twisted up. "He doesn't mean me. He means Nottingham. He means Rob," I said, and my voice broke to say his name.

"I feared the same, my lady," Allan said low.

"We're still days away," I said. "We have to leave now."

David stood. "Yes, my lady."

—‿—

I gathered my things as fast as I could, making half excuses to D'Oyly and Essex. We rode all night, and I weren't sure I were breathing the whole way there, or blinking, or had blood rushing through my veins. I were terrified of what would be at the end of this road, and strangely I were eager to meet it as fast as I could.

We stopped only for the sake of the horses, and when we dismounted to let them rest and drink, I were shaking. David and Allan were watching me close as we ate and drank and let the horses do the same, but they didn't question me. There weren't nothing to say if they did.

I opened my saddlebag, my fingers shaking as I pulled out the now creased and crumpled letters that I hadn't the will to open. SCARLET, 132.

My heart strummed loud through my veins as I touched it, the thought of opening it—of being with him in some small measure—thrilling through my blood.

I pushed it back inside. Not yet. I couldn't do it yet. Especially not if there were some chance he weren't alive in Nottingham to be found.

We smelled it long before we arrived. It were like the time we near lost Major Oak; even if the burning were through, it hung in the air, resting like ghostly fingers around the trees, the brush, anything it could hold on to.

Smoke.

The cloud of it were hanging in the air like a canopy, and it made my eyes sting and water. We rode forward, slowing as we neared the gates of Nottingham. David called my name and mimicked using his cloak to cover his mouth. I copied him.

The city gate were open, unguarded.

My heart hammered in my throat as we went slow into the bounds of the city. Nearest to the road, the houses and shacks that crowded to be counted in the walls were heaps of charred black.

Burned.

Prince John brought fire to my city.

There were a body in the ditch off the edge of the road. It were a woman, her dress and skin burned, her twisted, blackened hand covering her face.

I turned my face from her, looking up at the castle though I could bare see it in the smoke. My eyes stung fierce, and I let tears fall like they could soothe the pain in my eyes, but it didn't help.

Rob couldn't be alive. He wouldn't have let this happen without a fight, and if there had been enough men to burn a city, Rob wouldn't have been able to fight them. Alone. Without me by his side, where I were meant to be.

The fires weren't bare smoking now, almost out. The city must have been razed days before.

I knew I should have stopped, gone through the city and looked for survivors, for people I could help.

I went to the castle. I couldn't help myself. If he were killed, God only knew what Prince John would have done with the body.

The portcullis were raised, the gate open. I heard a noise, something I'd heard before and couldn't place, a strange, slow creaking.

It weren't till I were right beneath the gate that I could see through the smoke, and a low knock drew my eyes up.

The pair of boots hit the stone wall again, and then I heard the creaking of the rope that held them as the body twisted in the wind.

Bodies. At least five that I could see, hung over the outer wall of the castle and left to die, left to watch as the city burned.

Robin. Robin. Robin. It were all I could think as I dropped from my horse, running into the guardroom at the gate and searching for the staircase up to the parapet. I were shaking so hard I slipped twice when I tried to climb the stairs, like I couldn't make my wayward limbs obey. Like my hands and legs didn't want to bear me up, not if I were going to see his face hanging off the battlements.

I found the first rope and I half leapt off the wall, grabbing as low as I could and heaving up. The rope didn't move and the edge of the wall cut hard into my stomach. Anchoring my feet, I pulled my whole body back, pulling as hard as I could.

Dead weight. The true, horrible meaning of that struck me, and I felt tears run fast down my cheeks. I jerked hard on the rope and it fought against me, dragging from my hands and tearing my skin with it. I cried out, looking at the raw, bloody mess.

"Damn you," I grunted, setting back at the rope. "Damn you, God. This is *your* fault. You were meant to protect them. You were meant to protect *him*," I accused. The body moved the barest inch, and I planted my feet against the wall itself, heaving back.

Cold touched my neck, and I looked to the side, to see a tall man in a gray cloak pointing a sword at me. "Drop the rope," he ordered.

"The hell I will," I snapped back.

"You will not steal from their bodies," he growled, pushing the sword against my throat. I felt a trickle of wet run down my skin. "How dare you *touch* them."

"You have no idea what I dare. And this isn't a day that should see any more violence. Who are you?"

"My—" David called, cresting the stairs. He drew his sword quick. "Step away from her immediately, young man."

The man looked at me. "Her who? *Her*?" he asked, confused, jerking his head at me.

"David, please help me pull him up," I begged.

The man with the sword faltered. "Put it away," David growled at him.

The man obeyed, confused. David took the rope, shouldering me off gentle. "Let go, my lady," he whispered.

I did. David saw the blood on the rope and looked at my hands. "Pull him up, David. Please."

He turned back to his task, nodding. In a few short heaves of his long arms, David had the body up at the wall. I let out a tortured gasp—it weren't Rob.

Allan came up as David pulled him over the battlements, and I cut the rope, crossing the man's arms and pulling the noose from his neck as David went to the next one. Allan skirted past the body without words to help David.

"You're just—pulling them up?" the man asked.

"No one deserves this," I whispered to him.

The man went to the third rope and started pulling. "I know," he said to me. "That's what I came here for. To bring the bodies back."

The second one came into a view. It were a woman, and even though it weren't Rob, my heart still broke, and I started crying helpless over the bodies.

The third were a boy, so young I thought for a moment it were one of the Clarkes. When I cleaned off his smoke-sooted face, I didn't know it, and still I cried. It would have been easy for it to be Ben or Will or Jack.

"Rylan!" a voice called. My body ran still, my blood frozen in my veins.

Steps were loud on the staircase.

"Rylan, how—"

Rob's face appeared above the stair, and his eyes met mine like they were tied together, like there weren't anywhere to look but at each other.

He stepped up one more stair, blood draining fast from his face.

His chest heaved with sudden breath, and he looked at David and Allan and the man, who must have been Rylan. "No," he breathed. "You're not—is this—I'm not—"

"Robin," I said, and it came out a horrible, broken sob.

Half a breath later he had my elbows in his hands, dragging me up. His fingers were on my face, dirty with tears and smoke, and I dug my fingers into his shirt, trying to sink some part of me into him so deep we couldn't be taken apart again. His shirt caught the drying blood on my hands and I saw it there, bright on his clothes, blood that I put there. I couldn't stop crying.

Until he pushed my tears off and pressed my mouth to his. I heard Rylan murmur "*Oh*" behind us and didn't pay attention.

Rob were alive. Rob were alive, and I were home.

Whatever that meant in true.

Rob's arms shifted to hold me round my back, fortressing round me and pulling me tight to him. Our kiss broke and our foreheads pushed together, and then our cheeks, every little motion like a physical proof the other were there. When my forehead slipped into the bit where his neck met his shoulder, a shudder ripped through me.

"You're alive," I breathed against him.

His arms squeezed tighter. "I'm not the one who was meant to be dead."

I curled tighter. "This was meant to kill you, Rob."

"I know," he said. "And it didn't work. And you're not dead." He nudged my head up and kissed me again, then stared at my face. "Jesus, Scarlet," he whispered.

David and Allan pulled the last body over the edge, and I cringed.

"We should go," Rob said. "Rylan, I'm going to send Godfrey to help you. Get the bodies back as soon as you can."

"Yes, Sheriff."

Rob captured my hand and went to kiss it, but I hissed and he flipped it to see the burns and cuts from the rope. "Come. I'll bring you back to the forest."

I shook my head. "Rob, we came to help. Let us help."

He sighed. "Things are still burning. It looks like rain tonight, though. Hopefully by morning much of the smoke will clear, and the fire will be gone. Until then—we just came back to get the bodies today," he said soft.

I nodded.

"Here," he said, producing two leather gloves from his pocket. I winced as he tugged them down over my hands, but once covered, it hurt less, even in the caverns of gloves meant for hands like Rob's.

"Better?" he asked.

Pushing his forehead against mine, I twisted my hand in his until they clasped together like two pieces meant to fit.

He kissed me again.

Rob led us silent out of the castle, and David, Allan, and I mounted our horses. Rob glanced at the cart in the lane, being piled slow with bodies, and back at me.

I gave him a small smile. "You seem in need of a horse, my lord Sheriff."

He came close and I offered him my arm. He stepped in the stirrup and swung up behind me, holding my hips and sliding close against me, razing heat all along my skin. He wrapped his arms around me, and I leaned back a little, covering his hand that held onto me. I felt our hearts meet and match, finding the beat that they had in common and settle into it.

"My love," he whispered, putting his head on my shoulder.

I nodded against his head, and spurred the horse.

CHAPTER

FOURTEEN

Edwinstowe were abandoned. The houses were untouched, but there were a stillness that were absurd for the small working village. There were no animals in the pens, no children running 'cross the lane, no women creaking water from the well.

We rode through and into the forest.

The fresh hope of spring caught me up in its arms the moment we entered Sherwood. The trees were full and bright, sweet with sap and fir and pine. Weeds and grass and patches of wildflowers had shot up through the ground like they could pierce through the brush and clear away the death of winter.

We went to the caves. We'd stayed in one of the largest ones for many winters until the snows got too deep, and even on the nights when heavy rains forced us out of our tree-bound home. We rode up over the bank that protected the low, hidden clearing where several caves opened their wide mouths, and everyone froze.

Hundreds. Hundreds of people, easily all of Edwinstowe, and most of Nottingham and Worksop besides.

"You saved them all," I whispered.

Rob's hand clutched mine tight. "Not all. Not nearly all."

My heart stuttered. "Much?" I asked. "Bess?"

"Scarlet!"

I turned to see Much, very much alive. I swung off the horse before Rob could let me down, running down the hill to get to him. He laughed and caught me up in a fierce hug.

I pulled away from him to look at him in full. He were taller still, tall as Rob now, and he looked older in a way I didn't like. Sadder. Like he knew the sad things of the world.

Which, of course, he did now. We all did.

People started crowding round me. The Clarkes, the Morgan girls, the Percy family, everyone I'd known for years. Touching me, like all of the sudden they thought well of me. Like they'd missed me. It jumbled inside of me, with hurt and confusion and wonder that maybe that were the way of it—maybe they missed me. Maybe they loved me.

Allan set right about greeting the people he knew, and David waited for me to introduce him round, with a stern frown at Rob, who were still holding me close to him.

Robin were there, looking at me strange. People were all talking at once, and I felt so overtaken by all of it.

My people. They were my people now, in a way that had always been true but never so exact. I weren't this strange hero-thief that they misremembered. I were their lady now.

And they were hurt, and sad, and frightened.

"Will you tell us what happened?" David asked, coming into the clearing.

"Sit," Rob said over the din. "We can all eat together, and we'll tell you."

Rob took my hand and it felt like an anchor on rough seas. He tugged me toward the big cave; when we used to make this our shelter, we'd had one log chopped and laid out to sit on, and they'd brought more down so many more people could sit. It were near enough, and the children clumped together, bumping into one another, torn between playing or seeing what all the fuss were about. Their mothers sent them off to play. It were just as well. From the state of Nottingham, they didn't need to hear what had happened.

We sat on the log, and Rob let my hand go to sit, but I threaded my fingers back through his. His eyes met mine, shadowed but smiling.

His smile faded. "Prince John came through many days ago, and gave an urgent call for the knights of the shire to aid him in collecting the king's ransom. The knights went. Two days later, men on horseback came at dawn. Their only goal was destruction, and they made neat work of it." Rob's throat worked.

"Were they knights?" I asked.

"Yes and no," Rob said. "I'm fairly certain they were the same men, but they weren't wearing colors or armor. Our few remaining knights tried to keep them out of the gate. It didn't work, but it bought enough time, and people flooded to the castle, thinking I would be able to protect them there. The men started to burn the city, and then they came for the castle."

"He got people out through the tunnel," Much told me.

"The tunnel? I thought they blocked that," I said, looking at Rob.

He lifted a shoulder. "Not well. I opened it while I was sheriff."

My mouth tightened. Why would he have done that? I couldn't guess, but it felt like it had something to do with me. With me being away from him.

"He sent word to me," Much said. "And I got everyone from the villages to the forest before they could come for their homes too."

People squished closer to one another at this, like being close would prevent it from being true. Or maybe from happening again. Or both.

"Who were the people on the battlements?" David asked soft.

"Two of the knights that remained," Rob said. "The others were just people that didn't come to the castle fast enough." He shook his head, looking grim. "They just killed whoever they could get their hands on. Like life meant nothing to them."

"They didn't get their hands on many," said another voice, coming through the gathered people. "Thanks to you, Sheriff."

People moved aside to let Bess through, and I saw why. She were heavy with child, big and round and slow in the way she walked. Much stood, taking her hand and guiding her to him, and when she were close enough, he kissed her cheek. She gave him a gentle smile and sat down. He sat beside her, and she moved closer to him, leaning into his form.

Much's eyes closed for a moment, like it were a joy to have her close to him. And then they opened, and looked at me. "You remember Bess, Scar?"

Loosing Rob's hand, I stood and knelt by her so I could hug her. She touched my back to do it, and I stiffened but didn't pull away. "You look—you're . . ." I couldn't. I had no words to say to her, when all I could see when I looked at her were John, dead in the snow.

"I'm Bess Miller now," she told me. She fished a simple ring on a thread from around her neck with a smile. "I used to wear it on my finger but my fingers have gotten fat," she told me, holding her hand up like I could tell it were thicker. I couldn't.

Much took her hand, smiling at her, and it took me a breath to remember Miller were Much's family name. She were Much's wife. Much, who were bare a man. "Congratulations," I said, stunned.

She covered my hand with a watery smile. "Thank you, Scarlet."

"I'm sorry . . . I wish I had been here for the wedding," I said, looking to Much.

He shrugged, and his throat worked. "You were dead, Scarlet," he said. "Everyone said for months that you were. You're not, and that's more than I could have ever hoped for."

"We have had enough of death," Bess said. "Scarlet, please tell us *your* story. You cheated Death."

A stone settled inside my chest, and I could bare breathe around it. Cheated Death—no, I brought death straight to their doors.

"There's not much to tell," I said, shrugging and going back to Rob.

"Not much to tell!" Allan laughed. "I'll tell you her stories, if the lady won't. First, the prince stole her from the gaze of the queen mother, hiding her in prisons round the country. Then he ordered for her to be killed in true, and her valiant knight, Sir David, fought them off—and nearly got her killed in London, where I saved her from hordes of rioters!"

David scoffed and rolled his eyes.

"Why did he change his mind?" Rob asked, quiet, looking at me. "Why hide you one moment to kill you the next?"

"Prince John is going to try to prevent Richard from coming home," I whispered to him.

"What?" Rob asked, frowning.

"And then, determined to protect her father—"

"Enough, Allan," I said sharp. Everyone looked at me, and Allan looked hurt. "These aren't stories. This is my life. And I don't—I want—" My breath caught, and my hands curled tight on Rob. There were so many things to tell him, so many things I didn't want Allan to be the bearer of.

I found my breath wouldn't uncatch. I couldn't breathe, and I shook my head, standing. I leapt over the log and moved through the people. They let me go, stepping aside until I got into the deep, empty woods, and I couldn't hear people around me. I kept going, not knowing where I were headed.

"Scarlet!" Rob called, surprising close. I halted, and his heat touched me before his hands did, warm on my waist. "Scarlet," he said soft. "Where are you running to?"

I turned to him. "I'm not running. I'm walking. And I just . . . I just . . ."

"Needed to get away from us," he finished. "From me." He didn't sound angry. He sounded like he knew what I meant. Worse, he sounded hurt, and his eyes told the same.

"Those stories aren't meant to be told," I said, shaking my head. "Not like that. Not like I'm some damn hero for murdering people. Not like I cheat Death when all I do is bring it down on the heads of others." I put my hands on his chest, looking at them. "The thought of you, Rob—it was all that got me through. That got me back here. I'd never run from you."

His head pressed against mine. "You're alive. You're here. That's all that matters now."

"Is it?" I whispered.

"Yes."

"A lot has happened," I told him.

"Nottingham burned," he whispered to me, his voice rough. "Nothing will be the same as it was yesterday. So whatever happened for us both, we'll get there." His hands slipped onto my back, pulling me closer to him, and his lips lightly pressed over mine, bolting me through with lightning. "Come back, and rest, and we will start again in the morning."

Nodding, I let him lead me back to the camp.

CHAPTER FIFTEEN

Rob were right—it started to rain not long after sundown, and the heavy pour felt like Thoresby Lake had swept up over me, pulling things off me. Memories. Feelings. Wounds and blood. I wanted it. I wanted the rain to take everything I were away from me and leave something else in its wake.

It forced all the people into the caves, and I went with the younger women, lying down on a stuffed pallet in an echoing room full of people.

I couldn't sleep. Not with so many thoughts turning in my head, so many people and thoughts keeping me awake. I snuck out of the caves once the rain stopped, only to mount my horse and take the precious secrets in the saddlebags with me.

I went to Huntingdon House. After Prince John declared Rob's father—the old Earl of Huntingdon—a traitor,

Richard had given the lands to John and though he rarely came to this house, there were servants who lived there to maintain the place and keep the farmlands running. The properties I now owned made a tidy profit, and in the next few months I'd be a wealthy woman once it all started coming to me.

Riding up to the house were fair strange. I'd been there once before as a girl, and I remembered the road leading to it, but not the house itself. I'd been young.

The road led to a gate, and I saw two guards there, playing dice between them, not expecting any kind of company. They saw me and frowned, coming away from their game. "Move along, sir. The keep isn't receiving visitors."

"Good," I said, dismounting. I fished in my saddlebag for the paper from my father, and it came out with SCARLET, 132. "This is my keep now. And I'm not a sir. I'm Lady Huntingdon." I handed one the letter of creation.

They both gawped at the official paper with its loose hanging seals. They looked to each other, and to me.

I got back on the horse. "Open the gate, please. And send word out to all Nottinghamshire knights that they are to return to their garrison immediately."

They obeyed.

Because I were a powerful lady now, and more than that, I were a princess. Like it or not, people would obey me now.

Servants hurried to prepare a room for me, to feed me, to offer their obeisance, and I sent them away, lying in a bed that didn't feel like mine, and tried to sleep.

—∾—

The next morning, I went to Nottingham early. I'd wrapped my hands, thick enough that the burns and cuts didn't bother me. I wore fresh clothes—slightly crumpled from my saddlebags—and tied my hair back, still looking every inch a boy. If the servants in the keep noticed, they didn't comment on it to me. I didn't want to be the sort of lady that were feared, but at the moment, silence were easier than trying to earn their love.

I rode my horse to the castle. The rain had cleared much of the haze, but now there were a new smell, like water and death mixed together and left to rot.

"My lady!" David called, seeing me in Nottingham. "Where have you been? We couldn't find you this morning, your horse—"

"Investigating my holdings in Nottingham," I told him. I saw Rob at a distance. "I don't—I have to find a way to tell Rob," I told him. "It has to be me, not you." I frowned. "Especially not Allan."

He nodded. "Of course, my lady."

"Thank you."

Everyone that had been in the forest came, even Bess, bare any help at all in her state. It didn't matter. This weren't about pitching in, it were about being solid. United. Bricked up together like a wall so they could feel for a second like this might not be done to them again.

Of course, I wouldn't let that happen. I could protect them now, like I should have before. I were Lady Huntingdon, and I answered only to the king. Prince John had no business here.

We started to tear down all the burned things that were wrecks. Wood that could be salvaged were separated from wood that couldn't be. Every few houses, we found another body that had been trapped. The third one we found were a child, a little boy. When his mother found him, she broke apart. She dropped to her knees and picked him up, holding the misshapen, small charred body against her. His body made a sound like something cracked, and she wailed this horrible keening sound.

Women went to her. Some knelt in the rubble of her ruined house, some crowded behind her. They reached out their hands to touch her and pass on their love.

"*Lully, lullay,*" one woman began to sing.

"*Lully, lullay,*" the others answered.

"*The falcon hath borne my make away,*" they sang together.

Men joined in. We all knew the song from Mass, but it made me tremble to hear it here, outside the walls God watched over.

Monks came forward too.

"*He bore him up, he bore him down. He bore him to an orchard brown,*" they sang.

"*In that orchard there was an hall*
That was hanged with purple and pall.

And in that hall there was a bed:
It was hanged with gold so red.

And in that bed there lay a knight,
His wounds bleeding by day and night.

By that bedside there kneeleth a maid,
And she weepeth both night and day.

And by that bedside there standeth a stone:
Corpus Christi written thereon."

As she continued to weep, slowly the voices got louder, covering her grief over and letting her cry in peace as the rest tried to bear her son's soul to God's hands.

I pushed tears off my face and turned away from them. I wanted to honor her grief, but my pain didn't belong here. Instead, I turned and went up to the castle.

My castle now.

Memories flickered behind my eyes. I remembered when Gisbourne dragged me back from the gate when the people had been rioting, when de Clare near cut the hand off a young girl. I remembered walking, slow and numb, from the snow-filled bailey where Gisbourne's body hung, where John bled bright red onto the white snow.

I remembered how my knees hurt, being made to kneel before the prince in the snow, on the stone cobbles.

I remembered rage and hate and pain and death.

And I felt so weary of them now. Of the pain that never ended, of the death that never stopped taking, of the rage that didn't help anyone.

The prison where I'd almost lost Rob. The hall we'd tumbled to the ground, where I'd married Gisbourne, where I'd first met Eleanor.

I went up to the room I'd shared with Gisbourne, but all I could see were the way he threatened me, slammed me against the wall, trying to raise my skirts, trying to force me. I couldn't even cross the threshold, and tears were starting in my eyes.

Refusing to let them fall, I went down to one of the low rooms, nearest to the prison. The last I'd been here, Rob had been living in these rooms, waiting to fight, taking the punishment that Prince John passed down and rising triumphant and unscathed, like something God himself had ordained. Like a phoenix.

And now the city were a pile of ash, and I would give my people a way to rise again. Somehow, they would be whole again.

I sat on the bed, letting the unwrapped fingertips of my hand skim slow over the pillow.

"There you are," Much said, coming through the doorway. He went to the window, looking out for a minute before hopping onto the sill, looking at me. "Saw you come up here."

I looked at him, seeing the changes again.

He chuckled. "You've gotten very surly, Scar." I made a face, and he considered. "Well, I suppose you've always been surly. You're just quieter now."

I took a breath, looking at him. "I haven't any idea what to say, Much. To anyone."

He nodded solemn. "I understand that."

"You and Bess?" I asked.

This made him smile. "Yes. I couldn't do that to John—let his baby be born out of wedlock. It were Rob or me, and I couldn't let Rob do it."

This struck like ice in my chest. "Rob wanted to," I said.

He shook his head, frowning at me. "Really, Scar? Of course he didn't want to. When will you believe that he loves you?"

"I believe it," I said, touching the bed again. "I just don't know what it means. I think him loving me will always make Prince John hate us both. I think it's hard to act for love when you know there can be consequences."

He shook his head again. "Consequences," he scoffed. "Our overlord just ordered our city burned, and we have to pay a tax so high to bring our king home that we can't eat. And without our king, that overlord will probably manage to be the new one, and then what? What is ever without consequences, Scar?"

I looked at him, helpless.

"Nothing," he answered. "So don't be a fool and cast stones into a path that isn't meant to have them. Love Rob. Be with Rob. Keep each other safe, and keep each other happy."

I looked at him. "Is that what you're doing with Bess?"

He looked so sad as soon as I said it. "Yes, but I'm the stupid one there. She loves John—she always will. And I love her. And unfortunately, the best I can do is protect her and raise John's baby and make sure no harm ever comes to them. That's the only way I can love her."

Reaching out, I took his hand in my wrapped-up paw. "You're kind of hard not to love, Much. You'll win her yet."

"Maybe," he said, but I could tell he didn't believe it. "But you need to see to Rob, Scar. He's the sheriff of a city that just got slaughtered. And more than that, for once, and I thank God for this, he didn't run into the fray like he always has. He didn't put his life at risk. He put the people first, before his sometimes misguided sense of heroism, before his need to defeat an enemy. And while it was the right thing to do, I can't imagine that was easy for him. And losing you—Christ, Scar, that has not been easy on him."

I shuddered.

He rubbed my arm. "And I'm sure it hasn't been easy for you either. So why don't you take the tiny amount of solace that God offers you and stop being stupid and just be in love with him?"

I nodded. He were right about that, at least. "You're always the best of us, Much."

"Now that I'm not the only cripple, I might start to believe you when you say things like that," he said, holding up my half hand in his.

"Come on," I told him. "People need to eat. Let's raid the kitchens."

He stood and pulled me up by my hand, and I smiled.

"Turning into quite the gentleman, Much."

He lifted a shoulder. "I do my best, m'lady."

I opened my mouth, ready to tell him—him, if anyone—about my title, about being Lady Huntingdon, but I stopped. I just wanted to be Scarlet a while longer.

"What?" he asked.

I shook my head. "Nothing. Come on."

—∾—

We brought food, and several women went back into the castle to cook more food. I tried cutting salted pork, but it were clumsy and awful with my hands wrapped up. Hissing in frustration, I froze when familiar arms came around me and covered my hands. "Want me to do that?"

I shut my eyes, leaning my head against his for a breath.

Rob's head leaned against mine. "We need to talk, Scarlet."

With a sigh, I nodded. "I know."

"Let me," he said, nudging me aside.

I moved, leaning my hip on the table to look at him still. I crossed my arms. "I bare know where to start, Rob."

"Start where you left," he said, lifting his eyes to mine. "When I saw you last."

I drew a breath. "Prince John sent my carriage away from the others. He hid me, imprisoning me in castle dungeons. I never knew where I was." I stopped, the word feeling strange on my tongue, here with Rob, where I thought my hen-picked way of talking were the real part of me.

His eyebrows lifted. "You're talking different."

I tightened my arms round myself. "It wasn't like I didn't know how to talk before. Eleanor made me practice—but that's a later part."

He nodded, waiting for me to continue.

"He moved me round, and then one night he told my guards to kill me. One tried, and David killed him to save me."

"David was one of your captors," he said dark.

I nodded. "But before he tried to kill me, Prince John said Richard wasn't coming back."

"Which is the only way he'd try such a thing," Rob said, cutting the pork hard. "Coward."

"I had to tell Eleanor," I told him. He nodded. "It took a few days to send word to her, but she met me at Winchester—"

"Winchester?" he asked. "You were with de Quincy?"

I nodded. "He did me a great service, sheltering me until the queen came."

He frowned. "Go on."

My eyes dropped. "From there, I went to Bristol," I said soft.

"Bristol?"

I nodded.

"What was in Bristol?"

I looked up at him, swallowing hard. "A ship. Bound for Ireland."

He stopped cutting, looking at the food.

My mouth were dry. "I thought—I thought maybe running from Prince John would keep you safe. Would keep me safe," I said, and he looked at me, his eyes hot and full of things I didn't know to name. "I thought I could leave, Rob, I thought I could forget you, and forget the person I've become because of you. I thought—I thought so many things."

His throat worked.

There were water filling in my eyes. "I couldn't," I told him. "I heard Eleanor were in trouble—*was* in trouble—and I knew I couldn't leave. Leaving doesn't keep you safe. Leaving doesn't do anything but keep us apart," I told him. "I know that—" I kept on, but he stopped me, tugging me into his arms. Slow and careful, he pushed the hair off my face and tipped my mouth up to kiss him.

I closed my eyes and the water fell, but it didn't matter, not when I were hidden in Rob's love.

"My lord Sheriff, step away," I heard, and Rob's mouth left mine so that we could both turn and see David, his sword half-drawn.

Rob glared at him. "Sir?" he asked.

"David, what are you doing?" I demanded.

"My lady, I cannot allow him to dishonor you in such a way! The queen mother—the *king!*—would demand my life for less."

There were giggles around us, but David were fair serious.

"He may already demand your life for keeping his daughter captive," Rob snapped.

David's face went pale, but he didn't move or relent.

"She is—" he started, and my eyes went wide. "A lady of the court," he finished, nodding a touch to me. "The daughter of a king. You will not put your hands on her in such a manner."

Rob let me go, but he were still glaring at David. "She's my betrothed, sir."

"I am?" I asked.

"Then you should be more mindful of her reputation."

Rob crossed his arms.

"Oh, for Heaven's sake, what reputation do I have left?" I asked them. "I fell to my knees in the house of God covered with the blood of several men, and yet I'm not meant to kiss the man I have always loved?" I demanded.

Rob looked at me. "When did that happen?" he asked, turning to me—but still keeping his big, strong arms that I very much liked crossed round *me* crossed over his chest.

David sheathed his sword in full. "When the queen mother was attacked," he said. "My lady defended her valiantly."

And then I found I were Lady Huntingdon, I tried in my head. It were the most important thing to tell him.

"Was that part of Prince John's plot against Richard—to steal the ransom money? I can't believe he'd attack his own mother—though I suppose that would put suspicion off him."

I shook my head. "No—they were vagabonds seizing an opportunity. Well, I believe so, at least. I believe Prince John will steal the money, but he'll wait until it has all been gathered. He can't do much without a very expensive army."

Rob glanced at me. "And the nobles. His only power is that which they grant him."

My mouth opened to tell him I were one of those nobles, more than he knew, but I said, "And then we made our way up here. And he—he found me in Oxford," I told him soft, looking round to make sure there weren't others listening to me.

"Prince John?" he asked, leaning to me.

I nodded.

His hand gripped the cutting knife. "What did he do?"

I shook my head, putting my hand on his. "Nothing, Rob."

Rob looked at David. "He wanted to hurt her," David said grave. "But no one would watch him do it. And she herself turned him away."

The tears were in my eyes again. "Which is why he came here," I whispered. "He must have left me and come straight to do this. To kill you. To kill our people."

He looked full at me. "He didn't get me, Scarlet. And this wasn't something he did because of you. He did it because he's a vindictive, evil man. It wasn't something you could have stopped, my love. Not ever."

My shoulders raised up. "Your turn," I told him. "Tell me what's happened here since I left."

He nodded, but looked at the food. "Come," he said. "Let's get everyone fed, and maybe we can steal a moment to speak." He glanced at David. "Alone."

David frowned.

CHAPTER SIXTEEN

Rob and I worked with the rest of the people of Nottinghamshire until well after dark. Within a few hours we weren't finding any more bodies, which were a relief.

Rob opened the castle to anyone without a home to return to, and we brought as many blankets and pallets as could be found and stuffed to the Great Hall, feeding everyone what we could. It were strange listening to Rob give orders. He'd grown comfortable as the sheriff. He were born to it.

And I didn't tell him that those orders were now mine to give. I liked listening to him do it, confident in himself and his role.

I were sitting with Bess and some girl she knew, playing with the other woman's daughter, a sure-footed tot named Molly. The girl stomped around us with glee, reveling in her newfound ability to walk, and Bess tensed, hissing breath out over her teeth.

"Bess?" I asked, lurching forward.

The pain passed, and she laughed. "Just a rather hard kick," she said. "I swear, he's stronger than his father."

"He?" I asked.

Her shoulders lifted. "I don't really know. Some days all I wish for is a little boy, with John's eyes and shoulders, and every day he grows, it will be a little less like John died," she said, her voice hushing on the last word. "Then other days, that sounds like torture. And I hope for a girl."

Her friend squeezed her hand.

"Much wants a girl," she said, sniffing. "He'll be thrilled, either way, but he wants a girl. Some days—I know he looks at you lot, and wonders how he can be a good enough man if he's not like John, or Robin Hood. And that's not fair," she said, wiping a sudden tear from her eye. "It's not. He's a wonderful man all on his own."

I nodded. "He is."

She nodded hard. "Good. You tell him that, will you? He loves you."

"I will," I promised. "Come—you should rest, and I won't let you sleep on the floor in your state."

She nodded again, wiping away more tears, and her friend and I both conspired to pull her up gentle. I went and found an empty room—though a boy came in and I kicked him out, so maybe the chamber hadn't been very empty—and even with my awkward hands, I untied her dress and served as her maid to change her for bed.

"Thank you," she said when I were done.

I nodded, my mouth opening. I frowned, not sure how to say the words. "I'm sorry, Bess," I managed. "I'm so sorry. I got him killed."

Her shoulders jumped a little. "On my worst days, Scarlet, I blamed you. And Robin, and Much. Everyone there. But it's not your fault. Prince John killed him. That's all." Some pain came to her again, and I eased her onto the bed. "I'm just lucky he didn't take Much this time around. It was him that burned the city, wasn't it?" she asked.

"Yes," I said. "I doubt we'll be able to prove that, but I know it was."

"That's what I thought. So now . . . now I just pray he won't have the chance to hurt my baby, Scar."

Unsure, I touched my fingertips to her belly, and she pressed them there. I felt something move, and I shut my eyes. "No one will hurt that baby, Bess. I promise."

Tears leaked out the side of her eyes. "Is that a promise you can keep?" she whispered.

I nodded. "Yes." I tried to smile. "If nothing else, John will haunt me all my days if I don't."

She gave a tiny half laugh and nodded. "Will you tell Much where I am?" she asked.

"I will," I said.

She relaxed onto the pillow, as much as she could in such a state, and I left her, closing my eyes. God, I prayed that were a promise I could keep.

—⁓—

I found Much and told him, and he quit the hall in a breath, telling me Rob had gone down to the treasury. Smiling after him, I went down there. It weren't much—just a heavily locked room deep in the rock the castle had been built on. But the door were in splinters on the ground and the room were empty, not including Rob, sitting in a chair. The other chair and the table were broken too.

He had a coin in his hand, and he were staring at it, looking just as broken as the table.

"Rob?" I called.

He looked up. He drew a deep breath and held up the coin. "All that's left," he said. "All the county's money. All the tax for the ransom. This is it." He flipped it and caught it. "You asked me what's happened here since you left, and it has been the hardest thing I've ever done. Being the sheriff, imposing a tax that breaks my people even though I want my king home more than most—these months have been brutal. I've never felt so responsible, so aware of the sacrifice I'm asking them to make. And while I was trying to keep everyone alive, they came and stole our money. The people will be dead anyway, and I'm just a fool."

"You're not a fool, Rob."

He shook his head, looking down, leaning over his knees. He were broken. "It doesn't matter if I am or I'm not; the people don't have the money left. They'll starve as it is." He held up the coin again. "This is all that stands between us and Prince John, Scarlet. Our overlord just stole our damn money so he can beat us within an inch of our lives."

"Not our overlord," I told him, looking at the splinters on the floor.

"What did you say?" he asked.

"Prince John isn't our overlord anymore," I told him.

I looked up at him. Our eyes met, and held, and I didn't know if I could say the words.

"I am. I'm the Lady—" I faltered, looking down again. "Of Huntingdon."

"But you can't be," he said, and he sounded so confused it hurt. "Richard would have had to . . ." He trailed off, and I looked up, still hugged against the door, nervous to come into the room full. "And Eleanor would have asked him to do it the moment Prince John imprisoned you. Hell, she probably wrote to him from Nottingham."

"Rob," I said, coming forward.

He stood up before I got to him, and picked up the chair he'd sat on and heaved it against the wall, shattering it.

I jumped back. "Rob!" I yelled.

"Dammit, Scarlet!" Rob yelled back. "All this does is place *you* squarely in his sights. Now *you're* the one who won't pay the tax. You think he won't bury you for that?"

"I think he will try to kill me just about every which way he can," I snapped back at him. "With or without a title. The only thing it changes is that maybe, if we have enough alliances, we can stop him. We can be more powerful than he is."

His jaw worked, muscles twisting and bumping out, and he shook his head. He walked close to me, and I watched him, wary. He touched my cheek, and his lips pressed against mine, almost dry. I tilted my head, and he kissed me better, deeper, but he didn't touch me anywhere else. I raised my arms to put them around him, but he broke the kiss and stepped away from me. "Good night, Scar."

Frowning, I watched him walk away from me.

—∾—

I went to the Great Hall to sleep with the others, but Rob weren't there, and it weren't easy. Everywhere around me, I saw the death and pain that had brought us to this point.

I saw Ravenna, soaked in her own blood on the dais. I saw Rob in a gibbet. I saw Gisbourne and Prince John and the ridiculous excess of the feasts at Christmas that led these people to starvation now.

It were the dead of the night when I woke up, going out to the courtyard. It were a warm spring night with bare any breeze, and I crossed the way, going to the spot by the bailey that I remembered too well.

Someone had pried up the rocks that had been darkened with blood, and now the rocks there were too bright, a pale gray compared to the darker ones around them. Mismatched.

I stood there, looking at the place where John had died, until my legs started to sway, and I went back inside to sleep until the sun rose.

—∾—

"My lady," David called, shaking my shoulder. "My lady?"

Allan started playing some music damn close to my ear, and I frowned, opening my eyes. "Christ, Allan, stop that," I snapped, putting my hands on the strings. I glanced around at the other, still-sleeping forms on the floor. "People are trying to sleep."

"My lady, the Earl of Winchester is here," David told me. "We thought you should greet him."

"David thought," Allan corrected.

"Yes, no one would accuse *you* of thinking, would they?" David drawled.

I sat up. "Very well. Where's Rob?"

"Just left for the gates. He didn't want us to wake you."

I frowned at that, and stood.

Running quick for the city gates, I caught up with Rob as Winchester and a small company of knights came through. He and Winchester shook hands, and they both stared at each other with solemn faces. He turned, and I saw Essex behind him.

Christ. It were like three men all practicing how to scowl together.

Coming closer, I tried to straighten myself. I were still dressed like a man, not quite looking the lady. For Winchester and Rob I didn't think it mattered much, but I were still fair sure Essex didn't like me.

"Your Grace," Essex said, sighting me first and bowing. Winchester followed suit, and Rob looked at me like he didn't know me anymore. After a moment, he bowed too, and it stung.

"My lords," I said, dipping to them, which I'm sure looked fair foolish in breeches.

"We couldn't spare many men from the queen," Winchester said, looking between me and Rob, "but I brought what I could. And Essex volunteered to help." Winchester clapped Essex on the shoulder, and Essex looked stern at this.

"I wrote to Winchester for aid," Rob explained. His throat worked. "After they burned the city. Before . . . everything."

Winchester's eyes darted between us. "And we have knights to help you recover. As I said, not many, but surely any hands will help."

Rob's mouth tightened, and he looked at me.

Because I were the noble now. I were the one in power, not him. "Thank you," I told them. "Any help is needed. I'm still waiting for the Nottinghamshire knights to return from the prince's company."

Winchester grimaced. "That won't go over well."

I lifted my shoulders. "Little does."

"I was sorry to see you leave Oxford so quickly," Essex said to me. "I hope your wound is much improved."

Rob's eyes cut sharp to me at this, and he crossed his arms.

"Yes," I said flat. "Thank you. Come along, we will feed you and get to work," I said.

They nodded, leading their men into Nottingham. I went toward Rob, but he turned to Essex and began speaking with him.

Winchester offered me his arm with a gentle smile. "My lady," he said, dashing his head.

I took it, though I felt silly. "Your aid is very much appreciated," I told him.

He shook his head as we started to walk up to the castle. "Think nothing of it," he told me. He lifted a shoulder. "Besides, the queen told me to alert you that she will come as soon as she can. I figured it was an excellent way for me to see Margaret again."

This made me smile. "Why haven't you married her already? You're an earl; surely her father would agree. And you both are absolutely terrible at hiding it."

He grinned like a child. "I know. She has asked me not to ask for her hand until her brother returns from war. She believes—correctly, as I understand it—that her father would certainly agree, and press for a quick marriage as well. She doesn't want to be married without her brother, if she can avoid it. And I confess, I would do just about anything she asks."

I looked at Rob. "You're a very good man, Winchester."

He smiled at me, but we began walking through the worst of the city, and his smile left him. "This is Prince John's handiwork?" he asked.

"Not that he will admit it, but yes."

His throat worked, and we were quiet for the rest of the walk.

CHAPTER SEVENTEEN

That afternoon, the knights were making fast work in the city, and Winchester, Rob, Much, and I talked about what to do about the tax.

"We can't tell them," Much said. "It will break the people after all that they've lost."

"They won't be surprised," Rob said. "We had barely a quarter of the amount we were called for. But that's all the people had, and now that's gone too."

"I would give it to you," Winchester said, "but not even I have the kind of coin you're talking about. Not after covering for the people of mine that couldn't pay. It took everything I had."

"I'll sell my property," I said.

Much frowned. "Leaford? But then you'd be putting people out of jobs and robbing yourself of any income that comes in. Not to mention that I think the Lord and Lady Leaford would have a few concerns about that, which even if they aren't actually your parents, I would think you'd consider. And set all of that aside, no one has the kind of money to buy something like that. No one."

"She's not Lady Leaford anymore," Rob said sharp. "She's Huntingdon. She has all the Huntingdon lands, Much."

Much blinked, looking between us. "Oh."

"Maybe Eleanor will help," I said. "She'll stop here on her tour."

"Marian, she'll have already put every spare cent she has to bring Richard home," Winchester reminded me.

I sighed, leaning on the edge of a table. "It was much easier when we could just steal things," I said.

"No one left to steal from," Rob reminded. He raised his eyebrow in my direction, and I frowned.

"Sheriff!" a page yelled. I turned to see Will Clarke run into the room in the garb the castle servants wore.

"Yes, Will?" Rob asked.

"The prince is coming, Sheriff! He sent word that he's returning Nottingham's knights."

"Get everyone into the castle," Rob ordered. "Immediately. Will, start spreading the word. Winchester, take half your knights to the city gate and have the rest guard the castle. Tell Essex the same. Much, go out to the towns and warn them."

Much and Will left, but Winchester hung back. "You're the only one with the power to send him away, Marian," he said.

"I know. And I will. He has no right to be here."

"Whatever you do," Rob warned me, "keeping you safe is the most important thing now. If anything happens to you, he can lay claim to the shire again."

I raised my chin. "Then don't let anything happen to me."

"Don't ask that from me, Scar, unless you mean it," Rob told me, his eyes dark.

I drew a slow breath, looking at him. Wondering if my being a noblewoman would mean constantly putting him back in this place.

"No one will let her be harmed," Winchester said, nodding at Rob.

Rob nodded once at me.

—~—

The city gate weren't near as well fortified as the castle, but if Prince John were ever to transgress against us, we'd make it hard as we could. We shut and locked the city gates and Winchester and I sat mounted on horses, the knights around us. Rob were on the city wall behind me, an arrow in hand, true to his promise to keep me safe. I even wore a dress for the occasion, taken from my old things, which Rob had fetched out of the room for me.

I wanted to look every inch a formidable lady like his mother when I faced down Prince John.

Because of the rain there weren't much dust to rise, and we just felt the trembling in the ground as Prince John rounded the bend with a legion of Nottinghamshire knights. I held my breath, and a breeze kicked up, flapping my cloak to the side.

Prince John signaled his men—*my* men—to halt, riding a few paces up. My stomach curled hard when I saw his companion—de Clare, the cruel bully who'd taken great joy in hurting me the winter before.

But it were spring now, and this were my castle and my shire and for the first time in my life, I had the right to defend those things.

"Lady Huntingdon," de Clare greeted me with an oily smile.

"My lord Prince," I said, clear and loud over the quieting roar of horses' hooves. "Welcome to Nottinghamshire."

"Lady Huntingdon," he said, glaring at me with a sick, pleased smile. "Winchester, Essex," he said, nodding to each. "Marian, don't you just have a stable of men about?"

"Earls," I corrected, lifting my eyebrows. "And yes, I've found the nobility to be most supportive of my new role."

"Oh, yes, I'm sure an unmarried woman with a significant amount of land would become very popular," Prince John sneered.

"And a widow at that," de Clare said, his eyes skipping over me. "No need to be concerned with maiden honor."

There weren't a sound.

Prince John chuckled. "Well. I've heard you had trouble here," he said, all innocent. "I heard the town was sacked."

I glanced round. The gates were shut and unharmed; you couldn't see the burned town beyond. "No. You must have been misinformed."

He sniffed. "I can still smell smoke."

Smiling, I glanced at Rob. "We had a feast and a bonfire to celebrate my creation. It was quite the affair."

His smile grew more tense, widening to show his teeth. "My mother thinks she's very clever too, Marian, but she ended up in a tower for sixteen years for annoying my father with her willful mouth. You would do well to remember there are punishments for even the highest of the nobility."

I drew in a breath to speak, but Winchester were faster. "Before you dare to speak of punishment to her, I suggest you look to your own actions and wonder what the king might have in store for you when he returns. Besides, you may be a prince, but with the loss of the Nottingham lands, your holdings are less than hers—and, I would remind you, mine."

The prince lowered his gaze like a dog, glaring at Winchester and baring his teeth. "Those are bold words, Winchester."

"Bold, perhaps," Essex said. "But true."

The prince sniffed. "Holdings come and go, but royal blood is inalienable."

"Yes," I said, raising my chin. "Royal blood is inalienable, isn't it?"

"And where is the dashing sheriff?" Prince John asked, a smug grin coming over his face. "I'd heard he didn't fare well in the troubles."

My blood roared in my ears. No such thing had happened; it could only mean that Prince John had ordered it so.

He wanted Rob dead.

"Forgive my failure to greet you, your Highness," Rob called from his spot on the wall. I didn't turn to look, watching Prince John's snarl instead.

He didn't say anything for many moments. "Very well. Congratulations, Lady Huntingdon, on your incredibly swift rise from bastardy. If you can simply deliver the tax for your shire, I will be on my way."

"No," I said.

His horse pawed closer. "What was that?" he growled.

"No. You are not the overlord responsible for this shire, and considering our history, I will deliver our tax to the queen mother, or straight to London. The servants at the Huntingdon holdings have been alerted to the change and any personal items you may wish to recover, please write to me and I will handle it as I see fit."

His chest rose. "May I remind you, nobles whose shires fail to pay are held responsible," he said.

"We'll be sure to remind Eleanor of that. For now, I believe you are needed elsewhere, my lord Prince. Anywhere but Nottinghamshire, in fact. You may retain de Clare, but I require these knights."

Prince John's lip curled. He looked at each of us in turn. "This has been a very memorable visit," he said. "Rest assured I will treasure it for a long, long while."

He spurred his horse, and de Clare hesitated a moment, then followed along behind him.

When we couldn't see their horses anymore, Winchester's men began banging their armored hands on their chests, clattering with noise in a knight's version of a cheer.

The rest of the men didn't quite know what to do, and I called for the gates to be opened so we could be let in. I sent Essex and Winchester on ahead, and saw Rob watching me as the knights filed in.

The knights stopped and dutifully dropped their heads to me.

"I lied before," I told them. "There have been troubles here. Men came through, very well-organized and purposeful men, and burned much of the city. We are struggling to rebuild, and I need your help to protect these people and give them their homes back. I know some of you have been garrisoned here for a while, and some of you may be new. I look forward to your help and your service."

I didn't wait for their reaction. It were important, whether they respected me as their lady or not, but I knew that were a slow process, and a man wouldn't wait for them to approve. They would do their jobs, and I would win them over as soon as I could.

I sent them to different tasks within the city, and Rob waited for them all to ride past me before coming up to my horse. I dropped off the horse's back, taking a moment to arrange the skirts of the dress that caught up around my legs.

When I looked up, Rob were close to me. His bow were over his back, and his arms were crossed over his front. "You did well," he told me.

"Thank you," I said, looking at him. "You're not happy about this, are you? That I'm Lady Huntingdon."

He paused, but he shook his head slow. "I don't know what to think, Scar. I just need more time."

"I don't understand," I told him.

His shoulders lifted. "Those were meant to be my lands, Scar," he said.

Slow and careful, I reached for his hand, threading his fingers through mine where they weren't covered with bandages. He smiled at the strange sight.

"Your hands are a little ridiculous, love," he told me.

"Rob, they can be your lands again," I told him with a whisper.

"If we marry," he said, his eyes meeting mine, heavy and dark. "I know," he said, looking at our hands. "I just don't know that I deserve them. That I will ever deserve that title."

"Rob—"

"And more than that, I don't know that you can marry me, Scar." His hand pulled away from mine. "Prince John isn't wrong about that—you can marry any unwed man in the kingdom. Your father won't approve of you wedding a sheriff."

"I don't care about that!" I said, my heart starting to beat faster.

"Don't you?" he asked, looking at me. "You spoke of alliances. Do you know what the best way to ally yourself with another powerful lord is? What the best way to protect *Nottingham* is?"

I stepped back, close to the horse, and the horse tossed his head. "You want me to marry someone else?" I asked, my voice a bare whisper; I didn't think I were breathing.

"I want to keep you *alive,* Scarlet!" he yelled at me. "There's no way in hell I want to see you marry another man. *Again.* I've been through that torture once, thank you. But you are a noblewoman now, and there is a different set of rules. Protection and safety aren't things you can purchase at the tip of your knife."

"No—they're things I should purchase with my *body*?" I yelled. I couldn't breathe, and there were tears blocking my eyes.

"You survived Gisbourne," he said soft. "Surely he was the worst you could hope for."

I shrank back farther, and the horse trotted away from me. I shut my eyes and Gisbourne were there again, pushing me against the wall, clawing at my skirts, pulling them up. Hurting me.

"*Scarlet,*" Rob said, touching my arm. I turned away, hitting the ashen remain of a wall, and he caught my shoulders. "Scar," he said again.

I pulled away from him, and the tears shot out.

"Scarlet!" he said.

I shook my head, grabbing for the horse's reins and starting to walk toward the castle.

"Scarlet!" he yelled.

I didn't stop. And he didn't follow me.

CHAPTER EIGHTEEN

We all ate dinner in the Great Hall, sharing whatever we could for food, but we were running low. I sat by Rob, our food spread on a linen on the floor. There weren't near enough tables to seat all the people we needed to feed, and I never had a problem sitting on the ground.

Rob took my hand, and I looked at him, watching him, as he unwrapped the bandage on one, looking to see how the cuts were healing.

I wanted to pull away. If he were going to touch me, I didn't want it to be to check a wound, some necessary thing. I wanted it to mean something more.

That didn't mean I'd rather him not touch me at all, though.

"We should hunt tomorrow," I told him, eating a bit of cheese. "We don't have any meat left."

He looked at me, the corner of his mouth rising. "Guess we don't have to worry about a lord catching us poaching."

"They're royal forests, not shire forests. The only person who has the right to truly punish someone for poaching is the king."

He flipped my hand over, stroking his thumb along the beating vein in my wrist, making the blood rush faster. "Then we'll hunt happily. Everything seems easier in the forest, anyway," he said, and his voice were rough.

"I don't know if I can shoot anymore," I told him soft.

"You haven't been gone that long," he told me, brushing my wrist again.

Wondering if two could play such a game, I took his hand and traced my fingertips over his palm, edging one finger, then the next, then the next. He sucked in a hard breath. "Not because of the time," I admitted, unearthing my half hand from where I'd hidden it in my skirts.

He took this hand, unwrapping it and really looking at it for the first time. The scarred stumps were discolored, almost black, and tough and rough to the touch. Hard. Flipping it over, the palm were red and scraped up from the rope. He lifted my hand, kissing a bit of the uninjured pad at the base of my thumb. "Your hands have seen far too much pain. But if you want, I'll teach you to shoot like I taught you the first time."

I pulled away from him with a gasp. "*The first time!*" I yelped, outraged. "You never!"

He grinned. "You couldn't shoot a horse's ass when I found you," he boasted. "I taught you everything you know."

"You taught me some things," I said, lowering my voice. He raised his eyebrows and leaned closer to me. I pushed him back with a grin. "And none of them have anything to do with weaponry."

My eyes dropped to his mouth, and lingered there for a long breath.

He sighed and stood. "Scarlet, we should—I should—" He stopped, and he shook his head.

I stood as well. "Rob, I shouldn't have walked off this afternoon."

He looked at me, waiting for me to speak.

I lifted my shoulders. "I know you were trying to say something reasonable, but all I heard—" I stopped, looking down, and he stepped closer to me. "All I heard was that you don't want to marry me anymore."

He looked at me, meeting my eyes in that way that made me feel strange things sparking like kindling inside of me. He glanced away, looking round the hall. "Come," he said, holding out his hand. "I'd rather not speak about this here, but there is much to say."

My chest felt tight as I looked at his hand.

"And none of it has to do with me not *wanting* to marry you, Scar," he told me, his voice a low, private rumble. "Come to my chambers, and we can discuss it all."

I nodded, putting my hand in his.

He held my bandaged hand and brought me up through the castle. When I thought we'd continue up the stairs, he started tugging me down the hall. "You don't stay in the lord's chambers?" I asked. They were the nicest rooms, where Prince John stayed when he were here.

He shrugged. "No. I couldn't much stand the thought of him, and besides . . . ," he said, trailing off as he tugged me down the hall. As we grew closer to the room and he smiled broader, I felt the blood running out of my face. "I wanted to stay in the only room that reminded me of you. With your things in it, no less, so I could pretend like any day you'd appear again."

He loosed my hand to open the door, and my heart were pounding at the thought of going into that room, like it could bring Gisbourne back to life, like he would be there, putting his hands on me again.

Rob turned back to me and frowned, taking my hand. "Scar, we don't—"

I pulled away, so hard when he let me go I hit the wall and jerked with pain as my back hit rock. I shrank from him.

"Scarlet!" he said, frowning and confused.

I could bare breathe, and Rob came to me, standing before me, hesitant to touch me.

Like he thought it were him I didn't want to be touched by, like he couldn't see Gisbourne's ghostly hands reaching out for me, grasping at me.

"Locksley!" Winchester shouted down the hall. "Have you—Marian! Come quick, Bess is asking for you."

I pulled round Rob. "Bess?" I asked. "What's wrong?"

He grinned. "She's having the baby."

My eyes went wide. "What am I meant to do?" I demanded, panicked.

He chuckled. "I think she wants a friend there, Marian."

With little idea what I were doing, I went. Maybe to run from telling Rob so many truths, and maybe because even if I weren't sure I were yet, I wanted to be Bess's friend. I wanted to protect that baby from the moment it were alive in the world.

—∞—

I rushed back to the room I'd left her in. Much were outside, his arms crossed, looking fair tortured and grim. "God, Scarlet . . . ," he started, shaking his head.

Jumping forward, I kissed his cheek. "I'll take care of her," I told him. It were a silly promise to make—I didn't know the first thing about women and babies and care. But I promised it to him because he needed to hear something from his friend.

I heard her yell, and Much flinched. I opened the door and went in. Women were in there already, four of them, piling linens and getting water and doing it all without a word.

"Scarlet!" she wailed, and I froze, terrified.

She held her hand out to me from the bed where they'd moved her around, and said my name again. I lurched forward, crawling on the bed to sit beside her. She grabbed my wrist and I grabbed hers, bound together, strong and linked.

"It hurts," she sobbed against me. "No one says it hurts this much."

"No," one of the women told her, patting her knee. "They all forget once they have the babe. It's a quick mess of pain for a lifelong joy, my girl." She smiled. "Besides, the pains will get much, much worse. We're still early on."

The worst of the pain passed, and Bess curled against my chest, crying free. "Damn him," she whispered. "Damn him for leaving me like this. Leaving me alone to do this."

I squeezed her wrist harder. "You're not alone. You have a whole family outside that door. And in," I added, looking at our hands. "He left you with a whole damn family."

She kept on crying, but she nodded, and I reckoned that were good enough.

"You've got a long while to go, Bess," the woman near her knees told her. I reckoned she were the midwife. "Rest if you can between the pains. And you—" she said, nodding to me. "Don't let go of her hand. When she needs to squeeze, she needs to squeeze hard."

I nodded, like this were a solemn duty. It were, to me.

The midwife passed me cloths soaked in cool water, and I patted them on her neck, her forehead, cooling the sweat. She relaxed a little, tangled against me. "Hush," I said to her. "Rest. I'm not leaving you."

Bess nodded.

—⁂—

I never knew how long a birth could take. How much punishment it gave the mother. Bess labored for hours and hours, such pain that she screamed and cried and I were surprised there were still water in her to cry and sweat. The pains started with minutes between them and grew closer until it never broke, just kept coming and coming and coming. She cried and hurt so much that I cried with her. It weren't my arm—though that were red and sore in her grasp—it were the strangeness of it.

Pain never meant much to me. It weren't the beginning or the end—it were an ever-moving mark that never served a purpose, never bore a reason, never changed things except to make people more afraid.

But this pain—I cried with her and I cursed God for His cruelty. I thought He meant to take Bess from us—surely this amount of pain weren't natural, weren't expected, even though the midwife stayed calm throughout. I thought Bess were dying, and I were meant to hold her hand and watch because Death and I knew each other so well.

But then the baby started to come, and the pain started to mean something. Every push Bess gave became an inch closer to new life as the little one struggled to get out of her body.

The head came first, and it were a quick thing to pull it out once the shoulders appeared, like a strange and humbling magic, from Bess's body. The midwife caught the baby in clean linen, toweling off blood and mess. She cleaned the face, and the tiny eyes didn't open and the mouth didn't move.

"Sarah?" Bess whined. "Sarah?"

"Hush," the midwife said. Holding the baby in the linen, she swatted the rump.

And the tiny, perfect thing screamed. It screamed so loud and hard its lips trembled and shook.

The midwife laughed. "Bess, you have a beautiful, healthy baby girl."

Bess burst into tears as the midwife passed the bundle up. There were a fleshy cord tying the two together, and the midwife motioned to me. "Perhaps you and your knives could be of service?" she asked.

Silent and wide-eyed, I moved forward, away from Bess, my body hot and sweaty where she'd been pressed against me. I drew one of my knives, burning it in the fire to make the wound clean. I felt utterly strange at having a weapon so close to a brand new thing, and the midwife showed me where to cut.

In a breath it were done, and the tether that bound the two of them together became something less easy to see, less easy to touch. But it were there nonetheless, as she stared at her daughter and her daughter quieted, looking back up at her through bare-open eyes.

I stood before them, lost, captivated, as the women cleaned and piled things to hide the blood and the muck and all the things that had come out of her that no one wanted the men to know about. She just stared at the little baby, and the midwife showed her how to feed her.

"Scarlet?" Bess asked soft.

Nodding, I stepped closer. "Will you bring her out? I don't want the menfolk in here just yet."

"Yes," I said, my voice rough. Bess held her up a little but she weren't strong, and I picked up the baby, holding her at arm's length and staring at her as she stared back at me. The midwife laughed and took her from me, holding her like a loaf of bread I were meant to cradle.

"Like this," she told me, putting her into my arms.

I followed her instructions, but the baby turned and wiggled until she were in the crook of my arm, against my breast. The midwife smiled. "Just like that. Make sure to hold her head," she told me, positioning my other arm.

"I've held babies before," I said. "She's just . . . *tiny*."

The midwife beamed at me and nodded me toward the door.

One of the women opened it for me, and all the men were there, looking like they hadn't moved in hours, big broad shoulders and tall heads overfilling the space. I knew I were meant to look for Much, but I saw Robin first, and he came close, grazing his fingers on her little cheek and looking back up to me.

He kissed me, and I knew how it could be. Us, with a family, with little babies just like this. Our family.

"Is that . . . ?" Much breathed beside me.

I pulled away from Rob, showing Much the baby. "Your daughter," I told him.

His throat worked as he looked at me. He didn't deny that it were his. The way he looked at her, even if John were the father, she were Much's daughter. "Let me hold her," he told me.

I nodded, and Much slipped his arm along mine, catching her up in one hand and using his other arm to hold her underneath. He nodded at the door, not looking away from his daughter. "Open the door, Scar," he murmured.

"She doesn't want—" I started.

He grinned at his daughter, then glanced up to me. "Let me go be with my wonderful, miraculous wife, Scar," he said.

I opened the door for him.

Rob caught my hand and tugged it. "Come on. You need some rest," he said, kissing my temple.

Taking his hand, I let him pull me away from the other people, but I stopped him when we were alone. "I don't want to go back to that room, Rob."

He stared at me. "Will you tell me why?"

Nodding, a small sigh escaped me. "I just—later. I will tell you later. Is that enough?"

He kissed me again. "Yes."

There weren't any other rooms without people in them. Rob took me outside into the late morning, to the stables, nodding to the stable hands.

"Don't tell anyone," he whispered to me. "But I come up here to think sometimes. It reminds me of the Oak, in a way."

I wanted to tell him his secrets were safe with me, but he knew that already. And I were too tired to form the words. He led me to a ladder and we climbed up it slow.

There were a door in the hayloft to pitch hay down from, and Rob opened it, letting the sun and fresh air in as he arranged bales and loose hay. He brought me to it, kissing me and pulling me down to lie on his chest.

I laid my cheek on his chest, drowsy, bare able to keep my eyes open. "I love you," I whispered.

"I love you too," he told me, threading his fingers through mine.

CHAPTER NINETEEN

I woke up only a few hours later. It were still daylight and Rob were breathing deep beneath me, chest rising and falling under my cheek, his heartbeat drumming light and steady in my ear.

"I can tell you're awake, you know," he told me.

I lifted my head, and he opened his eyes. "We have to get to work, don't we?" I asked.

His nose nudged along my cheek. "I'm more interested in you telling me these secrets. Particularly the ones keeping us from sleeping in a bed."

I pushed off him, sitting up.

He sighed, sitting up too. "Work it is, then."

We joined the rest of the shire in the city, laboring along just like we'd done before. As we got to houses that were ruined but still half standing, we had to get the bigger men to do most of the work. Most of the women went to cook and prepare food, look to the little ones, and tend to a hundred other tasks that had to be done now that the knights were with us and stronger men could do the bulk of the hardest work.

Robin set them all to tasks, and I watched, as I'd become a bit useless too. My muscles were sore and I felt the grime of days of sleeplessness and sweat and pain upon me. I went to see Bess. She smiled when she saw me, and I sat by her on the bed. The tiny little girl were in her arms, silent and sleeping.

"She's peace itself," I said.

Bess laughed. "Until she starts wailing for something. Sometimes I don't know what she wants. But she's beautiful, isn't she?"

She blinked her eyes open like she knew we were talking about her, and she looked at her mum, then over at me. Her eyes watched me steady. "The most beautiful," I told her. "What's her name?"

She sniffed. "I wanted to call her Hannah, but Much—he insisted we call her Maryanne."

"Why?" I asked.

"It was John's mother's name," she told me soft. "He wanted her to have a piece of him to hold on to. Always." A tear slipped from her eye and she wiped it off. "And we both liked the closeness."

"Closeness?"

"Maryanne," she said, smiling. "Marian."

A warm rush swept through my body. I'd never heard my given name sound so beautiful, so lovely before. "Maryanne,"

I whispered. I touched her cheek, and she blinked but kept staring.

"She likes you," she told me. "Do you want to hold her?"

I nodded, earnest.

She handed her to me, and it were easier to take her than yesterday. My hands were still a little sore, but I didn't mind the soft weight. She wriggled a bit and settled into me, shutting her eyes again.

"It's strange," Bess said with a sigh, leaning back. "To see you as a noble lady, and with a baby. A year ago I wouldn't have known such a thing could happen with Will Scarlet, the village rascal."

I wrinkled my nose. "I wasn't a rascal."

"You had a lot of ladies sighing after you. The lot of you did. Everyone fancied they were in love with one of you." She laughed. "I remember telling Ellie at Tuck's that I thought Robin must have been of the wicked sort, the way he looked at you."

I laughed too. "Easy to say that now! Rob and I couldn't tell how we felt about each other; how could you?"

She shook her head. "Do you remember that night when Gisbourne came to Tuck's, and he was looking for you lot?"

"When he killed that boy," I said soft.

"And nearly killed Much," she breathed. "And you shot up into the trees like a squirrel and Rob were on the ground. He were right near me and he looked—" She shook her head. "That look, I've never seen the like of it. I was sure that he loved you then, boy or not. You can't look like that at someone—worry about someone like that—without loving them true."

I sighed. "He does love me. I just don't know if that will ever be enough for us."

"What do you mean?"

My shoulders lifted, and Maryanne opened her mouth and shut it. "John were the first one who told me love isn't enough. You have to choose that person, over and over again, every day. And Rob—we don't choose each other first, not like John chose you. John put you above everything else. And I don't know that Rob and I will ever do that." I shivered. "I don't know that I *can* do that."

She smiled. "John told me that. It was what finally got me to agree to marry him—he told me he'd choose me, every day. Of all the women he'd ever been with, he'd choose me. Day after day. Moment after moment." She shook her head. "But the bad things—you don't choose those, Scarlet. You deal with them. And if I've only ever listened to one moment of everything Much has ever said, you two make each other strong. Strong enough to make choices that the rest of us can't make."

"What if we had a family?" I whispered, looking at Maryanne.

Her hand fell on my knee. "Then maybe *we* would get the chance to protect *you*," she told me.

—∾—

I left her when Maryanne slept, and Bess wanted to sleep as well. I shut my eyes as I closed the door, trying to hold on to the feelings that I had while I had that baby in my arms, to tie them round my heart in some secret way.

"My lady," someone called.

I opened my eyes to see one of the Nottingham knights there. He were tall, red bearded, and without his armor. "Yes?" I asked.

"There's a problem in the forest, my lady," he said. "I was told to fetch you."

"The forest?" I asked, frowning and going with him. "Do we need horses?"

"It's just beyond the city gates, my lady," he said, bowing his head. "I don't believe so, unless you would prefer."

"No, we can walk," I said. "Take me there, please."

He bowed his head again. "My lady."

We walked through the main street, and I smiled at him. "I know you've just arrived," I told him. "But I've seen how dedicated you are. You and your fellows must have cleared four houses yesterday."

He didn't look at me. "It's my duty, my lady. I'm happy to serve."

I nodded. "Still. I want you to know your service matters, and that it's appreciated. Most knights I've met are not so hardworking."

He looked at me for a moment and nodded. "Thank you," he said.

I saw Rob, meeting his eyes as I walked past. He smiled, and I smiled too, following the knight.

We were almost at the gate when I saw Essex coming in. I frowned. "What's wrong?" I asked him.

He frowned back, looking at me and looking behind him. "What do you mean?"

I glanced at the knight. "I was told there was a problem in the forest."

"If there is, I don't know of it. Do you want my aid?"

"Certainly—" I started.

"It's for your eyes only, my lady," the knight said.

"What exactly is the matter?" Essex demanded, scowling at my knight.

"It's a *woman*," the knight said. "From the village. A woman . . . problem."

"Oh, good Lord," I muttered. "Is someone else having a baby?"

"You do seem to be popular with your people," Essex allowed me. "New though you are to the title."

"New to the title, but I am hardly new to the people," I told him with a shrug. "But I hope they don't start to think me a midwife," I said, scrunching my nose. "I have many skills but this is not one of them."

To my surprise, he smiled a bit. "Return soon, my lady. Unless you would still like an escort?"

I looked to the knight; if a woman felt uncomfortable with a man there, I wouldn't betray that. "No. I'll be well enough, but thank you."

The knight looked grim at Essex, and Essex gave him a good scowl in return.

We walked out through the open gate, heading into the forest. We seemed to be walking straight in, rather than off toward Edwinstowe.

"Where are we going?" I asked the knight, glancing back behind me to where he stood.

"Just a little farther, my lady," he said.

I turned forward again, and just as I did I heard the whisper of metal sliding.

Turning back once more, I gasped and ducked as the knight swung his heavy blade at me. I ducked and he swung wide, and I ran past him, trying to grab at my knives. With my hands covered, I couldn't draw them out.

He turned and raised his sword again as I yanked at the bandages, tearing one with my teeth. He swung his blade toward me again, and I dived behind a tree. The metal bit deep into the wood, and I earned a moment.

The tear were enough to unravel the bandage on my full hand, and I grabbed for a knife as he came at me again. He lunged at me, and I crossed my body to push the sword off with my good hand, leaving me off balance.

He saw this and grabbed for my hair, but I were quick and he didn't get me. He tripped me at the same moment, though, his foot hooking round mine while I tried to escape him.

I fell hard to the forest floor, and his sword thrust down, glinting in the afternoon sun.

Rolling to miss it, I got my hands under me to push up, but his foot smashed down on my back, pressing my face into the dirt.

"*Stay,*" he growled.

A roared yell came from behind us, and the knight—if he were such—turned. I heard metal scrape on metal, and I scrambled to my feet to see Essex fighting him, swords flashing bright.

"Stay out of this!" the knight yelled at Essex.

Essex hammered a hard blow. "What is *this*?" he demanded.

The knight moved fast, parrying and lunging, forcing Essex back. "No business for an earl," he returned.

"You are a traitor," he accused. "Trying to harm your lady!"

"She's not my lady," the knight snapped. "I owe allegiance elsewhere."

"To whom?" Essex demanded, but I already knew, and the knight wouldn't tell Essex that.

Essex were *excellent*. He had perfect form, and a practiced speed and precision most nobles were far too lazy to develop. I already knew the knight were quick and skilled, but they were a surprising good match.

With a hard blow, Essex disarmed him, and without a moment's breath, ran him straight through. My breath stopped and I covered my mouth.

"My lady, are you hurt?" Essex asked. He pulled his sword out and the man fell; Essex bent down and used the man's tunic to wipe his blade clean before he sheathed it. "My lady?"

"No," I said quick, shaking my head. "Let's get back to the wall."

He nodded, and I walked to him and we went to the gate. I looked back once, seeing the man's body lying in the woods.

Once the gates were shut tight behind us, Essex kept walking, but he turned to me.

"If you ask me if I'm hurt once more, I swear I'll flatten you," I warned him, walking faster.

He glanced at the gate, then back at me. "You're bleeding," he told me.

I touched my face. The side of my face were scratched up good, and the skin above my eye were cut. I swore, and he looked at me. "Oh, for Heaven's sake," I grunted. "Don't look at me like that. I think you've rather discovered I'm a different sort of girl than Isabel."

He looked ahead. "In some ways," he told me. "Yet I think if she found a way to break free of court, she'd be rather similar to you indeed."

This thought startled me, but I thought it better not to say anything to that.

—∾—

We reached the castle and the knights set running about, and before we reached the upper bailey, David were there with Allan behind him, and Rob were striding across the courtyard.

"My lady!" David cried when we were closer. He dropped to one knee. "I didn't think—I should have thought to protect you, my lady. I cannot ask for your forgiveness."

"Forgiveness isn't needed, David. Please stand up."

"What happened?" Rob asked, shouldering past David. "They said you were hurt."

I turned my face to him. "A few bruises and scrapes, Rob, nothing serious." His hand slid into my unbandaged one, unthinking, like it belonged there.

"A man, either one of the Nottingham knights or dressed to look like him, drew her outside of the city and tried to kill her," Essex explained, his face ever stern. He were watching me, and watching Rob, and looking at our hands.

Rob's hand tightened on mine. "He's dead?" Rob said, looking at me.

I nodded. "He had me," I admitted. "I wasn't expecting it, and he nearly got me. Essex stopped him," I said, looking to the earl.

"How were you there?" Rob asked him.

"I saw them going out. The knight refused my escort of the lady, and the more I thought about that, there was no good reason he would do such a thing. So I followed you," he told me.

Rob's frown turned grim and dark. "Prince John tried to assassinate you."

"Again, it would seem," I told him. "Who else was with these knights and wants me dead?"

"I should have been there," David said.

"Yes," Rob said. "You should have."

I pulled my hand away from Rob's. "Rob!" I snapped.

"And I should have been there," Rob snapped back, turning away from me with a curse. "If he can get to you here, Scarlet, you will never be safe."

"Oh, stop, the lot of you," I said, glaring at each in turn. "I'm not safe. I was never *safe*. Of course he wants to kill me. He also seems to want his brother dead, and I will not let that happen." My eyes rested on Rob. "If you want me to be safe, we need to pay the tax, protect the money, and bring Richard home."

Rob sucked in a breath, shaking his head. "How about we start with cleaning you up, and then we'll save the kingdom."

I crossed my arms, then winced when it made me feel a bruise on my side. "Fine."

Essex bowed to me. "My lady, I should go speak with Winchester, but we should speak tomorrow. I have a matter I'd like to discuss with you."

I nodded. "Very well. Thank you for your valor today, my lord."

He straightened, and nodded once.

Rob brought me inside, fixing me up, cleaning the scratches on my face. Nothing needed stitching, and he didn't speak to me until he were finished.

"Tomorrow," he said. "Will you hunt with me?"

I looked at his face, his handsome face, and nodded. "Yes."

That night I slept in the hayloft, half hoping Rob would go there looking for a place to sleep, but he didn't. I slept alone, cold and wary as the night crept on.

I woke in the early morning, and before I found Rob, I found Essex in the Great Hall, eating bread. He saw me and stopped, coming from the table to me.

"My lord," I said to him, inclining my head.

"My lady," he said, bowing. "Do you have a moment for us to speak?"

I nodded, glancing at Rob as he entered the hall. "Yes. Why don't we walk down to the tournament grounds?" I suggested. It were the only part that were close to the castle and still far enough to allow us privacy.

He nodded once, and offered me his arm. I hesitated for a moment, but I took it.

Once we were away from the noise of the others, he glanced at me. "I've been frank with you thus far, my lady. I'm hoping that's a trait you appreciate."

My eyebrows pulled together. "Yes. Quite so."

"I support your efforts to curb the power of the prince," he told me. "And I believe that I can help you win Isabel's favor. But as yesterday clearly demonstrated, you are vulnerable."

"I will always be vulnerable," I admitted.

He looked at me. "Not necessarily. You command a tremendous amount of land and wealth now; if you were to ally with another earl, your power would be greater than that of the prince."

I stopped. "Ally."

He drew a breath. "Before I left her, the queen mother asked me to consider whether you would be a suitable wife for me."

I stepped back. "I told her no. Yet over the past days, you have impressed me, and that is not easily done."

"My lord, I—"

"You care for the sheriff," he said low. "And you have already guessed my affections lie elsewhere. But both of those are people we cannot have, Lady Marian. And I do believe we could be friends, which is more than I've hoped for in a match. More importantly, it would protect us both against Prince John. And your grandmother would be very pleased."

"Stop, please," I said.

He looked at me, with his same stern expression. "Consider it."

I shook my head slow. "No, my lord. Thank you—you're right that it would be a wise decision. We'd be powerful beyond measure, and maybe that would stop Prince John. Or perhaps it would make him more angry, and more desperate. But I won't let Prince John steal my choices or force my hand. Especially not concerning this."

His mouth opened, but I shook my head.

"You cannot marry Isabel because she's already married, but I can marry Rob. I will marry Rob."

He nodded once. "Does he want to marry you, Marian?" he asked me. "He cares for you, that much is clear. But he's an honorable man—and though he was born a noble, he's not one now. He knows better than most what a marriage could purchase you. Will he marry you, knowing what he will be keeping you from?"

I stared at him, horrified that I didn't have a sure answer for that.

"As I said, Marian, this would be a match of friendship and gain; if he will have you, I wish you the best." He stepped closer to me, catching my full hand and bringing it to his mouth. "I must go attend to the queen. I'll leave in the afternoon, but should you find yourself in need of a husband, my offer will stand."

He kissed my hand, and let it go.

CHAPTER TWENTY

I were quiet and stunned as I returned to the Great Hall. Rob were there, ordering people into groups to hunt. He led us into Sherwood, glancing at me but not saying anything. Allan had declined to come, so I were with Rob and David and Godfrey, and we walked into the forest, toward a clearing in the woods where we'd always had good luck with hunting before. In the undisturbed deep of the forest the animals were out roaming, young ones hobbling along beside them, frighting as we came through but sure to return as soon as we were still.

"Scar, you and I will go up," Rob said, pointing to a good tree with a wide, stable heart where we could sit for a long while. "David, Godfrey, lie in the brush."

David looked to me and I nodded, and he and Godfrey went off to obey. I swallowed as I looked at the tree. "Rob," I said soft.

His eyes met mine.

I turned my hands over, touching the stumps of my fingers. "I don't know if I can climb anymore."

He looked me over, looked at my hands. "We'll see."

"Rob—" I started, but he went toward the tree.

My face flushed. I didn't want to fall down the damn thing in front of him. I didn't want to be this girl, who didn't know much of what she were good at anymore. I crossed my bow over my shoulders and followed him with a sigh.

He stood next to the tree. The first branch were just above his head, and before it wouldn't have been a thought to jump and grab it, curl my legs up into the tree, gaining one branch and then the next, climbing fast.

He stepped aside and I jumped for it. One hand held fast and the other slid right off, leaving me to swing, my shoulder burning with the effort. I grunted, letting go and frowning at him.

His eyes met mine. "Again," he said, nodding at it.

"Rob—" I started.

"Again," he said gentle.

I shook my head, but I did as he asked, and as my first hand fell he grabbed my knees. I looked down at him, and he nodded up again. He pushed up, and I could change my hold on the branch, with my palm on top to get a better grip.

My arms were weaker than they'd been before, but I pulled myself up with a huff. Rob came up right behind me.

"It doesn't count as climbing if you're doing half the work," I told him.

He shrugged, standing on the branch and pulling me up with him. There were more branches now, like stairs in the tree. "Then what does it count as?" he asked.

I frowned, unsure.

"Come on," he said. "I'll go up first. And if you need help, I'll help."

Simple. But not simple at all.

He started up the tree, and it were easy to follow him. My feet could do most of the work with my hands only guides and balances, and I tried to go faster, to keep pace with him.

He made the heart of the tree before me, and he turned back and held out his arm. I grabbed it above the wrist and he pulled me up, close to him. "You beat me," I told him.

His head tilted. "Were we racing?"

"No," I said. I were the only one racing, it seemed.

"Where should we set up?" he asked, looking about.

"There," I said, pointing to a wide branch with sturdy branches below it. I went to it and crouched, letting my legs hang off either side and catch the lower branches for stability. Rob sat a bit behind me, and we both took out our bows and arrows.

Nervous, I started to test mine. I tried holding the bow in my whole hand and the string in my half, then reversed it. Then reversed it again.

I felt Rob's eyes on me, and turned to look at him. He looked up at my face. He'd been watching my hand.

I turned away from him, feeling my stomach twist, feeling ugly and scarred and weak.

"Can you use a knife with that hand?" he asked.

I pulled one from my belt, showing him.

He tested the grip, his fingers molding over mine and pushing, and nodded. "Impressive."

I looked at it. "I practiced with a rock. It's not as strong as the other hand."

"Of course it isn't, Scar. You lost two of your fingers. But the fact that you can hold a knife at all is incredible."

My eyes dropped to the bow, miserable. "I can't do this, Rob."

He slid closer behind me, kissing my cheek quick before drawing his arms round me. He pressed my whole hand against the shaft of the bow, and slid my other hand on the string. He took an arrow, wedging it careful between my two remaining fingers, and I shifted my thumb to hold it against the string.

He let go, and the arrow dropped, clattering slow through the tree. Birds flew off at the noise. "Dammit!" I snapped, trying to pull out of his arms.

But we were on a tree branch, and he were blocking me, and I couldn't get free without knocking him off. And considering the path the arrow took, I weren't keen to do it just yet.

"Hush," he said against my ear. "Try again."

I twisted hard to glare at him. "What, Rob? You want to hear me say I'm some strange crippled girl and I'll never shoot the bow again? That—that—without being able to hold these weapons I'm not sure of *anything*? What do you want?"

His mouth hooked up. "I want you to try again," he told me.

He didn't guide my hands as I clutched the arrow, trying to draw it on the string. I could hold all the parts, but I couldn't aim it—I couldn't even hold the damn thing straight, and my hand were cramping.

I unstrung the arrow, shaking my hand out. "Hurts?" he asked.

"Yes. Is *that* what you want to hear?" I grumped.

He took the hand, rubbing the muscles.

I pulled away. "I can't do this, Rob."

His shoulders lifted. "Very well."

I frowned.

He nodded into the clearing. "There's a deer. Someone should probably shoot it."

"Go ahead."

He leaned back, crossing his arms and watching me. "Don't feel like it."

"Don't feel like it? Robin!"

He lifted his shoulders again.

"You'd really starve your people to prove a point?" I snapped.

"Would you?" he returned.

"Fine!" I snapped. I strung an arrow and aimed it. I let it fly, and it went so wild the deer didn't even spook. "Fantastic," I told him. "I hope I didn't kill Godfrey. If they're not laughing themselves to death down there."

His arms were around me again, guiding my hands. "Like this," he said, shifting my fingers a bit. "Listen to your bow.

Mind your breath. Find the moment, Scar. You can do this," he whispered in my ear.

I drew in a deep breath. My hand hurt holding the arrow, and I knew it were sweating I were holding it so tight. I let the breath out, waiting for the lull between heartbeats, and I let it go.

"Hey!" Rob yelled, pointing as the arrow landed in the rump of the deer. It started, frightened and hurt, and it were disoriented enough that Godfrey could leap over and cut its throat.

"I hit the *ass*," I grunted.

"Well, you're acting like an ass, so that's perfectly fine," he told me.

"*I'm acting like—*" I started to yell at him, but he ducked closer, tilting my chin to kiss him, feeling like maybe, hidden in a tree and acting like our old selves, the rules of the world didn't apply. I only let it go a few moments too long, before pulling away with a frown.

"You hit the deer," he said soft. "You did it."

I glanced out. Godfrey and David were trussing the deer so they could move it from the clearing. "I hit the deer," I allowed.

He rubbed my cheek and turned my face back to his, waiting, and with a sigh I kissed him, twisting on the tree to have an easier time of it. He rubbed along my legs as we kissed, drawing one up and hooking it round his waist to pull me closer. I drew a breath through my nose, not breaking the kiss—with both of us in pants, it felt *close*. Very close. Bending my knee pushed him harder against me, and our lips broke as we both drew a ragged breath.

"I love you, Scarlet," he told me, his eyes dark and shimmery blue in the green shade of the trees.

"I love you too," I told him, not looking at him. He reached to kiss me again, and I leaned back. "We never finished that talk 'bout whether or not you want to marry me," I told him, not looking up.

He drew a breath, leaning back too. "I want to," he said.

I looked up at him, but he were looking out over the forest. "Talk or marry me?"

His mouth twisted up. "Marry you, Scar."

"But."

He looked at me. "But you're a noblewoman. I can't forget that."

"I'm a bastard with royal blood and royal favor," I told him. "You were the one born a noble."

"You can protect Nottinghamshire if you marry, Scar. You must realize that."

I crossed my arms. "I do. Essex just offered for my hand this morning, in fact."

"He *what*?"

"Yes. Said that would be the best way to protect me, and protect Nottinghamshire."

Color crept up Rob's face. "Essex? Winchester says he's Isabel's lackey. You'd marry him?"

"Who else did you have in mind? Winchester's not married. Should I wed him? How about de Clare—he's not an earl, but he'll inherit an earldom," I taunted. "If I don't mind a cruel, twisted man for a husband, of course."

"Scarlet!" he growled at me.

"What?" I demanded. "You want to toss me to another man like I'm some thing that can be traded for power and wealth? You think that will protect Nottingham? You think *that* will stop Prince John?"

"You need to think!" he snapped.

"No!" I snapped back. "*You* need to think. Like a thief—like a girl. Like all the people that get their power and their choices taken away from them. I won't be one of them. I will hold the earldom as my own if I have to."

"And I have no doubt you can. But it will be easier—"

"With a man I don't love and don't want and don't care about, touching me, making me have his children, silencing me? That won't be easier."

"And you think I'm such a prize?" he shouted at me. "You'd take me over an earl? You think I'll make it easier, with my nightmares, with my scars?"

I pushed forward, taking his face in my hands. "I have scars, Rob. I'm not frightened of your dreams. I love you, and you make me stronger. You make me stronger than wealth or power. And together, if you just choose to be together, we can save Nottingham."

He were breathing hard with anger, staring at my eyes, his chest rising and bringing him close to me. With a grunted noise he pushed forward against my hands, our mouths meeting. I thought it would be some frantic thing to match the anger in his body, but it were deep, and slow, and full like everything he felt were unspoken on his tongue.

I heard a rustle and turned my head, looking out in the clearing as his mouth shifted with me, moving under my ear. He swept my hair back, tasting my skin. "Rob," I whispered. "Stag."

He nodded, and I grabbed his bow, putting it in one hand and an arrow in the other. He kept kissing my neck, and I felt him fumbling with the weapons behind me.

"Rob, I should—" I started.

"Stay still," he murmured, straightening to look at my eyes. He glanced once—*once*—over my shoulder into the glen. "Kiss me," he said.

Thinking it were for good luck or some such thing, I did, and his mouth captured mine, tilting and twisting and opening, dragging me away into it. I didn't know when he let go of the arrow, but I felt the bow brush my back as his hands touched me slow and careful, wary of pressing too hard and hurting me where the bruises were.

Threading my arms round his neck, I broke the kiss. "Rob, the *stag*," I reminded him.

He nodded toward the clearing.

Godfrey and David were trussing it up, but there weren't no need to cut its throat—Rob had shot the beast through its eye.

Its eye.

I pushed him back with a grin. "Posturing braggart, show-off peacock!" I accused.

"If by that you mean I'm the best damn archer you've ever seen and you'd like to reward me with a kiss," he said, drawing me back to him. "Then I accept. And yes, I will continue to give you generous lessons to achieve my epic—nay, *legendary*—skill."

I kissed him.

He were, in fact, the best damn archer I'd ever seen.

—w—

Getting down the tree were worse than getting up. I thought it would be fine, but while I were searching for one of my first footholds my hand lost grip and I fell to a lower branch. Rob were there quick to catch me before I fell lower.

From there he guided me down, stepping first, holding my waist as I followed.

At the bottom, he jumped from the tree and held out his arms, and without hesitating, I jumped into them. He caught me, like I had absolute faith that he would. My match, my bandmate in all things.

He put me on the ground and I felt the breath run out from my lungs.

My match.

"You have the strangest look on your face," he murmured to me, brushing my hair back. "What are you thinking about?"

Shy, I smiled, but I turned away from him. Godfrey and David took the animals back to Nottingham to dress and cut to give to the kitchens, and Rob and I went about gathering up arrows. I found my first—though sadly not last—stray buried deep into a tree trunk.

I tried to pull it out, and it wouldn't budge. I twisted, pulling harder, and wedged my foot against the tree.

The arrow popped free, and I fell back, only to see the head—the hardest bit to replace—were still lodged in there.

"Damn you," I cursed the tree. "Give that back or I'll chop you down!" I threatened, wrapping my sleeve round the arrowhead to pull at it without cutting myself.

"I mean it!" I growled, tugging harder. "I will cut you up and sell you for firewood!"

I gasped, letting go of the tree and staring at it.

Staring at all of them.

Hundreds of trees. All in the *king's forest.* "Rob!" I yelled.

He were looking at the arrowhead already, and strode toward it. "If I pull it out do I become King of All the Britons?" he teased.

I shook my head as he balled up a bit of his cloak and wrapped it round the arrowhead. "No, Rob, the trees!"

He looked frightened for a moment. "Did they threaten you back? I've heard things about the Green Man." Then he grinned at me, teasing again.

"Dammit, Rob, the forest. The trees, the deer, the peat—there's no one with enough money to buy a manor, but firewood?

Wood for building? Meat to feed their families, peat to make a fire?"

The arrowhead gave and Rob held it in his hand, staring at it. He twisted round, taking it in the same way I had. Adding tree upon tree upon tree. He took a deep breath, his eyes wide.

"Good Lord, Scarlet."

"It will take us a few days, a week at the most, with all the knights and the men from the villages," I said.

"A day or two more to sell it," he said.

"We'll have the full amount before Eleanor even arrives. Prince John won't be able to touch us," I told him.

He didn't say any more. He just caught me up and kissed me.

He leaned me against a tree, kissing me, and my mind spun out, thinking of being alone with him, of marrying him, of touching him in a way I were so curious about.

I pulled away from his kiss. Before any of that, there were something I had to tell him.

He looked at me strange, but I ducked out of his arms, walking away from the clearing.

"Scarlet?" he called. I heard him move behind me, his steps slow and even, following where I led. He could have caught me easy, but he didn't—he let me lead.

Deep into the forest, it seemed he grew impatient, and I heard his steps coming closer to mine. Never looking back, I started running. This were what I wanted, to run away not from the good things, but the bad ones, to always be able to feel a tiny speck of free and unfettered and still keep the things I loved.

Still keep him.

"Scarlet!" he yelled, confused, but he ran after me.

He were faster and he ran up beside me, his face worried and frowning, but I just kept running, and he ran beside me.

It had been too long since I'd run in the woods. My feet knew their way over the wood floor—thank God I hadn't lost that, for it were fair hard to learn back—but the rest of my body'd forgotten. My lungs hurt and my legs burned.

I ran faster. I were never afraid of pain.

Sweating hard, I knew we were close and I ached for my destination. Stumbling a bit to do it, I tore the tunic off over my head. Rob were staring at me.

I started to untie the shirt, and Rob tripped on a log, flattening on the ground with a loud curse.

Laughing, I slowed for a moment but continued on. He could catch up.

I kicked off my boots, and Rob were struggling to regain his lost ground and drop his clothing at the same time.

My men's pants fell off me, and I jumped onto the big rock that jutted out into Thoresby Lake. The loose, long men's shirt just bare covered the important bits of me.

Tearing with my teeth at the bandages on my hands, I cast them off and dived into the water as Rob made the rock.

The lake were still cold as winter, the near-ice of it stealing my breath and slamming through every inch of my skin. I hung under the water for as long as I could, willing the cold to strip away all the awful things that had happened since I'd been here last, all the pains and new marks on my body, till I couldn't feel them.

I felt Rob's entry into the water, and came up for air as he did.

He whipped his hair out of his eyes, leaving it to splay across his forehead like a hedgehog's spines. I swam to him, smoothing his hair back.

He kissed me. "Why did you bring me here, Scar?"

"Because I love this place," I told him. "Do you remember when you brought me here? When you told me I should marry John?"

He frowned. "Not my finest moment."

I grinned. "No." I touched his cheek, then pulled back to use my hands to tread water. "But you brought me here when I was hurt and confused. Like you knew how much I loved it."

He nodded and caught one of my hands, looking at the healing cuts and swollen burns. The cold water felt awful good for them. "Are you hurt and confused now, Scar?"

I ignored that, taking a deep breath and kicking harder against the shivers. "There's something that I need to tell you," I whispered to him. "Something I won't ever tell another man. Not ever. So if you decide you don't want to marry me after this, I'm not marrying Essex. I'm not marrying anyone, do you understand?"

He looked confused and a bit frightened, but he nodded. "What is it, Scar?"

"That night before Gisbourne were found dead," I told him, and he looked at me, eyes bluer than the water we were in. "He changed his mind."

Rob frowned. "What do you mean?"

"He decided he didn't want the annulment anymore," I said fast, in a rush. "He decided he would make me stay his wife, because he could use me to gain influence from Richard."

Rob's arms were well underneath the water, and though I could feel his legs kicking, pushing water round, he looked still. "Make you."

"And I were hurt," I said, raising my hand like it were an excuse. "And he pushed me up against the wall—" I stopped, shaking for reasons that weren't cold and feeling like I were going to cry.

Rob gathered me up, his body warm in the cold water, and I felt like I could breathe again. His breath rushed over me, harsh, his eyes closed tight, trying to ward off the things I were telling him. "I will never make you set foot in that room again," he whispered.

"I got my knife," I continued, talking to the crook of his neck.

He hugged me tighter, kicking for the both of us, and his hands held me up, curled on my back. "You did?" he asked.

I nodded. "And I managed to call for Winchester. And he kept Gisbourne away from me."

Rob took my chin from his shoulder. "You mean—he didn't—"

There were bare enough time to shake my head once before Rob kissed me, soft and gentle, so distracting sweet that we both stopped kicking, and our heads slipped under the water, such cold on my skin and such heat on my lips.

Rob pulled back, kicking hard to bring us up, holding me against him. He held me tight, kissing my shoulder as he hugged me. "I'm sorry," he said. "You knew I'd be too angry—I would have killed him. I'm sorry I wasn't in a state to protect you. I'm sorry you had to call for Winchester, and not me."

I shivered. "I thought you'd be angry."

"At myself, love." He kissed my shoulder again. "At myself."

Sighing against him, I looked round, realizing it were growing darker. "Sun's going down," I whispered to him.

"One hundred fifty-six," he said absent-like, letting one arm loose of me to start to swim toward shore.

"What?" I said, tugging on his hand.

He looked at me and grinned. "One hundred fifty-six."

I'll wait. Every sunset, every day. I'll count them all until you're mine. My perfect wife. My only wife.

"The numbers. The letters—you were counting the sunsets," I said as I realized.

His grin grew broader, wider, fuller, like he were pulling stars down from Heaven and tucking them into his smile. "You got the letters."

"Only recently," I whispered. "I haven't . . . I haven't read them yet. I saw the numbers, but I didn't know."

And then he kissed me, and stars flooded through me, glittering and dancing and heating me with their fire as he pulled me to shore. He pulled me up onto the rock, and he kissed me until it were dark.

CHAPTER TWENTY-ONE

When we got back to the castle, I went to Bess's room. She let me hold the baby, and said she were feeling much better, and when I asked her, quiet, how one goes about planning a wedding in secret and in a few days' time, she shrieked and covered her mouth, laughing with me.

The next morning the work started in earnest. I were out of clean clothes and Rob gave me some of his to wear. There were something about wearing his clothes that felt even closer between us, and I smiled again with my secret that he weren't much aware of yet—I would marry him. I were ready to marry him.

We rode out to the forest, Rob and I sharing a horse and snugged close together on it, his hand spanning my waist and keeping me to him.

I covered his hand and threaded my fingers through his. I always wanted to be close to him.

Most of the shire were there already by the time we arrived, but many more people were drifting in on the roads. We met in Edwinstowe at the heart of the forest, and Rob and Much stood together and started doling out tasks.

Many of the women and children were sent to the places where peat grew, thick layers of rich-smelling moss that would burn in a fire for near as long as a wooden beam. It could be cut out of embankments and sold in bricks. Peat were expensive stuff, and always sold well at market. It weren't heavy or dangerous to pull it out either, so the women and little ones were good for it.

The biggest men were sent to pull down a few trees, away from the rest of us in case they happened to fall wrong. Godfrey went off with them.

And then there were the hunters. Rob nodded to me with a grin for this, and I smiled back. The Clarke boys cleaved quick to me, and even Missy Morgan ran over to me, eager to hunt with me. I laughed. "We have to split up," I told them. "Teams of two, a good shot and someone to carry the animals."

"I'm better at skinning them," Missy said.

I smiled. "That can be a separate job too."

Rob slid his arm around me. "Hunt with me?"

Putting my hands on his chest, I pushed him off a bit with a teasing grin. "That's not a good idea."

"You're a better spot and I'm a better shot, and you can practice your shooting," he said. "Besides, I think it's fairly well known we're an unbeatable team," he said, darting in for a quick kiss.

"Kissing doesn't count as hunting," Will Clarke said. We turned to him, and he were frowning serious.

"Exactly," I said, trying not to grin as I pushed Rob off.

"Rob!" Much yelled. "Scar! Try setting a good example, please?"

Will were still in front of me. "Why don't you and your brothers go with Missy, Will?"

He turned to Missy and his face turned redder than the ribbons I liked. "Fine," he grunted.

—⁂—

The peat and wood were loaded up on carts to be taken to market, but the meat were sold off to butchers in the neighboring towns who could resell it on their own. The hunters all ended a bit early, and the little ones took some of the meat back to the castle. Rob and I took the rest to sell, getting back to the castle as everyone were eating, tired but looking less frightened than they had in a long while.

It felt like sun finally breaking through storm clouds.

Rob went back to his room with a glare toward David, and I took Much (Bess insisted, since she still needed to rest and couldn't help) and Missy Morgan aside and asked them to come with me to the forest.

David strode over to us, frowning. "What's going on?" he asked.

"There's going to be a wedding," Missy crowed.

"A *secret* wedding, Missy," Much reminded her gentle.

She blushed and blinked her eyes slow at him. "Sorry."

"A wedding, my lady?" David demanded. "The queen—"

"Won't know," I told him. "Now if you're my knight, I need you to help."

He frowned again. "As you wish, my lady. But surely this is women's work."

I frowned too. "Perhaps, I just . . . I don't know many women. Fondly, at least."

"I can take care of that," Missy told me, smiling.

"Remember it's *secret,*" Much and I said at once.

She laughed. "I know. Let's go to the forest, then!" she said.

We did. Before we were done the first night, Missy also got Ellie and Mariel, Bess's two barmaid friends from the inn, to help out. Though Ellie gave me a bit of a saucy wink, she never made fun of the things I didn't know as she started to order us all about.

—w—

We hunted one more day, and then didn't hunt the next. The butchers round Nottingham wouldn't be able to buy more meat so soon, and we let the littler ones hunt small animals to feed the workers. Rob went to help with the tree folk, and I went to cut peat with the women and children.

Down in the mud and muck my knife kept slipping from the weak grip of my half hand and I gave up, hacking at it with the full hand only. I had spent so long in the stillness of prison, I'd forgotten just how much I needed this hand for. I'd forgotten just what Prince John had taken away from me.

It were late in the hazy warm of the afternoon when we heard a crack and a boom. The women all lifted their heads and turned like a pack of gulls, and I sprang up and ran for the sound.

Much and a whole group of workers got there 'bout the time I did, called over by yelling men. Everyone were hollering, throwing their hands about, and pointing at one another, gathered round a downed tree that had taken two others in its path, and from what I could see, landed on at least three men.

"Rob?" I cried. "Rob!" I hated the girlish shriek there were in my voice, but I couldn't help it none as I scrabbled round the trunk, looking for him.

"Scar," he said, hands catching my shoulders as I turned.

Relief choked me as I hugged him overtight, clinging to him. "Christ and his Saints, Rob," I breathed into him.

He kissed me quick, and we broke apart, looking at the damage. Two men were close together and the third were farther down. "Cut the trees," he ordered. He started barking men's names and indicated the three sections to cut so that the trunks would be small enough to lift. "Much!" he said, pointing to the men. Much nodded and moved quick, overseeing the cuts the axes were aiming for.

The men were crying out with every hack of the ax, and I turned to the gathering women and young folk. "Rocks," I said, pointing. "And the logs they've already cut. Wedge them next to the men so the weight's off a bit," I told them, grabbing an armful of wood myself. We built up little walls on either side of the pinned men, pushing and heaving till it pressed the trunk up, ever so little.

My heart kept pounding hard right up till it were late at night and the last man came free. The first two had broken their arms, I reckoned, but he were the worst. He could bare stand.

"Here," I said, and looped his arm round my neck, hugging close to him and holding him up. I held him tight and he groaned, slipping from my arms.

I yelped as he fell to the ground, and Rob and the others tried to haul him back up. He resisted, and coughed once. A gush of blood came from his mouth. I dropped to my knees and the other men stepped back a bit. Trembling, I rearranged myself around him and knelt by his head, laying his head gentle on my knees. I wiped the blood from his mouth, dashing the red on my legs and wiping his mouth again.

His name were Thomas Percy, and he were so young. Bare twenty-and-two, only a few months older than Rob. He were handsome—all the Percys were, their hair like corn silk and their eyes so soft and brown they looked like a puppy's. "Rob. Robin?" he said, and his voice were thick, caught up in his throat and wet.

"Right here, Tom," Rob said, kneeling. Emma Percy, Tom's little sister, gave a yell and came over to him, sitting on Tom's other side. She grabbed his hand, crying a terrible fuss.

"Rob," Tom said again. "I'm so sorry. I didn't mean—I was trying to help."

It sounded young and pitiful to my ears, and I stroked his hair back as tears slicked down on my cheeks. Rob clapped Tom's hand in both of his and nodded solemn to Tom. "You did well, Tom. You did very well."

"Tom, *no*," Emma said. "No!"

He touched her cheek, but there were a bit of his blood on his fingers and it smeared over her face. "You'll be all right, Emma. Connor will take care of you. He loves you, Emma."

She gripped his chest, crying hysterically and tugging him as if she'd keep his soul from flying out. "No, Tom," she said, over and over.

Tom coughed again and spat out blood, but more caught in his throat, shining at me in the dim light from the torches someone'd lit. "I'm sorry I won't be there, Emma. To give you to him. You'll do it, Rob," he said, looking solemn at Robin. "You'll give her away?"

Rob nodded, and I saw water in his eyes, not falling down, like it were his will alone that kept it in.

"There, Em," Tom said, but it were more a gurgle now, quieter too. "You won't be alone."

She wailed and clutched him, but I felt it, the moment when his eyes lost their light and his body went still and slack. I felt tears leaking into the seam of my mouth, and I kept petting his head, like if I never took my hands off him he wouldn't have died.

But then the monks came, and villagers came with a cart, and they took him away. And soon everyone else went away, and it were just me and Rob in the forest still, with blood on our hands. He were in front of me, and then he were pulling me up. "Come on, love," he said to me soft.

I clung to him, and tears started coming out faster. Not moving more, I sagged against him, and he clutched me tight, letting me cry on him like I weren't much used to doing. I weren't used to tears being a thing I could share with anyone, but there in the woods with death still lurking round us, I wanted to give them to Rob.

"We can't win, Rob," I whispered after a bit. "We can't never win. All of these people—they look to us for hope and help and all we do is get them killed."

"Yes," he grunted. "And how many more would die if we weren't here?"

I shuddered, and he gripped me tighter.

"John died," he breathed in my ear. "But it wasn't our fault. He was innocent, and the prince killed him. His death isn't our fault. It's our banner. Our cause. Our reason to fight, always." His head nuzzled against me. "And yes," he whispered. "He's also the reason I want to give up every damn day. I miss him, Scar. I miss my brother."

Rob shattered me. I broke into a million tiny pieces, crying in his arms like I never cried my whole life. I cried for John, who hadn't gotten near enough of my tears. And I looked around the forest and wondered if it would always be like this, tired and broken beyond all putting back together. Every day we lived, and every day it felt like we had a little less to live for.

—~—

We went back to the castle, a place it were dangerous and easy to start calling home, and Rob drew me aside, holding my hand.

"Stay with me tonight," he asked. "I don't want . . . after today, I just want you in my arms. Any way you'll have me."

I thought about how I loved sleeping against him, wrapped into his heartbeat like I could be tucked into his heart, and I shut my eyes against the temptation. In the dark behind my eyelids, I thought again of when I got to the tree and didn't see him, and had thought for a moment that he were dead. Dead and gone from me forever.

Opening my eyes, I shook my head. "I know," I said. "But David will have a fit, and soon enough, we will be married."

"When?" he whispered. "I know we should finish raising the tax, but Scarlet, if we're going to do it—"

"Eleanor will be here in a few weeks' time," I told him. "Maybe sooner. And we should wait for her blessing."

He sighed. "You're so adamant about *not* acting like a noblewoman, it's a little strange you care so much about her blessing."

I wanted to tell him. But I wanted to surprise him more than I wanted to tell him. Especially after a day that were so awful, I wanted there to be something wonderful left. More than anything, I wanted to give him this gift.

"Soon, love," I told him. "Good night."

He watched me go, and I went outside and into the forest.

—∞—

The next days were awful. We were all slow moving, slow from all the work our desperate, scarred hearts had pulled from our bodies the day the tree fell. I ached everywhere, and more than that, there were a sadness that had drifted down onto us like a mist. Cutting peat we were all quiet, digging our hands into the cold, hard earth, and we stumbled home at night without much to say about it. Missy, for her part, had told more and more people about the secret wedding, and I couldn't even fault her. It were clear on the faces of those that knew, shoring them up like holy water.

By the third afternoon, the sun had scared away the chill of the morning, and the woods were warm and bright. One of the women starting singing something, a song I'd heard before but didn't know the words for. The rest of the women began to take it up, and the children too, leaving their tasks to dance with one another in the sudden compulsion that little ones have. The women kept singing as one of the little boys took a loose clod of dirt and threw it at a girl and she shrieked, and the dancing turned to running and chasing.

I heard a whistling and a low chorus to the song, and some of the women laughed as the men bundled up the road on the cart to load up the peat, responding to their song. Rob came to me and I stood, his body fitting against mine so easy, my shoulder tucked under his, his hip against the curve of my waist. I looked up at him, and he ducked his head to give me a soft, gentle, easy kiss.

It were a husband's kiss, I rather thought. It weren't the first kiss, a thing of hunger and new tastes. It weren't all our sad kisses of leaving and coming back, full of desperation and scared. It were just a kiss. A kiss that felt like he'd done it before, a kiss that knew he could do it again.

Then again, it also sent lightning crackling down my back, and I remembered there were ways we weren't husband and wife just yet. I felt a blush running up my face and he stroked my cheek, kissing me again.

"I don't know, Sheriff," Bess said. I broke away from Rob, surprised. She hadn't been here a minute ago. She had the baby with her, and Much weren't far off, but she had a wicked smile. "Keep kissing her like that and I think we'll all have to go to your wedding fair soon," she said.

To my surprise, this raised cheers from the women and hollers from the men. I felt myself burn red, glaring at her for even teasing at our secret, and Rob tucked me closer to him. "Mind your business," Rob said, grinning. "Isn't there a tax to pay?"

"You'll never get them to the altar," Much said, winking at me as he took the baby. "Unless it were up in a tree. Or a prison. Then Scar might attend."

"Nonsense," Brother Benedict said, hefting a stack of peat bricks onto the cart. "Lady Huntingdon spends more time in a pew than the rest of you."

"Leave Scar alone," Rob said, rubbing my back. "Benedict? Much? How are we doing?"

Benedict rubbed his forehead. "I think we're coming along."

Much tallied the bricks with a frown. "If we split the cargo to two different markets we'll do better for price. Considering that, we're a little over the tax amount."

Rob started. "Over?"

Much nodded. "Well, given our luck and the nature of thieves here about, we really have to consider that we'll lose some of the money somehow. Fortunately, we're well ahead of the deadline and we have a lot of forest yet."

"Still, let's not use that opportunity if we don't have to. One thing we certainly know is there's always another tax." Rob looked around. "I know everyone isn't here, but those of you that are, gather close for a moment," he called.

People drifted in, and children whooshed past me, bumping me closer to Rob. He kissed my temple.

"Our work is done," he proclaimed, and everyone whooped and cheered. He grinned. "And now, we need to take all this to market and receive our bounty in coins. But before that," he said, and people sighed, crestfallen. "I think we need to celebrate."

Everyone cheered again, and I laughed.

"Anyone who can hunt, you can have one more day to hunt the royal forest, and we will feast tomorrow in Nottingham. Anyone in the shire who wants to come is welcome. We will share what we have, and then we will see what the sustenance of this noble shire really is—hope. And love. And caring for the fate of your fellow man." He nodded solemn. "We will honor the lives of those we've lost and we will toast to those new lives who have just begun."

Much held up Maryanne in answer as the people cheered.

"Let's do it in the forest," I said quick and loud, catching Much's eye and nodding. Winchester saw this and looked confused.

"Yes," Much said. "The forest gave us all this, it can host the feast!"

"And Rob, you and I can ready things at the castle."

"Shouldn't we be in the for—" he started.

"And Winchester will help us in the forest. You're not needed, Rob," Much said, nodding him off.

Rob started to smile and looked at me with a shrug. "I confess I don't know what's going on, but I will definitely take a few moments with you, my love," he told me, putting his arm around me.

"Well, I think we will both have much to do," I told him, smiling. "But I'm sure we can find a few moments."

"And maybe," he whispered into my ear, "with Sir David in the forest, you can stay with me tonight."

I elbowed him off, beaming at him. "We'll see about that."

He grinned. "As long as there's a chance, I'm a happy man." I smiled at him, but he grew serious, tugging me closer again, flush against him. "I mean it, you know. Whether you're never ready, whether we never beat Prince John, whether this never ends—as long as there's a chance, as long as there is some kind of hope for us, I'm happy."

I touched his face. "I'll be ready. And we'll beat Prince John, and this will end. We deserve more than a chance, Rob. We deserve a happy ending."

His mouth grazed over mine, like a ghost of a kiss. "Strange words from you."

"You inspire them," I told him, rubbing my nose on his. "You inspire me."

No sooner did his mouth fit over mine than I heard, "My lord, my lady! I must *insist!*" from David.

Rob twisted me in response, holding me careful and tight in his arms while he dipped me and gave me an awful dramatic kiss.

CHAPTER TWENTY-TWO

I went to the forest as soon as I were able, and Missy and Ellie near jumped on me to keep me from the place we'd been setting up for a wedding.

"Well, what are you two up to now?" I asked. "I thought this was my secret."

"Not anymore," Missy said. "Come on, my mum says there's much to do with you."

"Your mum?" I asked. From railing against my thievery to thinking I were corrupting her daughters, Mistress Morgan hadn't ever been so keen on me.

"Yes," Missy said. "And Bess has a present for you!"

This eased me a bit. At least Bess, I were sure, would prevent Mistress Morgan from poisoning me or some such thing.

"Ladies," I heard. We turned to see Much and Winchester there.

"His lordship has been quite the help," Much told me, and Winchester smiled.

"Mr. Miller isn't aware that I have other motives," Winchester said. "I seem to rely on Lady Huntingdon's help to get my own lady to the altar."

I beamed at this. "She'll be arriving any day," I told him.

"And you don't want to wait for her?" he asked. "Or more importantly, Eleanor?"

My face fell a little. "I'd love for her to be here. But I don't want to wait a day more to be Rob's wife."

He nodded. "Maybe then you'll start to call me Saer."

"He calls you Quincy, not Saer," I told him with a grin. "Only Margaret calls you Saer."

"Yes," he said. "Ladies I hold in high esteem may call me by my given name."

I nodded. "I'll consider it, Winchester."

He smiled and bowed to me. "Very well; I will take it as my solemn duty to distract the unwitting groom."

I laughed. "Thank you!" I told him, and the girls tugged me fast away to Edwinstowe.

Missy brought me back to her house, and it seemed the small home were filling with females. Mistress Morgan scowled at me, looking me over from head to toe and back again. "Well," she said. "Ellie, fetch some water, and I'll start scrubbing."

I looked at my hands, caked with dirt from digging out peat.

Mistress Morgan saw where I were looking. "Trust me, your hands are the least of your worries, young lady."

"Yes, ma'am," I told her.

She nodded. "If it matters, I've long since owed you an apology. I shamed you for stealing, and all you ever wanted was to help my family. I'm sorry for that."

My heart swelled up. "It's never needed," I told her. "But it means a lot, all the same."

She gave one final sharp nod. "In the morning, we'll send the girls for flowers. Perfect time of year for it."

"Flowers?" I questioned, but she already went to the kitchen, and Bess sat me down.

"You heard her," Bess said with a smile. "Time to scrub!"

—~—

They were at me for hours. I had little idea what they were doing, only that I had no modesty by the end of it. Bess cleaned my hands careful, especially the half hand with the damaged stumps. I told her she didn't have to, that she should rest, and she just smiled and pushed off my protests.

I'd lost my sister far too early in life, and in running from home with Joanna, I'd given up my only chance at a mother. I'd never had this, females that wanted to be part of my life. That wanted to be part of *all* my life.

"Thank you," I whispered to Bess. "Thank you for . . . this."

She beamed at me. "Don't be silly," she told me. "We're family now. We'll be family as long as you want it."

"Even though I'm some stuck-up lady now?" I asked her.

She laughed. "In truth, you're a lot nicer now than when you were a thief pretending to be a boy. So if it's the ladyship part of you, I'll take it." I frowned, and she laughed again, gentler. "I think you just have so many more people that care for you than you've ever been willing to admit, Scar."

It were strange, and wondrous, and made water push up behind my eyes, that maybe she weren't wrong.

Missy popped her head round the corner into the kitchen. "Is she done? It's done!"

I frowned. "What?"

"Yes," Bess said, toweling my clean, soft hands dry.

Missy hopped into the kitchen with a dress. My dress, sort of—it were made from a blue dress I'd worn the night Rob became sheriff, that last happy night with him—but it were different, the light blue underskirts repurposed to make the whole dress, and the old velvet overlay changed to just bare edge it in dark blue, shot through with silver. The skirt were layers of soft blue fabrics that must have come from still other dresses. The whole thing shimmered and looked soft and sweet.

My breath caught. Were this meant to be something I could wear? Could I be soft and sweet? Were I meant to be, once I were a wife?

"Look," Missy told me, flipping it round. She stuck her finger through two small loops. "For your knives!"

I laughed. I laughed so hard I started crying, and I hugged her close to me.

—

When they finally let me rest, I curled up in a chair by a dying fire. There, in the slow-darkening light and quiet, I finally pulled out Rob's letter.

SCARLET, 132.

I wish I could paint. I'm awful at it, and I'm sorry. Or even sketch. I'll try with words, pale though they are.

I left the castle early today. There was frost on the ground, hopefully our last, and the cold made my breath plume out in these big clouds. It seemed like a fairy story, or like Avalon, shrouding me in mist. Like if I just kept breathing, I could will magic into being. I could make things change for us, or I could make you appear to me.

The frost made everything glitter. It was one of those perfect frosts, where every blade of grass looks special and beautiful because of ice like lace on it. Even with the frost, the forest is green again, and this was like a crystal green, like a prism around the green.

We buried John in the graveyard of the monastery, and this morning—like many others—I went to visit him. To talk. To tell him he was right about us all along. He knew I loved you from the first. He said I was being an ass and should just tell you, and I told him to stop meddling—which led to a rather massive fight. You'll remember it, that first winter—you and Tuck and Much had a hard time pulling us apart. John slugged Much in the face by accident and you wouldn't speak to him for a week. You two thought we were fighting about one of the tavern girls, and that started the fight—but really, we were fighting about you. And what I should do.

I never told John that I'd said you should marry him. Mostly because I thought he'd take me up on it, and once things were good between us, I never got the chance. So I confessed it to his tombstone. That it should have been him to love you, to marry you. He would have taken you away from Nottingham and gotten started on a family with you straight off.

He would have been alive; you wouldn't be hidden away, in whatever hell Prince John is keeping you in. Maybe then I could have forgotten you.

Maybe not. You're not easy to forget, Scar.

The point of all these sketches is that I know you're not coming back. I have faith that Prince John won't hold you captive forever; you'll find a way out of that prison. You will beat him, because you never give up hope. But you won't risk returning here and bringing his fury down on Nottingham.

And it's not just Prince John, is it? I know you won't risk hurting me. You won't risk maybe hurting yourself. Because every day, when I'm a little more certain that you won't return, part of me is furious and despondent, but part of me is so relieved, Scar.

I'm scared of the ways you hurt me. I'm scared of the ways that you make me feel things—confront things—think things—that I never wanted. When you're not here my life is only half of what it can be, and, coward that I am, I sometimes find comfort in that ease.

What do I give up? Only the good things—those moments when you look at me and I'm robbed of breath. Those moments when you touch me and my mind is taken from me. Those moments when you forgive me, heal me, and I find my heart has been utterly stolen. By you. In ways that I only hope to deserve.

So stay away, Scar. I don't blame you. I understand. I will continue to live my half life, and I'll only mourn how it might have been when I see the sunset, and I can't prevent myself remembering all the things I feel for you in that half world between light and darkness, between the end and the beginning.

Wherever you are, just remember you have my heart in your keeping, and as long as that damn sun goes up and down, I won't be able to completely lose hope that you'll return to me.

When I slept, it were only after the words were formed within my heart, and my eyes were so tired I couldn't see.

CHAPTER TWENTY-THREE

The next morning, the girls woke me early, dressing me, braiding my hair round my head and sliding tiny white flowers into the twists. They took the fresh-bloomed wild roses from the forest and crushed their petals into my skin.

"Scarlet!" Missy yelped, coming into the house just past midday. She sprang away from the door. "Hide!"

"No!" I returned. "Is it Prince John? What's happening?"

She laughed, pulling me into the kitchen. "No! Rob's coming."

Bess caught her cloak and threw it over me. "Go out the kitchen when he comes in the front," she ordered.

I nodded, and Missy took my hand, laughing.

We started to do as she said, but I fast saw the flaw in her plan—the door out the kitchen were in sight of the front. And too quick, Rob opened it, and Missy and I hid off the side.

"—went to the castle, Rob," Much said.

"No," he said hot. "She didn't. She wasn't at the castle last night or this morning, and she was meant to be. Bess, Scar is missing. Have you seen her?"

"She stayed with me last night, Rob," Bess said in her soft way. Maryanne made a noise. "And you lot should know better than to burst in here with a baby about."

Rob sighed. "Thank God. Where is she now?"

"Much is right. She left here and went to meet you at the castle."

Bess, bouncing Maryanne, glanced at us in the kitchen and saw our problem. She moved to the far side of the room, and laughed. "Oh, Sheriff, the baby's watching you."

He took the bait, and Missy and I slipped out the back door, leaving it open so he wouldn't hear it shut.

I knew we had only a few minutes, and Missy and I started to run. Rob ducked out the back door and Missy shrieked, pushing me onward while she sought to stop Robin. He darted round her, close enough that I could see him frown at me. "Scarlet, what the hell!" he yelled at me.

Ducking through narrow straits between houses, I broke into the main square and saw Winchester.

"Winchester!" I cried, smiling. "Stop him!"

He whipped his head back around and saw Rob turn the corner behind me. Without a thought, he held his arm out and Rob ran straight into it, were knocked off his feet, and slammed onto the ground on his back, still.

I stopped with a gasp and Winchester winced, ducking down. I covered my mouth.

Winchester stood with a smile. "Still breathing!" he said.

"Good Lord, Winchester. I'm telling Margaret about that."

He shrugged. "Go hide. We'll send him in the right direction when it's time."

I nodded, turning and running at an easier pace.

"Anyone have any rope?" I heard Winchester ask.

—∞—

I planned to go straight to the clearing, but I knew I had hours yet and my feet didn't take me there. Instead, I found the road that cut through the wood, the one we'd given a reputation to as lawless and dangerous.

Following it down, I found the arch where two trees knitted together, where we'd robbed many a traveler of their goods. Where we'd started, where we'd honed our skills.

It weren't my destination. I went onward, off the road, going on the path that were worn in by pilgrims, marked by crosses in the trees. I picked wildflowers as I went, and by the time I arrived I had a big, messy bunch in my hands.

I didn't go into the monastery proper. Last I'd been there had been when Rob hurt me in his sleep, and those memories weren't far enough away. The pains in our love were never far below the surface, like the blood in the bruises they left.

Besides, there were enough pain to face. I turned into the graveyard, and it didn't take me long to find the new, simple stone that bore John Little's name.

Careful of my pretty dress, I knelt down, placing the flowers on his grave. "You're a father, John," I told him. "I imagine you're watching over her already, but she's perfect. Just perfect. Even considering she looks like you, which is something."

Drawing a slow breath, I pressed a hand to my stomach.

"I'm marrying Rob today." I smiled. "Much is giving me away. I can only imagine that if you were here you would have insisted it be you. I hope, at least. I hope after everything we went through, you didn't really love me the way you thought you did. I hope you didn't die because you loved me like that, not when I didn't feel that way for you." I looked down, sniffing. "Not when I kissed you when I wasn't sure if I meant it."

A tear jumped from my eyes.

"You died because of me, John. You died because of me and I'm sorry. There's no reason, there's no getting around it. I'm sorry. I'm sorry, I miss you, and I will always love you."

I brushed the water off my face, I kissed my fingers, and I pressed the fingers to his gravestone.

"Good-bye, John," I whispered. I crossed myself, shutting my eyes.

In the dark behind my eyelids, I could see him there, standing, watching me. He sat on the gravestone, rubbing his thumb over where I'd kissed it.

Good-bye, Scar, he whispered back.

—ᴡ—

The sky were just starting to glow with color when I made my way toward the clearing before Major Oak, and when I saw it, my eyes filled with tears.

All week long, we'd been fashioning ladders out of wood so that the townspeople—and me, to be honest—could get up into the branches of the old tree, stronger and healthier than ever after the fire last winter that were meant to destroy it. But my friends had gone further, and in the branches were draped long ribbons of cloth and garlands of flowers, making the whole tree alive with color and bits of things moving in the wind.

Missy and Ellie were running around, lighting candles at the base of the tree. Well, sort of candles—little stubs of things that were waiting to be melted down and wouldn't burn long. But the whole thing started to light up, and they smiled at me from their work.

I covered my mouth, touched, as tears started to course down.

"You can't cry on your wedding day," said a voice in my ear. I turned round and gasped to see Margaret, who ran to me with open arms. I caught her, hugging her tight. I saw Eleanor over her shoulder and let go of Margaret, going over to her. And losing all my words.

She raised her chin and her eyebrow both.

"Scar," Much said, coming over. "He'll be here soon. If I'm going to give you away—"

"Don't be foolish," Eleanor snapped, glancing at him. "She isn't yours, young man. You cannot give her to anyone. She is my granddaughter, and I will be the one giving her away."

Much's eyes damn near jumped out of his skull. "Christ!" he yelped, dropping to all-fours on the ground. "Your royal, serene, um—holy? Highness," Much stammered.

I laughed. "Much, get up. Much, Eleanor of Aquitaine, Queen Mother of England," I introduced. "Much Miller."

Her eyebrow arched up again, and she watched as Much got to his feet, brushing himself off. "One of your fellow vagabonds?"

"The best of my fellow vagabonds," I told her.

She gave him a regal nod. "You may address me as 'my lady' or 'my queen,'" Eleanor told Much.

He turned red. "Yes, my lady. My queen. My lady Queen. And I didn't meant to—um—steal her from you, or imply—anything. Sorry. Sorry, *my queen!*" he babbled.

She touched his shoulder. "Thank you for your service, young man. You have honored me and my granddaughter. Why don't you join the rest of the wedding."

Much looked like the Pope just canonized him, and he bowed deep to her. "Yes, my lady!" he said, turning and near running for the tree.

"He does know *you're* royal, doesn't he?" Eleanor asked.

I laughed, watching him go. "Sort of royal. How did you know about this?" I asked her.

"Oh, for Heaven's sake, how do I ever know anything? Between Margaret and Winchester there isn't much gossip I don't hear." She took my hand, and drew a breath. "I will give you away, if you'll have me."

I hugged her.

Townspeople were starting to come, climbing the ladders we'd made to get up to the branches and sitting in the tree.

Nervous, I took up one of the candles, holding it in my hand as the sky grew pinker and he weren't there yet.

I pushed the wax about. It were almost out. Raising my head, I stared into the forest.

Hearing someone coming, everyone went silent, and my heart stopped beating.

Winchester appeared, and he went to Margaret, taking her hand and kissing it before turning to me. "He's right behind me," he told me with a wink. He kept her hand and led her into the tree.

More people had come than could fit in the tree, and they just stood round the clearing, waiting. Waiting like I were waiting.

And then more footsteps crunched, and when a body rounded the tree, it were Rob. Allan took up his strings, playing music with a bright smile.

Rob stopped, seeing all of this before him. Seeing me before him.

I put the candle down, and it doused. He were dressed well; I reckoned Winchester must have somehow managed to talk him into that. It set my heart to hammering, seeing him so handsome, standing before me, piecing it all together.

A slow smile dawned on his face, and his eyes darted past me for a breath. "My lady Queen," he said, bowing to Eleanor.

She nodded, and he stepped closer to me.

"What is all this, Scarlet?" he asked.

I were shaking, and he took my hands, surprised. "I choose you, Rob. I will always choose you. And I may not be good at it just yet, but I will choose you every day of my life. Over and over and over until I do it the best of anyone. And together, we'll be strong enough to take on our enemies. We'll be strong enough to take on our demons."

He squeezed my hands, rubbing his thumbs over my knuckles, his smile sliding off to the side. "And you couldn't have just told me this? This lot has sent me over half of Nottinghamshire looking for you."

Grinning, I told him, "Our love has always been the grandest adventure, Rob. I couldn't let our wedding be any different."

He blinked, and I saw water edging his bright eyes. "Our wedding." He lifted my hands to his mouth. "Scar, you'll finally marry me?"

I nodded, and a tear shot down my cheek. "Yes. Finally."

He wiped it off. "Our last sunset apart," he said, looking to the trees as they were soaked in orange and pink.

He started to turn us toward the tree, but Eleanor stopped him, pushing at his chest. "I'll thank you not to take another step, young man. I have something to say."

He dropped his head to her.

"When Richard comes back, he will beat the stuffing out of you for marrying his only daughter without his consent." Rob's face dropped. "But I give my consent, and my blessing, which will have to be enough for him. And, of course, the more evident it is to me that you adore her, the easier he will be to mollify."

"You and your minstrels, you mean," I told her.

She lifted a shoulder. "Who doesn't like a good song. Now just one more thing—" she told me. She turned to me, untying the cloak from under my chin. She pulled it gentle from my hair, and my shoulders, and Rob just looked at me. He looked at me like he were lost, and found, and like he loved me. I couldn't look at him, couldn't remember this face, and ever doubt that he loved me.

He took my hand in his, kissing it, and walked me forward to the tree.

I led him up one ladder and then another, everyone in the tree holding it steady, as we went up to the strongest part of the tree, where the priest teetered, unsettled by the height.

"The heartwood," Rob murmured, looking at me. "You wanted to marry me in the heart of Major Oak."

I beamed at him, grateful that he understood.

"And Scar," he whispered.

I leaned in close.

"Are you wearing knives to our wedding?"

Nodding, I laughed, telling him, "I was going to get you here one way or another, Hood."

He laughed, a bright, merry sound. Standing in the heart of the tree, he reached again for my hand, fingers sliding over mine. Touching his hand, a rope of lightning lashed round my fingers, like it seared us together. Now, and for always. His fingers moved on mine, rubbing over my hand before capturing it tight and turning me to the priest.

The priest looked over his shoulder, watching as the sun began to dip. He led us in prayer, he asked me to speak the same words I'd spoken not long past to Gisbourne, but that whole thing felt like a bad dream, like I were waking and it were fading and gone for good. "Lady Scarlet," he asked me with a smile, "known to some as Lady Marian of Huntingdon, will thou have this lord to thy wedded husband, will thou love him and honor him, keep him and obey him, in health and in sickness, as a wife should a husband, forsaking all others on account of him, so long as ye both shall live?"

I looked at Robin, tears burning in my eyes. "I will," I promised. "I will, always."

Rob's face were beaming back at me, his ocean eyes shimmering bright. The priest smiled.

"Robin of Locksley, will thou have this lady to thy wedded wife, will thou love her and honor her, keep her and guard her, in health and in sickness, as a husband should a wife, forsaking all others on account of her, so long as ye both shall live?" the priest asked.

"Yes," Rob said. "I will."

"You have the rings?" the priest asked Rob.

"I do," I told the priest, taking two rings from where Bess had tied them to my dress. I'd sent Godfrey out to buy them at market without Rob knowing. "I knew you weren't planning on this," I told him.

Rob just grinned like a fool at me, taking the ring I handed him to put on my finger.

Laughs bubbled up inside of me, and I felt like I were smiling so wide something were stuck in my cheeks and holding me open. More shy and proud than I thought I'd be, I said, "I take you as my wedded husband, Robin. And thereto I plight my troth." I pushed the ring onto his finger.

He took my half hand in one of his, but the other—holding the ring—went into his pocket. "I may not have known I would marry you today, Scar," he said. "But I did know I would marry you." He showed me a ring, a large ruby set in delicate gold. "This," he said to me, "was my mother's. It's the last thing I have of hers, and when I met you and loved you and realized your name was the exact color of the stone—" He swallowed, and cleared his throat, looking at me with the blue eyes that shot right through me. "This was meant to be, Scarlet. I was always meant to love you. To marry you."

The priest coughed. "Say the words, my son, and you *will* marry her."

Rob grinned and I laughed, and Rob stepped closer, cradling my hand. "I take you as my wedded wife, Scarlet. And thereto I plight my troth." He slipped the ring on my finger and it fit.

"Receive the Holy Spirit," the priest said, and kissed Robin on the cheek.

Rob's happy grin turned a touch wolflike as he turned back to me, hauling me against him and angling his mouth over mine.

I wrapped my arms around him and my head spun—I couldn't tell if we were spinning, if I were dizzy, if my feet were on the ground anymore at all, but all I knew, all I cared for, were him, his mouth against mine, and letting the moment we became man and wife spin into eternity.

CHAPTER TWENTY-FOUR

There were so many people around us I couldn't count them all. I didn't much care to either—there were no hunger or thirst, no pain or weariness. Rob and I danced and kept dancing, close in each other's arms, as the light of the sunset gave way to the torch-lit dark of night.

I had no way of knowing what the time really were, but at some point Rob and I stole away a little, and he leaned me against a tree, kissing me until my whole body shivered and burned in the same strange moment.

"You look so beautiful," he told me, pulling out one of the flowers that Missy had braided into my hair. "The most beautiful bride I've ever seen."

"You're awful handsome yourself," I told him, running my hands over his chest. "Too handsome by far. We'll have to make you much uglier now you're married," I told him. "Make sure all the ladies want to keep their hands off."

He grinned and kissed me. "I'll let them all know how fond my wife is of knives."

My belly fluttered and a shiver ran through me.

"What?" he asked, his voice a low soft groan by my ear.

"*Wife*," I said. "I'm your wife."

"In almost every way that counts," he told me, squeezing my hips. "And I like the way your eyes look when you say that."

Blushing, I tried the word again. "Wife," I murmured, gazing at him.

"Husband," he growled, and that sent another shiver tumbling through me.

"Let's go back to the castle," I whispered. "Or the manor. Or somewhere. Please?"

"Scarlet," he said, very serious. "I'll tell you this once and don't go using this power for ill purposes, but when you say 'please' like that, I'll agree to damn near anything, all right?"

I laughed and he turned, dragging me against him and walking me backward to the feast tables and dancing.

Kissing my neck, he murmured, "Christ, I know I left a horse around here somewhere."

"Sheriff!" called Ellie. Missy and a few other girls were standing there, holding the reins of a beautiful gray horse.

"There it is," he said, only letting go of me enough to hoist me onto it. He swung up behind me, tugging me tight against him, and Ellie held on to the reins. "Ellie?" he asked. "Can I have the horse back?"

"No," she said, smiling. "We have a surprise for you two."

Rob looked at me and I raised my shoulders. He kissed me, wrapping his arms around me. Much handed us a cloak and Bess waved up at us, and others began to cheer and hoot at us. Rob wrapped the cloak around me and tucked his arms round me tight. "All right, Ellie. Lead the way."

Missy and a few of the other girls carried candles, and it felt like we were following fairies deep into the woods. The horse moved slow and careful, led along by the girls who looked back at us to giggle every now and again.

When we stopped, I realized where we were. "The cave?" I said, looking to Rob in question.

Rob's shoulders lifted, and I looked at the girls. Two of the smaller ones with candles rushed inside, and a dull glow began from within.

"You saved our lives by bringing us here," Ellie told us, looking down. "So start your new life here too."

Rob clutched me tight, and I looked at him. He nodded once, taking my chin and kissing me.

I nodded. Rob dismounted and helped me down, and I hugged Ellie. "Thank you," I whispered. "This is perfect."

She hugged me. "Hopefully you'll feel the same in the morning," she laughed, and swatted my rump as I let her go.

The little sprites inside the cave ran out, and I kissed Missy's cheek and thanked her too. Then Rob took my hand and I forgot all about them as he led me inside.

They had lit a fire, and instead of our old pallets there were a new one, fresh stuffed and bigger, with furs and blankets heaped on it and flowers strewn all around the place. Rob's hand ran up my spine to my neck, and I shuddered. He came in front of me, kissing my neck, and then my cheek, and then the corner of my mouth. "Do you remember what I told you that night?" he whispered, switching his kisses to the other side.

That night. That night in this cave, when he'd told me—everything. Everything for the first time. "That I changed everything."

Another kiss, and my clothes started to feel overtight, like my skin were burning, my whole body trying to burst out. "What else?" he murmured.

His lips sucked on my neck, just beneath my ear, and my knees buckled. I gripped him with a gasp. "That you'd keep my heart," I moaned.

His mouth hovered right over mine, grazing whisper soft over my lips, not giving me what I wanted, what I burned for. "What else, my sweet Scar?"

"That we'd be free," I said, pressing my lips to his.

His mouth were fire hot, aggressive, powerful, his tongue moving into my mouth and filling me with taste and touch. He gripped my hips and pulled them flush against him, and I pulled my mouth away from his, gasping for breath. He moaned, lips reaching for mine again.

"Rob," I breathed, panting.

He gave me a kiss-drunk nod.

"Take my dress off," I asked him. Smiling and dropping a teasing kiss on his mouth, I whispered, "Please."

Holding me tight, he twisted me around in his arms, trying to untie the knot in my laces Mistress Morgan had tied. With an impatient growl, he yanked and the thing tore. I gasped, but with one hand he pulled my shoulder close to him, kissing my neck as he undid the whole bodice until it gave way, and he tugged the blue kirtle off over my head.

It tore out some flowers with it, and he seized on this new task, dragging his fingers through my hair and plucking out one after the other.

His fingers drew the string of the knot holding my underdress together at my neck until it gave, sweeping my hair over my shoulder. For long seconds, he didn't touch me, and I knew my back, scarred as it were, were exposed before him.

He took a breath and dragged his lips along the long scar Gisbourne had given me. I shivered.

He found another by my spine, and pressed his lips there.

He kissed every mark. He stood, pressing his head into my hair. "I hate that I can't protect you from the pain you've already faced, Scar."

I turned. "You do," I told him. "You make it go away."

He kissed me, pressing me tight, and bunches of new sensations flared and sparked in me with only the thin barrier left between my body and his. I started tugging at his tunic and he let me drag it up over his head, and I pulled the shirt beneath with it.

His chest were bare beneath it, and I felt like my body must be running on something other than air. I couldn't catch my breath, couldn't remember to try, and still I were moving, alive, more alive than ever before. I put my hands on his chest, knowing I weren't the only one with scars.

"Turn around," I told him.

He didn't move, looking at me, nervous and mournful, and I took a breath, moving around him.

His back, once punctured and pierced with metal spikes, were a mess. Some were neat circles, but most were craggy dips and ragged tears of healing and infection and pain.

Tears sprang to my eyes, and I ran my hands over his shoulders. He turned, looking at me, shaking his head. "No, my love," he whispered. A tear fell and he wiped it away, kissing my mouth.

He broke away, touching my cheek.

"I'll never regret those scars," he told me, pressing our foreheads together. "I'll always remember that as the day I knew you loved me."

He kissed me again, and I wrapped my arms around him.

He pulled the longer kirtle and the plain underdress up together, and my legs felt the rush of cold. I shivered, and he stopped. "Scar?" he asked, his chest heaving against mine. Waiting. He nudged my nose with his own.

"Please don't stop," I told him.

Stepping back, Rob pulled the dresses all the way off and pulled me against him, so quick he hadn't even dropped the balled-up cloth and it were pressed like a pillow to my back. He kissed me, and shy and slow, my hands trembling, I pushed the rest of his clothes off him.

And then we were skin to skin, heat to heat, breath to breath.

He pulled me down gentle to the pallet, and he showed me the mysteries of my body that I'd never understood, and it felt like my world came apart and rebuilt again slow, brick by brick, to form a whole new life. And lying there with him by the fire, his body curled around mine and our fingers and legs twined together, I realized what he'd meant, all those months ago.

Nuzzling against his head, I whispered to him, "This is freedom, Rob."

Using our twined hands to tuck our arms close around my body, he murmured into my hair, "*You* were always my freedom, Scar."

CHAPTER TWENTY-FIVE

I woke up in his arms, the fire cold beside us. I tugged the furs higher, not wanting to move from him yet. My chest were pressed into his, and I could only feel one heartbeat. I didn't know if his body matched mine or mine matched his, but somehow, in the night, they'd fallen into one beat.

One soul. Two bodies.

Married.

"Married," I whispered out loud, my head on his shoulder.

"That did happen, didn't it?" he said, his chest rumbling beneath me. I could hear the smile in his voice without looking up.

I grinned and kissed the bit of skin nearest to my mouth. "Yes, *husband*. It did." I raised my head. "Oh—not just husband. *Your Grace.*"

He looked at me, his brows tightening together. "I'm the earl now."

I nodded, and he brushed my hair back. "Is that a good thing?"

He sighed, and I rested on his chest again. "I don't know. I'm not sure I was meant to have that title, Scar."

"Of course you were."

"I don't think it was a coincidence that I'd done all those horrible things in the Holy Land and came back to find that I wasn't responsible for anyone anymore. It felt like justice, and I've spent so much time trying to atone . . ." He shook his head. "I never thought I'd be in the position to get any of that back, Scar."

Tucking my head lower, I didn't dare look up at him when I asked this question. "And now?" I asked. I held my breath.

He drew a deep breath. "Now." The breath ran out of him, and he rolled up onto his side, laying me on my back and looking at me. "If we're going to be Earl and Lady Huntingdon, Scar, we will do it right. Together. We'll protect the shire."

"Make it prosperous again," I told him, running my hand up his arm as his thumb stroked my waist. "Make it so there are stores and reserves and these things won't affect us in the future."

He nodded, his eyes navy and serious. "And if we have any children, we are going to protect them. Watch them grow. Not let them run away to holy wars or London."

I couldn't help but smile. "Do you really think any children of ours won't be awful troublemakers, Robin Hood?"

He shook his head, smiling. Hair fell on his forehead and I brushed it back. "Last we spoke of it, you didn't sound keen about the idea of children," he said soft.

"It terrifies me," I whispered.

"Why?" he asked.

"If a child ever got hurt because of me—" I started, but the awful thought choked me and I stopped, shaking my head. "But I trust God. If He wants us to have babies, Rob, I swear I will find a way to protect them with everything we have. With every*one* we have."

He nodded, pulling me up to him and kissing me. "We should probably leave this cave at some time, shouldn't we?" he asked between kisses.

"We have to talk to Eleanor. But not yet," I told him with a smile.

He grinned. "Remind me to petition Richard to have this cave attached to the Huntingdon lands," he murmured.

I laughed, and he kissed me.

—~—

We left the cave in the noon sun, and it felt strange to put on the same clothes as the day before, like I couldn't wear the same thing when I felt like a different person. Rob held my hand tight and kissed it. "Let's go talk to Eleanor," he said.

I nodded.

We brought the horse but walked together. It were like stealing a little extra time for ourselves, refusing to go fast back to the world. When we reached the castle people saw us and shouted, hugging and kissing and giving us their good wishes. Even the knights came to us, pledging themselves now to Rob as well.

It were late afternoon by the time we made it to the keep itself. There we found Eleanor, holding court in front of the fireplace, looking very grand. Margaret were sitting with her, but she were staring at the ground, and Eleanor were holding her hand. Winchester were pacing, his arms crossed over his big chest, glancing back at Margaret.

"What's wrong?" I asked, looking at Rob as dread crept over my heart. We hadn't even been married a whole day yet.

Eleanor and Winchester both looked at Margaret, and she lifted her head to show me tears tracked all over her face. Rob squeezed my hand, but we didn't move.

Margaret held up a letter in her lap. "My father," she whispered. "He's ordered me to travel to London. To marry the future Earl of Hertford."

Winchester made a low growling sound, like a wolf, and I looked to him. "*De Clare*?" I demanded. "She's meant to marry *de Clare*?"

"Yes," Winchester gritted out. "The man who arguably took the most pleasure in the prince's cruel treatment of you. Yes, I'm sure he'll be a suitable husband."

Rob looked fast at me. "Quincy, come with me. Let's take some air."

"Air?" Winchester snapped. "*Air*? Prince John is doing this because of me!" he roared. "You think de Clare just woke up and decided to be married? No. '*Bold words*,' he said. Prince John is ordering this and I swear to God I will see him bleed for it."

Eleanor stiffened, and Rob pushed at Winchester's shoulders. "Outside with you," he ordered, and then, much quieter, "You're scaring her, Quin."

He glanced at Margaret, who were looking at him with wide, lost eyes, and he hung his head. He let Rob push him out of the room.

I went to them. "All is not lost," I told her, kneeling in front of her.

"It is," she sniffed. "My father won't change his mind. He's going to meet me in London within a fortnight and the marriage will happen within the month."

"Winchester will change his mind," I told her. "Let him ask for your hand."

"Winchester is right," Eleanor said soft. "I can't imagine this happened without my son's urging. And if my son has promised your father something, it may be difficult to match." She looked at me, and back to Margaret. "Particularly," she added with a sigh, "if your theory about his plans for Richard is correct."

Margaret drew a breath and it came out with tears. I caught her hands in mine. "No," I told her. "I won't let this happen. I promise. The only way you'll marry de Clare is if you damn well want to."

She shook her head. "I don't. But my father—"

"We'll deal with him."

"You must escort her down to London," Eleanor told me.

I shook my head. "I can't leave Nottingham. Not now."

"You must," Eleanor told me. "I gave you the option of a strong, protective alliance, and you chose your own path," she said, her eyebrow arching up.

"You never thought I'd marry Essex," I scoffed.

The eyebrow dropped. "Well. Still, you need more of the nobility at your side to quell John, Marian."

"What, and show them how Prince John has repaid Winchester for his aid? No one will help us then."

"Really?" she said. "They don't have wives and daughters? People they wish to protect? People they love?"

I frowned.

"Whether it makes them bold or not, the other nobles need to see that Prince John is acting out against their way of life. And besides, if you're in London you can protect the silver we're sending down there."

"No," I told her. "I can't leave Nottingham. Not when Prince John has already proven he can strike within these walls."

"But that's it exactly—he can strike within these walls. He can strike you anywhere. If you're only concerned with your corporeal body, you will lose. The battle you are fighting now, Marian, is not one of physicality. Your knights can stay here and protect your shire, but you need to wage a much more subtle war, of diplomacy and shifting loyalty. Go to court, and perhaps you can stop him, once and for all."

"Please," Margaret said, squeezing my hands. "Please come with me. If you're there—I'll feel so much better if you're there."

Frowning fast at Eleanor, I looked to Margaret and nodded. "Very well. I'll go with you. I won't let you go alone."

The door opened behind us, and Rob stepped inside. Winchester followed him, crossing his arms again.

I stood, turning to them, and Margaret wiped her face. "I'll go with Margaret to London, Winchester. I'll make sure this doesn't happen."

He nodded. "I'm coming with you," he said. "If your father is headed for London, I'll meet him there. And you can be damn sure I won't let this marriage happen," he promised, looking at Margaret.

Rob were looking at me, and I met his gaze. "Maybe you should stay here," I told him.

His mouth tilted up, and he chuckled. "Not a chance, Scar," he told me, and it sounded the same as when he said he loved me.

I nodded. "We'll leave for London as soon as Nottingham is sorted."

—∾—

We stayed in Nottingham for another week. For the time, we arranged for people whose houses had burned to live in the castle and with families in Edwinstowe. Most of our people were farmers, and the spring were a busy time they couldn't afford to miss. Some knights were sent to help, and several others stayed behind to start rebuilding the homes in Nottingham.

I weren't keen to leave Nottingham. It felt like we were finally home, and more than that, home in a way we could defend and protect. We had built up our walls and turned back our enemy, and now we were leaving to ask for more.

Or so it seemed. God knew it were hard to look at Bess and Maryanne and not remember why Prince John had to be stopped and King Richard had to return safe.

Despite any worries or fears, we prepared the carriage, full of nothing but riches, and I stood in the courtyard with Rob, Winchester, Allan, David, and Margaret as people gathered to see us off. Much and Bess were there, and she let me hold the baby, like my touch might bless the girl.

"I hope you'll hurry back," Bess told me. "Things won't be the same until you return."

A shiver ran down my neck. "No. And if there's any sign of trouble—"

"We'll hide. In the forest. Much will take care of everything, I'm sure."

She looked at him then, drawing in her breath, and I saw something different in her eyes. Bess loved John, that were true, but looking at her then, I didn't think Much's heart were in poor keeping.

"He will," I agreed. "But I knew that already, and Rob agreed with me."

She looked confused. "What do you mean?"

I nodded toward Rob, and waved Maryanne's little arm at Much.

"My dear people," Rob said, standing on the step of the carriage. "Some of you are aware, as the new earl, I can no longer be your sheriff."

A murmur ran through the crowd, and Much, standing beside him, frowned.

"But Scarlet and I must go to court, and we want to ensure your safety and your protection while we are gone." He nodded to me.

I kissed Maryanne's cheek. "You could say Rob and I know something about what it takes to protect this shire," I said with a smile, and people chuckled. "So there was only one person we could appoint as sheriff, if he'll take the position."

Much looked at me, then looked round.

"Much Miller," Rob said, beaming with a wide grin, "will you be the Sheriff of Nottingham?"

His throat bobbed, his mouth slack and open.

Bess laughed, going beside him and kissing his cheek shy. "Say yes, Much."

He looked at her, his eyes full of wonder. "Yes," he said to her.

Rob grinned. "Repeat this oath, Much," he told him.

Much kept looking at Bess as Robin said the words, like he were saying his wedding vows over again.

"By the Lord, I will to King Richard and the Office of Sheriff be faithful and true, and love all that He loves, and shun all that He shuns, according to God's law, and according to the world's principles, and never, by will nor by force, by word nor by work, do aught of what is loathful to Him; on condition that He keep me as I am willing to deserve when I to Him submitted and chose His will."

Much repeated it, and he drew a deep breath and kissed Bess. Her shoulders raised for a moment, but then her arms went round him and the people cheered.

Maryanne squirmed against me, and I looked at her. "Your papa's a hero," I whispered to her. I brushed my nose over her cheek, then laid a kiss in its wake. "Both of them."

CHAPTER TWENTY-SIX

We arrived in late afternoon, five days after we'd set out from Nottingham. Margaret and I rode in a carriage, and I held her hand most of the way there. She were pale and would bare look at Winchester.

The men flanked our carriage, Rob and Winchester ahead and David and Allan behind.

Wending through the squalor of London, it were like we were meant to see the dirt and grime of the city long before we saw the beauty of Westminster Palace. And then the city began to fade and turrets of the long rectangle of the palace came into view, teetering on the edge of the river, and you remembered the riches, the glory, and the power that England held tight in its palm.

Servants rushed out to greet us, and we dismounted in the wide courtyard. The wind were snapping off the river and it made me feel taller, more royal, than I expected.

"Your Grace," a well-dressed man said, coming forward and bowing to Winchester.

"Sir," Winchester frowned, "we have contributions from the queen's efforts; please have your men help us bring it to the treasury."

"The treasury is in the White Tower, your Grace. I will have knights escort it over immediately."

"What?" Winchester asked. "It wasn't a few weeks ago."

"The prince ordered it," the man said. "He was afraid the palace wasn't secure enough."

"And the White Tower is better?"

"Forgive me, your Grace, I cannot think to guess at the prince's motivation for his decision. We can have someone escort it over immediately."

"Absolutely not," I said.

The man looked to me like I weren't supposed to speak. "My lady—"

"No," I said. "We will escort it there immediately."

"My lords—"

"I wouldn't contradict her," Winchester warned.

I turned to Margaret, kissing her cheek. "Go in and rest. Get settled. We will return very soon."

She nodded, looking to Winchester, and I nodded to Allan.

Allan came over. "Stay with her," I told him.

He dismounted with a gallant smile. "I have just the song to cure a lovesick lady," he told her. She frowned at this.

I took Allan's horse. "I don't know if de Clare is here yet," I told them, "but Allan, do not allow an audience with her if he is."

Allan nodded once to me.

I mounted the horse without aid, and Winchester and Rob did the same.

"One of our knights will lead you—" the man started.

"I am familiar with the White Tower's location," I told him.

He didn't speak more.

Rob sidled up next to me. "You don't have to come," he told me. "We can do it."

Glaring at him, I said, "I'm coming. For Heaven's sake, I put on a dress and you lot think I'm a girl."

Winchester frowned at me. "I confess, my lady, I often don't understand you at all."

Rob took my hand and flipped it over, kissing the palm. "Woman, maybe. Girl, never."

I shook my head with a smile.

David nodded once to me, solemn. "My lady, we should go. It's already late and as you remember, London can be . . . rough."

Rob glanced at me at that, more questioning, watching me like there were more secrets he wanted to peer into. "Let's go," he allowed. I nodded to David.

We left the palace with the carriage, taking the road along the river. The city were bright with lights and dark with the shadows that clung to the edges of them to our left, and out on the right, the river stretched wide, still and deep, never showing its dark secrets or the ways it moved under the surface. Breathing in deep, it weren't the lush green of the forest; there were smoke and mold, too many bodies and wet.

I looked at Rob, trying to fill my mind with forest and ocean and sun instead, all the things I saw in his eyes and his face and his hair.

The White Tower were almost full dark, but for a lantern above the wooden staircase leading to the elevated door. The gate were shut, and a guard only appeared when we came close.

"The Earl of Winchester and the Earl and Lady Huntingdon," David said to the guard. "We're here to contribute to the king's ransom."

The knight looked us over and nodded to us, opening the gate.

At this signal, ten knights came out of the keep, and David approached one as we all dismounted. "We have silver for the ransom," he told him.

The knight looked at David but didn't respond.

"Yes, sir, we will take care of it," said another knight, and David turned to him.

David frowned, listening to his accent. "French, sir?" he asked.

"*Oui*," the knight answered. "Prince John called for us from France—I believe so more of his own knights could defend the queen mother."

David nodded. "Very well. Yes, empty the carriage."

The French knight bowed his head in agreement.

"We need the amounts—we have Eleanor's record but not yours," the French knight said, nodding toward a little man with his head out the door.

Rob nodded, and we went up the staircase. Inside, we didn't go up to my former rooms, but down, into the bottom of the keep. In a large room there were near fifty chests, arranged neat behind a small desk where the man recorded our sums before going out to the carriage.

I went over to the chests, chills running up my arms. It were a grand fortune, to be sure.

It were even enough of a fortune to steal the throne of England from my father and place Prince John on it instead.

—w—

We didn't speak until we had unloaded our contribution and left the walls of the White Tower. Even then, we were silent for many moments more, our horse's hooves loud on the road.

"French," I said finally. "He had Frenchmen guarding English money."

"It doesn't bode well," David agreed.

"If you needed to raise an army to steal an English crown, where's the first place you would go?" I asked, shaking my head.

"France," Winchester said. "Especially if you're the son of Eleanor of Aquitaine." I nodded.

"The time doesn't work out," Rob agreed. "If Prince John sent for them when the queen mother was attacked, they would barely be boarding a ship by now, not guarding the silver for weeks already."

I glanced back at the White Tower, formidable and tall, its pale gray stone bright with only the moon upon it. "Then Prince John already has stolen King Richard's ransom. And we need to steal it back."

—w—

The next morning Rob and I woke, and called for the servants that dressed us. I watched him as they went, tugging and pulling and tying both of us.

He had changed, just a bit. The way he stood, the angle of his chin—these were like they were when I'd known him first. When the luster of nobility hadn't been taken away from him, when he hadn't been brought low and humbled.

He caught me looking and grinned at me. "Thank you," he said, with an authority that really meant they were dismissed. His servants bobbed to him and left, and mine hesitated.

"Milord, her dress—" one said.

"I will serve her Grace," Rob said, smiling just at me.

The girl bobbed and left, leaving my dress half-laced in the back.

"Now," he said. "What was that look for?"

Placing my hands on his chest, I let my fingers trail over him. The fancy shirt and expensive tunic, the sharp way his strong neck came up out of the clothes. I touched the hollow of his throat, drawing in a breath.

He sucked in air, and his throat moved against my finger.

"You were born for this," I whispered to him. "Being a noble again. This was where you were always meant to be."

There were a rumble in his chest, like a purring from a cat. I looked up and he were looking at me, staring at me, his eyes peeling everything away until he were left with whatever were at my deepest core.

The way he'd always looked at me.

"I didn't deserve this—I couldn't do this—until you, Scarlet. So if there's something I'm meant for, it's you."

Looking at me like that, his words that rushed through me, it were better than any of his incredible kisses. It were the feeling of hope, that we might be able to win through this. I nodded, like he knew my thoughts. "Time to begin."

He nodded back. "Time to finish this."

—∾—

Westminster Palace weren't properly part of London. A short walk outside it, it were considered its own town, and the nobles took full advantage of that to keep themselves from the squalor of the city. Just outside the palace walls, there were long greens where the nobles flocked to now that the sun were warm and they had all gathered here to hide from the unrest of the country.

We went out, my arm in Rob's like I were some proper lady, and my fingers curled into his arm within the first few feet of the palace walls. Margaret walked alongside me, close enough to reach for me.

I had faced fires, weaponry, and marriage, but nothing seemed quite so terrifying as facing down a field of bored nobility.

"There he is," Margaret whispered.

I followed her gaze, and saw de Clare laughing at something an older gentleman said. The man looked stern, if not outright offended.

Margaret's gaze also drew his notice, however, and de Clare clapped the man on the back and came over to us.

Rob took a small step forward as he did, positioning himself between de Clare and me in a tiny little way. I frowned at him.

Rob's eyebrows lifted. "You think I don't know the way he spoke to you last he was in Nottingham?" he told me soft. "The man's damn lucky I don't put an arrow through his eye."

"There she is," de Clare said, loud, still a step or two away. He came closer still, reaching for Margaret's hand. She tried to step back but he caught her, bowing over her hand and kissing it. "My future wife."

Margaret went stiff and still, curtsying to him. "My lord de Clare," she said quiet.

He looked at Rob and me. "And Lady Huntingdon," he said, releasing Margaret to drop his head to me, not near the full bow my rank required. "And the Sheriff."

Rob didn't so much as incline his head. "That's the Earl of Huntingdon, de Clare," he said. Rob took my hand and kissed it.

De Clare laughed. "Well, the prince was right about men lapping at the teat of power, wasn't he? Well played, Locksley," he said.

Rob's face were flat, and he stepped forward, close enough that de Clare stepped back. "'I can find her in the castle, alone, vulnerable. I can do whatever I want to her.'" Rob's voice were a low, measured growl.

I frowned at Rob, confused, and de Clare looked much the same, glancing from me to Rob and back.

"Is that not what you said to my lady wife once?" Rob asked. "You seemed to insinuate that it is easy to get a person alone. To pay them back for any perceived threat with the promise of punishment."

De Clare's face went a little more pale.

"Don't speak to her. Don't speak about her," Rob said, glaring hard into de Clare's eyes. "Ever."

De Clare stepped back, but the slick, smug smile returned. "Come along, Margaret. Why don't we get to know each other a little better away from such company?"

He reached for her hand again, but she stepped back. "You will address me as Lady Margaret, until such time as we are wed," she told him, her voice quiet and strong. "And though I will obey my father, I will not go anywhere with you now."

His face twisted. "Fine. But do not let these people give you any delusions, *Lady Margaret*. You will marry me, and when you do, you will not enjoy the same disgusting prideful tendencies as she does. You will be a proper wife."

She drew a breath. "Does that mean you will also be a proper husband, my lord?" she asked.

"Yes," he said, his upper lip lifting in something caught between a smile and a snarl. "I will do what I please, and I won't be questioned by my wife. Think on that, Lady Margaret."

He turned away, and Margaret looked at me, her face grim and her chin raised.

I saw Winchester. He were standing close, close enough to hear, and he watched her. She saw him, and he smiled at her, proud and loving, and she drew in a deep breath, nodding once to him.

Rob rubbed my hand, still captive in his, with his thumb. "Isabel," he murmured.

Isabel, Princess of England and wife of Prince John were there in her full glory, a small crowd of her ladies around her. She saw me, and looked at Rob and frowned. She raised her chin in a poor imitation of Eleanor, looked at us, and waited.

We moved forward, Margaret trailing behind us. I curtsied and Rob bowed. "My lady Princess," Rob greeted. "It is excellent to see you again so soon after midwinter."

"And you, my lord Sheriff," she said, frowning in my direction. "Or is it my lord Leaford now?" she asked, her lip curling a little. "I'm so relieved to hear you haven't perished, Lady Leaford."

"Thank you," I told her stiff. "And you can address us as Earl and Lady Huntingdon."

She didn't look much surprised, but it were the ladies behind her that gasped. "So Richard has created you."

"Yes," Rob said, smiling. "But my lady, we never got a chance to speak in Nottingham. And you know, as we were riding down here we saw the most beautiful Welsh ponies—do you remember that pony you had as a child?"

She looked at him. "Tulip? Why, my lord, how strange that you would recall that."

"Of course," he said. "I remember when my father was in attendance at court and we visited Gloucester. You were an accomplished rider even then."

Her eyes lit. "Oh! That's right—you kept sneaking her sugar cubes and she got sick," she recalled.

He laughed, and she smiled with him. "Your father was furious," Rob said.

"And you wouldn't let me take the blame," she said, nodding. "I remember."

He lifted a shoulder, and I wondered if that were his intent all along, to remind her of a debt she owed him, even in such a small way.

Margaret came forward and curtsied low. "My lady Princess," she greeted soft.

"Lady Margaret, welcome," Isabel said, with something that I thought were rather close to genuine affection. "Why are you not with the queen mother? She has not been imperiled again, has she?"

"No, my lady Princess," Margaret said, rising. "My father wishes me to marry."

Isabel smiled, her eyes finding Winchester. "How lovely! We need a wedding to raise our spirits. What a delicious idea."

"To my lord de Clare," Margaret said, softer, meeting Isabel's eyes.

The joy went out of Isabel's face, and her ladies behind her murmured. "Oh. That will not suit," she said.

Margaret shook her head, red flushing her cheeks.

"Is your father coming to court?" Isabel asked.

Margaret nodded. "Within the week, my lady."

"Hm. We shall see what we can do to convince him otherwise," she said, glancing to Winchester again.

"Thank you, my lady Princess," Margaret murmured, never failing to look the part of the perfect, demure lady.

Isabel's eyes raked thoughtful over Rob. "I heard there have been troubles in Nottingham," she said to him. "If your wife will excuse us, you should tell me how you quelled such forces, and Margaret shall come with us. She desperately needs a story of adventure."

Rob turned to me, touching my cheek for a moment, kissing where his hand were, and then kissing my hand like he couldn't let me go just yet. "I'll be a moment, my love."

I nodded, and his eyes spoke a warning—he may not be beside me, but I knew he would be watching me, and wouldn't stand for someone hurting me.

Like I would ever need such a reminder.

I nodded to him, and I caught Isabel's thoughtful, frowning gaze as she watched us. He straightened and offered her his arm, and her ladies closed behind them as they turned to walk along the river.

"Must be my turn," Winchester said, coming up beside me and catching my hand. He tucked it into his arm. "Your Grace."

"Your Grace," I returned with a sigh.

"Is she all right?" he murmured to me, his eyes drifting after Margaret.

I smiled, watching her walk. "Yes. She's made of strong stuff," I told him.

He straightened a little. "I know," he said. He sighed. His eyes darted away and back. "And here we go."

"Your Grace," someone said, and we turned to an older man. "Who is this beauty on your arm? You haven't gone and gotten married, have you?"

"Suffolk, I haven't ever enjoyed the kind of luck I would have needed to snare her," Winchester said. "Roger Bigod, Earl of Suffolk, may I introduce Marian Locksley, Lady of Huntingdon. Marian, you'll remember his son was one of the lords to answer Eleanor's call for knights."

He bowed over my hand with a cry of surprise. "Huntingdon, really? That's been created again?"

Winchester nodded solemn. "One of the final acts before Richard was captured."

Suffolk's stare became piercing, calculating. "You must be very important to him, my lady."

"She is," Winchester said, raising his eyebrows.

"Come, Winchester, you must be sporting and tell what you know," Suffolk said.

Winchester glanced toward me, and back at Suffolk. "Far be it for me to say such, my lord, but King Richard feels quite . . . paternal about her."

The man's eyes widened, and he turned to stare at me, taking in my face, looking me up and down, like there were pieces of the king hiding in my face, like King Richard would jump out of my skirts at any moment.

And then he smiled at me. "Hm," he said.

"I was most grateful to see Hugh in the north assisting the queen," Winchester said.

Suffolk turned from me and beamed. "Yes, he's a good son. Now if I can just get him married—you'd set an excellent example in that regard, Winchester."

Winchester's jaw tightened.

"But Locksley, eh?" Suffolk asked, turning back to me. "That was the old earl, of course. Excellent man. Clearly you're not *his* daughter."

I opened my mouth, but Winchester smiled instead. "Daughter by law," Winchester said. "You'll be interested to know Robin Locksley, her husband, is returned to court."

"Really?" asked Suffolk. "We have all heard such tales of his bravery. It is a credit to the peerage to have him back amidst our ranks."

"His valor and honor are barely done justice by tales and songs," I told him, able to speak at last. "It would be a happy task to introduce you to him."

Winchester beamed at me, nodding slight.

"When did this marriage happen?" Suffolk asked. "I find myself amazed that I have not heard of it."

"Just shy of a fortnight past," Winchester said. "A beautiful, joyous affair. I believe the queen mother had all of her minstrels attend to tell Richard of it upon his return."

His eyebrows shot up, like this were information of particular value. "Ah, a new bride then. We must find a way to properly *fete* you," he told me. "And your happiness."

A celebration—when England were on the brink of tearing itself apart. "Your Grace, your notice and happy wishes are certainly celebration enough. I confess I couldn't find greater happiness." *Except if your prince stopped killing people I love, of course.*

"Your Grace, you must excuse us; a new commodity at court must be widely introduced," Winchester said, like this were a roguish joke.

Suffolk chuckled. "Of course. Your Grace, it is a pleasure to meet you," Suffolk said. He dropped his head to me, and I bobbed a curtsy.

Winchester led me away. "You did very well," he told me, patting my hand in his arm. "He is the only earl to outrank you, and his approval will sway many others."

"Does that mean I can quit with the curtsies and silly garden walks yet?" I asked.

"Not nearly," he told me.

"Christ," I muttered.

"He's here too," he said, pointing to an abbot's hat. "The Abbot of Westminster. The abbey is not far from the palace."

"You're very sacrilegious," I told him.

He shrugged. "Ask him. I'm fairly sure he believes it."

Drawing a breath, I started toward him. Winchester lifted an eyebrow at me. "I don't know many things, Winchester, but if we're robbing the English Crown, we need Christ on our side."

He laughed.

CHAPTER TWENTY-SEVEN

By noon, I'd met at least thirty members of the nobility—the women in clusters, eager to fawn over Winchester and Rob, and the men ambling singly around for the most part.

Then the sun rose high and the men grouped, arguing about whether to shoot or hunt as servants brought out tables, piling them with food.

Lady Suffolk, the earl's elegant old wife, protested that they had to shoot so that the ladies could be within an appropriate distance to admire them.

Rob came to me and kissed me light. "I wonder if it's better to win or lose to someone important," Rob murmured with a grin.

I pushed him, grinning back. "Win, or I won't know who you are when you return," I told him with a laugh.

"I was hoping you'd say that," he told me, giddy like a child as his hand slid on my neck, bringing me to him for a dizzy kiss.

There were sighs behind us, and Rob broke off with a laugh as he saw the ladies clumped behind us. "Ladies, you must forgive my ardor. We've only just been married," he said.

There were murmurs and simpers of sighs and forgiveness, and he bowed to me and then to them as he went to join the men. I turned to them all, sitting on benches that had appeared under an awning that servants were affixing even as they sat, and for a moment I froze. There were no places left to sit.

Isabel met my gaze and lifted her eyebrows.

"Lady Huntingdon," said the woman beside Isabel, standing. "Please, you must have my seat."

Isabel frowned, but the young, tall girl stood, curtsying to me. "Thank you. What is your name?" I asked her.

"Lady Maud," she said. "My father is the Earl of Pembroke."

I pressed her hand. "Thank you. Your kindness is most appreciated."

She nodded, blushing, and went to a farther row where other young girls squished in tighter to make room for her.

"Lady Huntingdon," Isabel greeted, terse and tight.

"My lady Princess."

"Your husband is charming," she told me. "But don't think I will soon forget your rough manners and your cold, cruel heart. No matter your title."

"Cruel heart?" I asked her, surprised. "How can you—" I stopped, my voice fading.

How had I forgotten? She *loved* Gisbourne. It had been clear as day.

"You blame me," I murmured. "For his death."

She turned to me, glaring fierce but her eyes shining wet. "Who else is there to blame? If you could have loved him, cared for him at all—*he* would have been Earl of Huntingdon, and my husband wouldn't have punished him. He would have succeeded." She shook her head. "He didn't deserve what you did to him."

"Punished him," I repeated, looking at my hand. "How did he punish him?"

"You know already," she said bitter. "You know he—killed him." Her voice failed her on that awful word. "He made me watch. He put the rope round his neck and told him to say good-bye to me."

A tear skipped out of her eye, and she didn't wipe it off. She squared her shoulders, and I wondered if this were the only way she could ever mourn him, in public, with only the defiance of not wiping off a tear.

"Isabel," I whispered.

She shook her head. "Your fault. And you didn't even wait until his body was cold to marry *him*—the incarnation of everything Guy couldn't ever be," she said, nodding to Rob on the field. "I won't let people love him when they wouldn't love Guy."

My stomach sank, but worse, I didn't blame her. We all had our own rebellion, and this were the only one a girl like Isabel, beautiful and trapped, could claim.

—w—

When the shooting broke, the ladies all stood to take some of the lavish food the servants had provided, and I caught Maud looking at my hand, not fully hidden in my skirts.

"What happened?" she asked, her hand on her chest. As if I didn't know what she were talking about, she said, "To your hand."

I glanced at Isabel, and she were watching me. "I was punished," I told Maud.

"For what?" another woman asked.

Drawing a slow breath, I turned from Isabel's gaze. "Displeasing the prince," I said.

Lady Suffolk shook her head slow. "A woman should never face such treatment," she said.

"A noblewoman at that," another said.

"A favorite of the queen mother," another said.

The women began to whisper and talk.

Isabel's face folded down.

I went back to the benches.

—~—

We returned to our chambers to dress for dinner, and Rob smiled, coming to me. "We did well today," he told me, putting his arms round my waist and kissing my neck.

I smiled, twisting to meet his lips instead. He kissed me full, catching my back with his full strength and pulling me off the ground. I broke the kiss, then thought better of it, kissing the corner of his mouth. "We did," I agreed. "But I think you should go to dinner alone."

He put me down. "And where exactly will you be?"

"London," I told him. "Allan has a friend there—she helped us once. She'll have access to a ship, and she'll know people we can trust to steal the ransom for us."

He sighed. "I don't know about this plan, Scarlet."

My shoulders lifted. "We have to get the money away from him. If Prince John controls the ransom, my father will never return, Prince John will be unstoppable, and you and I won't survive. Nottingham won't survive. All this courting favor and being a good little noble—it won't matter. If we can't get the money away from him, we don't have a chance."

He nodded. "I know. I just cannot believe we are planning to steal from our country. And that somehow, that may make us patriots instead of traitors." He kissed my forehead. "I don't know if you should go to London alone."

"Allan and David will come with me," I told him. "You have to stay here and make excuses."

His throat bobbed, and he looked at me, still holding me close. "Scar . . . you have to be careful, all right?" he murmured to me.

My eyebrows pulled together, but I nodded.

"I've only just married you," he said. "I can't lose you now." His eyes shut, and his forehead pressed to mine. "You know there's a chance you're already with child, don't you? So just . . . just think about that before you run into danger, yes?"

I shut my eyes too. "All the more reason to do this now," I told him.

He nodded against me. "All right. Go. Be back as soon as you can."

I let go of him, digging through his things and finding a black tunic and pants, tugging on my leather boots and a heavy cloak. When I opened my door, Allan were smiling and David were slapping his hand away.

"My lady," David said, bowing to me.

"My lady," Allan said, mocking a curtsy.

"Let's go see Kate," I told them.

—~—

"No," Kate said, striding down the dock and away from us. "Absolutely not."

"Kate!" Allan protested.

She stopped, spinning on her heel to push her finger at his chest. "Are you *mad*?" she demanded. "Steal from the royal treasury? Steal from the king's ransom?"

"Not steal it as such," I said, peering round Allan on the narrow dock. "More like hold it until he shows his true colors."

"Until *Prince John,* the man who cut off the fingers of his own niece shortly before trying to murder her, figures it out, you mean?" She shook her head and stomped up the gangplank of the ship. There were children on board her boat, some older, most younger.

I started up the plank, but Allan put his arm out across my chest to stop me.

David pushed him off. "Don't touch her, Allan," he snapped.

"It's very bad form to board a ship without permission, lady thief," Allan told me.

Kate stood on the deck of her ship, her arms crossed. "Permission not granted," she told me. "You want all of us to risk our lives? You'd kill us all."

"You're awful cavalier with their lives already, doing what you do," I told her. "Don't pretend you lot shrink from danger."

She scowled. "I don't make decisions for them. We'll discuss it, and I'll let you know."

"We don't have long."

"There is always enough time to let people make their own choice," she said. "Or we're not doing it."

I sucked in a breath. "Fine. Let me know as soon as you can." I looked to Allan, and he nodded once. "Allan will come back for your decision."

She nodded, and didn't move from her ship as we left, darkness falling on our heels.

CHAPTER TWENTY-EIGHT

The next morning, Rob and I were bare dressed when Margaret sent us word that her father were meant to arrive within the hour. We went to her chambers together, and found Winchester stalking the halls before her room like a lion.

"Quincy," Rob said.

Winchester stopped. He looked like he hadn't slept.

"What are you doing?" Rob asked.

"Her father will arrive soon," Winchester said. "I'm just . . . thinking. What to say. How to convince him. What Prince John could have possibly offered him."

"Winchester," I said. "You must offer him a show of strength. He won't respond to your feelings for her—you know that. Or he would never have agreed to such a match in the first place."

Winchester drew a breath, his whole chest heaving up.

Rob glanced at me and stepped closer to Winchester, talking to him quiet with his hand on his shoulder, and I knocked at Margaret's door. A servant answered, but Margaret emerged a moment later.

She saw Winchester, and Rob stepped aside as she walked toward him. He bent to her, kissing her.

I heard the servant make a noise of surprise, but I glared at her and she ducked back into the room.

Rob took my hand as Margaret let go of Winchester, and he wiped a tear off her cheek, staring at her. "I won't let this happen," he murmured to her.

She nodded, kissing him quick once more. "You shouldn't be here when he arrives."

"I don't care. I will be anyway," he told her.

She smiled at him.

"As will we," Rob told her.

She looked at us like she hadn't noticed us before, and she nodded. "He'll be here any moment," she said.

I nodded, and Winchester offered her his arm.

We were all quiet as we walked through the palace to the courtyard where we had been received. To my surprise, Isabel were there, standing tall with her flock behind her as the gates opened and riders came through.

The Earl of Leicester rode up to us, taking a moment to look over the assembled people before dismounting. He weren't caked with dust from the road, so I rather thought he cleaned himself—or changed his clothes—before entering the palace.

He gave his horse to one of the servants that ran up to help him, and turned his eyes to Isabel. He gave her a deep bow.

"My lady Princess," he greeted.

She bobbed her head. "Your Grace," she said.

Margaret stepped forward and he embraced her, kissing her cheek. "Margaret, you look well," he told her.

"Thank you, Father," she said soft.

She stayed to the side of him, and he looked at Rob, but his gaze settled on Winchester. Leicester bowed his head, but didn't bow, and Winchester did the same. "My lord Leicester," he said.

"Winchester. Surprised to see you out here."

"I escorted your daughter from the queen mother's side to London," he said. "A happy task."

Leicester's eyes settled on Rob, and then on me. He looked at my scar, and I saw his eyes run down my arm to where my hand were hidden in my skirts. "You must be the Earl and Lady of Huntingdon," he said, his voice careful and even.

I curtsied to him, and Rob bowed. "My lord," Rob greeted.

He glanced about, though we were in a very open space and were the only ones there. "Where is young de Clare? He did not come to greet me?"

"Lord de Clare has little in the way of graces to recommend him," Isabel said.

Margaret looked down, and the earl took this in as well. "Hm," he said.

"My lord, my servants will lead you to a room to refresh yourself," Isabel said. "Or, if you would prefer, we would be honored for you to join us in the gardens. My ladies and I were just going for a walk."

"I would prefer to walk," he said, patting his legs. "Far too long in the saddle." He turned to Margaret. "But I will need a few moments alone with my daughter," he said.

Isabel gave a gracious nod and swept off toward the gardens. Her ladies followed behind her, and Isabel shot a glare over her shoulder at me.

"Come along, Quincy," Rob said. "We can't wait here for her."

Winchester's eyes were hard, watching Leicester. "No," he said, shaking his head. "No, this cannot go on a moment longer."

Rob reached for his arm, but Winchester shook him off, striding forward. "My lord, before you speak with your daughter, I must insist on a private audience with you."

Leicester looked at Winchester and paused a long moment. "Margaret, go with Huntingdon. I will meet you in the gardens."

I drew a long breath as Margaret came toward us. She raised her chin, walked forward, and though I couldn't say the same, she never turned round once as we walked out of the courtyard and into the gardens.

—w—

When Leicester came out, Winchester weren't with him. Leicester nodded to Margaret, flicking his fingers at her like a dog, and at his command, she went.

The first few words of their exchange were too quiet to hear, but she cried, "Father, please!" and everyone in the garden went silent.

"No," he said sharp. "You will obey me. You will marry de Clare. You will listen to your betters and do as I say!"

"But Winchester is a better man! An earl in his own right already."

"And you *care* for him," Leicester snarled. "Do you not think I've heard of your wanton ways? The prince himself came to me, telling me of your behavior. The queen has written to me to say she wishes to attend the wedding, and if that were not so, you would marry de Clare tomorrow, my girl. No more of your protestations."

"Father, please—" she begged.

He slapped her.

I ran forward, stepping in front of Margaret. She curled herself, sobbing free, against my back. "Lady Huntingdon—" Leicester started.

"Scarlet," Rob said, coming to me. "Take Margaret inside. Now."

I met Rob's eyes, and his blue oceans were hot with anger. I nodded once, glaring at Leicester.

Turning, I took Margaret full in my arms, and I hauled her out of the gardens. We bare made it inside the wall of the palace when her legs stopped holding her, and rather than drag her, I crumpled round her, trying to make my arms a fortress like Rob's arms were for me. I petted her head and kissed her hair, and she just cried on me.

"I thought—I thought I would have a happy end," she whispered, hiccoughing with sobs. "I loved a man suitable to my station, without a wife, who was free to love me too.

How did that end badly?" she said. "I did everything I was meant to."

"It's not the end," I told her.

—w—

I brought her back to her chambers, and stayed with her until she slept. When I returned to my own, Winchester were there with Rob. His nerves were gone, and in its place, a cold, hard anger.

He saw me and stood. "Locksley's terrible at this, Marian," he told me.

Rob stood too, frowning.

"At what?" I questioned, coming in.

"I need a plan," he said. "I'm going to marry Margaret one way or another."

"And this came for you," Rob said, holding a letter.

I came to them, sitting beside Rob and taking it. It were in Eleanor's hand, and I broke the seal. "Eleanor's coming with Essex and Bigod," I said, reading it quick. "With a considerable amount of silver."

"No," Winchester said. "I don't give a damn about the ransom right now. I'm not letting that monster lay a finger on Margaret."

"Neither are we," I told him, leaving the letter in my lap.

"You have to run away," Rob said. "That's your only option."

I rubbed my head. "Not your only option. But it is a good one. Goodness knows that's how Eleanor married King Henry."

"That was against her will, though. Margaret's willing, isn't she?"

Frowning, I said, "I'm not certain. She wants to honor her father's wishes. I can't help you if she doesn't agree to it."

"There's no way I'll be let near her," Winchester said. "Will you speak to her, Marian?"

I nodded. "Yes. But if she agrees to marry de Clare, you have to respect her wish," I told him.

His mouth twisted. "I don't know if I can," Winchester said, his voice rough. "But I'll try." Standing, he shook his head. "I'm going for a ride," he said. "I can't . . . I can't be here a moment longer."

He didn't even wait for good-byes as he quit the room.

Rob leaned back, draping his arm over me and staring up. "And I thought our love was fraught," he said.

I held up the letter. "If they're bringing more silver, we need to wait until it's here to steal it," I told him. "We can only make this play once, and if Prince John has enough to fill the treasury back up again the plan is useless."

Rob looked at me. "There's no way if Eleanor, a huge number of nobles, and de Clare are here for a wedding, Prince John isn't planning on coming. Especially since I'm sure de Clare has sent word that we're here by now. Prince John won't be able to stay away. Which means stealing the money when he's here. When he's watching."

"And when Winchester is either too drunk with grief or running off with his bride to help us," I added.

He drew a breath and closed his eyes, his throat working. "There are a million ways this can end badly, Scar."

I nodded. "There always were."

CHAPTER TWENTY-NINE

That night, I went to visit Margaret. She were awake in her room, staring out the window, quiet.

She turned to me when I entered. "Have you seen Saer?" she asked.

I nodded. "He's gone riding. I thought that meant an hour or two, but Rob thinks he won't be back until tomorrow or the next day."

She sighed. "That will clear his mind."

"He wants to run away with you," I said.

She looked at me with wide eyes. "He does?"

Sitting beside her, I nodded. "I told him I would help you both if you consented. If you wanted to overthrow your father's wishes."

She looked at me. "You did that, didn't you? Disobeyed your father. Ran away."

My shoulders lifted. "It turns out he was not actually my father, but yes. I ran away—without a man—instead of marrying Gisbourne, who my father wanted for me. I was young, though. Not ready in so many ways."

"And it was the right choice?" she asked.

I sighed. "Maybe. I think life becomes a fabric of choices, interwoven, all related. I think I had to run away then to be married to Rob now. But running away also cost me the life of my sister. It split my life into these two things, thief and lady."

"You aren't split. You're simply more than one thing at once."

I shrugged. "I don't think I would have chosen different," I told her. "But this path has been costly beyond measure, and fraught with darkness and pain. I would wish different things for you."

She stared out the window again. "I don't understand if the less painful path would be to marry de Clare and obey my father, or Saer. The man I love."

Shaking my head, I said, "I can't say either. But being married to someone you love . . ." I stopped, shivers running over my skin. "I never imagined I could care for someone like this. I didn't think I had that in me."

She took my hand, gave me a weak smile, and looked out the window as her smile faded. "I can't disobey my father," she whispered. "Not yet."

—∾—

Isabel called for a feast to be held the next evening to celebrate the engagement of Margaret and de Clare. Even in so little time, the palace cooks made a ridiculous spectacle of stuffed birds that looked frozen in flight, sugar confections that appeared as if from some kind of strange dream, and food enough to feed half of London.

There were minstrels called in, and I shouldn't have been a bit surprised to see Allan amongst them, but I were. Rob laughed beside me, grinning my way.

"I have prepared something exquisite for the princess," Allan said, bowing to Isabel.

She beamed at this. "Very well, minstrel," she said. "Play on."

Allan glanced at me with a wink, and I glanced at Rob, horrified and hoping I weren't the princess he meant. Allan swept out in another, fancy bow for Isabel, and he nodded to his fellows.

A bonny fine maid of a noble degree,
With a hey down down a down down
Maid Marian called by name,
Did live in the North, of excellent worth,
For she was a gallant dame.

For favor and face, and beauty most rare,
Queen Hellen she did excel;
For Marian then was praised of all men
That did in the country dwell.

'Twas neither Rosamond nor Jane Shore,
Whose beauty was clear and bright,

That could surpass this country lass,
Beloved of lord and knight.

The Earl of Huntingdon, nobly born,
That came of noble blood,
To Marian went, with a good intent,
By the name of Robin Hood.

With kisses sweet their red lips meet,
For she and the earl did agree;
In every place, they kindly embrace,
With love and sweet unity.

Rob kissed my hand, but I felt pale and weak and sick. This couldn't be a good thing, and I felt eyes on me, de Clare and Isabel at the very least.

The song went on, verse after verse, telling some silly false story of kisses and feasts and me getting wounded and Rob rushing to my aid. Which, I'm sure, were true in some way, but it felt strange and different, and I sounded like a simpering lady. Not one word of my knives, or the scrapes I'd saved him from. I felt myself scowl deeper and deeper at Allan.

"It isn't really about us," Rob whispered to me. "It's what they want to hear."

"They want to hear lies," I grunted.

He flipped my hand over. "Stories aren't about what's true; what's real and not real."

His fingers trailed over mine, and mine chased after him, fingertips touching, kissing, breaking. "No?" I asked.

"No. Stories are told to make you feel something, and they can tell ours over and over again, and every time it will be something different."

He drew a heart in my palm with his fingertip, and I looked at him.

He grinned. "Pay attention; Allan will be hurt if you miss it."

In solid content together they lived,
With all their yeomen gay;
They lived by their hands, without any lands,
And so they did many a day.

But now to conclude, an end I will make
In time, as I think it good,
For the people that dwell in the North can tell
Of Marian and bold Robin Hood.

He finished with a great big flourish of music, and Rob's hand slid full into mine. I looked at Rob, shy over my shoulder, and he were staring at me, drunk on me, leaning forward until our lips met.

All I could hear were the strange symphony of my breath and my heart and his heart until our lips parted, and then I could hear people clapping. I pulled away from him, frightened, but no one were cruel about it; they were smiling, laughing, clapping in a happy way, celebrating us.

Here. At court, where I'd only known games and claws and teeth.

I looked back at him. "I love you," I whispered.

He nodded. "I love you too. And that's the best chance we have," he told me.

The clapping died down, and de Clare, sitting between Leicester and Margaret, cleared his throat.

"Surely, minstrel, your tale is taller than most," he said.

Allan gave a fancy bow. "Nay, my lord, for the proof sits here with us."

De Clare tapped his finger on the table. "Yes, the subjects of your story are here. But you failed to capture many things I'm sure the prince would be most upset about."

"Please correct me, my lord, so I don't make such a mistake in the future," Allan said.

"You forgot the true hero of the story was the prince, triumphing over two fools who tested his patience and his generosity at every turn. They fought his knights, they stole his bread. The Lady Huntingdon even tried to kill him. You praise a traitor, minstrel." De Clare twisted his cup on the table. "I cannot think that the prince will look kindly on such."

"Lady Huntingdon is no traitor," Margaret said to him.

"Forgive me; she was a traitor and is now a high-ranking lady instead," de Clare said, taking her hand and squeezing hard enough that she winced. "Things change so quickly I can barely hope to keep up."

"My wife is an uncommon thing," Rob said, his deep voice rumbling. "Stalwart and brave in all things. It is the prince, and perhaps the law, that changes so swiftly, for she is like the evergreen forest, eternal and sure."

De Clare chuckled. "The prince will be here soon, my lord," de Clare told Rob, "and you'll see how he feels about your wife. And you." De Clare raised his cup to Allan. "You most of all, minstrel."

"Come now, de Clare, it was a lovely song," Lady Suffolk said.

"Yes," Suffolk said, beside her. "But perhaps we ignored our best source of adventure. De Clare, please, tell us of the goings-on in the north."

De Clare took a deep drink, enjoying the attention, and Rob's hand wrapped warm around mine.

"I will say," de Clare began, "that England has never been more resplendent, more proud and glorious. York was the first major city we went to, and the beauty we saw there—beyond compare." He glanced round, taking in the warm smiles before going on. "The redheads, the blondes—Lord on high, I saw one bit of fun with the best—"

"Enough," Isabel said.

De Clare laughed heartily.

"Quite enough," Isabel repeated. "Or do you need to be removed from the table, de Clare?"

"With so lovely a dinner companion—" he started, pulling Margaret's hand and trying to drag it to his mouth.

She pulled away with a gasp, and even her father glared.

"Don't *touch* me," he mocked. "Like you don't enjoy a man's hands on you." He shrugged. "You'll learn to like my touch soon enough, wife!" he crowed, drinking more wine.

"De Clare," Leicester said, standing. "You've had enough for one night. Why don't you absent yourself?"

De Clare got to his feet. He weren't drunk at all, just an ill-mannered brute. "Very well, Father. I'm sure you know best."

Leicester frowned. "Don't mock the bonds of marriage," Leicester said. "You will not refer to me as such until it's true."

De Clare laughed and turned back to Margaret. He leaned over her chair and took her chin, kissing her full on the mouth.

Leicester's scowl burned red.

De Clare let her go, and quit the hall.

CHAPTER THIRTY

Winchester returned, roaming the palace like a moody beast. Rob tried to keep him out of doors as much as he could.

Allan spent much of his time in London. He wouldn't tell me for sure that Kate agreed to our plot, only that he knew she would come through when we needed her. It weren't reassuring, and the days were passing faster.

We received word that Eleanor and her party would arrive by nightfall five days after Leicester. No one had heard when Prince John would come, but I could feel him drawing close like a gathering storm.

Leicester declared that his daughter would be married on Sunday, two days after Eleanor were meant to arrive.

Margaret didn't come to the gardens anymore. She didn't want to see de Clare, she didn't want to see Winchester. I rather thought she wanted time to grind to a halt before Sunday ever came, but that weren't in God's plan just yet.

The nobles gathered in the garden. Rob and Winchester seemed engaged in a serious debate with Suffolk, and I could no longer walk aimless in a strange place where nature were made careful and pretty instead of wild and free.

David followed me as I left the gardens, but I waved him off. I didn't want to be followed; I just wanted to be alone.

There were a little brook past the gardens, and I crossed it, walking through a field and making for a copse of trees ahead. The farther I walked, their tittering whispers faded out, replaced by birds talking animatedly to one another, flying and swooping above me. The blades of long grass in the field slid against one another, shushing me, and the sun beat down on all of it, making it glitter.

Inside the copse of trees, the air were cool and fresh, and I shut my eyes, wishing myself back in Nottingham.

Just a few days more, I promised myself. *And all this will be finished.*

As soon as the trunks of silver arrived with Eleanor, we could spring into action. Prince John or not, we could protect the realm, and we could be free.

I stayed as long as I could, hiding in the trees, trying to draw on their strength. Maybe Prince John wouldn't arrive until the next day, and we could finish this after Eleanor arrived.

As I crossed the brook to come back to the castle, riders on the road kicked up dust to come around the curve, slowing at the gate. My blood went cold and still as I saw Prince John riding at the forefront, and he saw me clear in the sun.

His horse and men stopped as the portcullis were raised, and I curtsied. "Prince John," I greeted, tight-lipped. "Welcome to court."

He dismounted, coming to me with a bright, false smile. "Lady Huntingdon. My God, you just keep on turning up alive, don't you?" He laughed like he'd said something funny, coming close to me. I backed up. "You know, it's simply so difficult to enlist able men these days. So next time I try to kill you," he said, meeting my gaze, "I'll be the one holding the blade."

I stopped backing up as the gate opened full and knights came out, taking the prince's horse and men inside, keeping people between us. Prince John gave me a grin and inclined his head to me, walking into the palace.

—∾—

Eleanor arrived within a few hours, and when she did, she called me for a private audience. "You did as I asked?" I said.

"Hello, my darling granddaughter," Eleanor said, embracing me. "So lovely to see you."

"I know you like your manners, Eleanor, but now is hardly the time."

She looked wounded. "There is always enough time for exquisite manners, Marian."

I rolled my eyes.

"And yes, I did as you asked. Since I'm certain it will all be for nothing, I prepared the chests for you."

Drawing a breath, I nodded. "Thank you."

"So you're going to steal this money?" she asked.

"Move it. To force his hand."

"Because there are French guards."

"He claims they're from Aquitaine, that he called them to protect the treasury so he could protect you with his knights," I told her.

"That is a very sensible reason for them to be there," she insisted.

"But the timeline doesn't work out—and consider the alternative, Eleanor. You yourself said he would need to buy armies. You said France would be the first place he turned."

"But these are not *armies*," she said. "If they're knights, you can't buy them, they're dedicated to someone. And if they're not Aquitanian, they belong to someone else. So they must be Aquitanian, because who else would offer him men?"

"Then there will be nothing to worry about," I told her.

She shook her head. "Of course there will. You are striking a hornet's nest, and I'm holding the ladder to let you do it." She frowned. "How is Margaret?"

"Miserable," I told her.

An eyebrow lifted. "And still here?"

"Yes," I said, confused.

"Oh, for Heaven's sake. That fine earl of hers needs to toss her out a window and run off with her. Why are they still *here*?"

"She wants to obey her father."

Eleanor drew a breath, and raised her stone chin. "Take me to her."

She rapped her jeweled walking stick on the ground, and I nodded, leading her quick out of the room to where Margaret were. I knocked on the door and announced Eleanor, and when the maid answered, she looked frightened. "My lady Queen," she greeted, curtsying. "My lady Margaret is not quite here."

"Not *quite*?" I questioned.

"Has she gone to the meal?" Eleanor asked. "Is she walking? It's after dark."

The maid shook her head. "Your Highness, she's not . . . here."

Eleanor's eyebrows rose sharp. "She left. The palace. Of her own free will?" Eleanor asked.

"Yes," the maid said quiet. "With . . . someone."

"With Winchester?" I asked, worried sudden. What if de Clare—or the prince—

"Yes," the maid said. "I'm not meant to say anything."

"Oh," said Eleanor, raising her chin again. "Next time someone asks you, you silly girl, tell people she fainted and needs her rest. Tell them she will be well by morning, yes?"

"Yes, my lady," the girl said, dipping and bowing her head, then retreating into the room.

Eleanor looked at me. "Good. That was easier than I thought. Now go do whatever it is you must do—the less I know the better, I imagine."

—~—

I brought David and Allan into the room with me. Rob were already there, and he stood as I came in.

"Well?" he asked.

"Winchester and Margaret ran off," I told him.

His face broke into a grin. "What? Really?"

I nodded. "And we need to do this tonight. Eleanor put the chests in place, just as I asked. Her carriage is full of them and waiting in the courtyard."

He drew a breath. "Very well. David, Allan, get horses and meet us by the carriage."

David glanced at me, ever loyal, and I nodded once.

They had just bare left when a knock came to the door.

Our maid opened it and announced Essex. Rob bristled as Essex came into the room, coming straight for me. His cheeks were filled with color and bright, and he looked wild.

"Is it true?" he asked. "Everything you hinted at—is Prince John a traitor?" he demanded.

"I don't know," I told him. "We'll find out soon enough. Why? What's the matter?"

"He struck her," he growled, and Rob came closer to me. "He struck her and he's going to annul their marriage."

"What?" Rob said.

"Isabel?" I asked.

"You'd think pain would count more than children," he said. "But it doesn't. He tortures her and she has yet to give him a child, so he will annul their marriage and marry Isabelle of Angouleme."

My breath caught. "Good Lord. The knights—they're her men."

"What knights?"

"The prince put the ransom in the White Tower. The men guarding it are French knights—he claims they're from Aquitaine, but they can't be."

He nodded. "That must have been what Isabel meant." He looked at me. "Please tell me you have some scheme to stop this, Marian. John Lackland will purchase a crown with his new wife's money. Isabel said he told her himself he's planning on sending the money to France to make sure Richard never returns."

Rob crossed his arms. "Scarlet. Her name is Scarlet," he snapped. He shrugged his shoulders at me. "I can't stand hearing that name on everyone's mouth."

"My name doesn't matter," I told him. "What they call me, the words I use—they don't matter. Our actions, and what we will do to bring the King of England home matter." I looked at Essex. "So yes, I have a plan."

CHAPTER THIRTY-ONE

"I look terrible in this," Allan whined.

David scowled at him. "The great trickster. I thought you could pretend to be whatever you wanted. Having difficulty pretending to be me?"

"But I look so much handsomer as *me,*" Allan said.

I frowned at them from the carriage seat. "You'd make a terrible knight, Allan. Try to look intimidating."

"David's not intimidating," Allan said, looking at David on his horse.

"Be thankful you haven't seen that side of me yet, Allan," David grunted.

The gates round the White Tower came into view, and David rode forward to trot abreast of the carriage with Rob and me on the coachman's seat. The French guards came out to greet us, looking wary.

"Open the gate," David ordered.

"On what business?"

"We have contributions from the queen for the king's ransom," David said.

They opened the gate.

There were more knights now; at least thirty, ambling around. They didn't help us as we rode the carriage close, and Rob and David hefted a chest between them. They walked it to the stairway, a wooden thing that led up to the entrance of the tower and could be rolled away if enemies approached.

The thing creaked as they went up, and I followed slow behind them.

They brought the chest into the treasury room on the lowest floor of the tower. They set the chest down and went back to repeat the task, and I stood watch over the room. The man of accounts came to me and asked the sums, and I told him.

He left, and I unlocked the chest that Rob and David had just set down.

A dirty face looked up at me. "Quick," I told him.

The young man leapt out of the chest. I went out to the hall and Allan were there. "This way," he told me, and he grabbed one chest while the boy grabbed another.

They disappeared into a smudge of darkness underneath the stairs.

Rob and David came down again with a chest.

I frowned. "Where are your swords?" I asked them.

"They keep hitting the stairs," David said. "We put them in the carriage."

Hairs raised on the back of my neck. "Hurry, then."

Rob gave me a solemn nod, laying the chest down.

Again, one of Kate's orphans sprang out of a chest, and he waited for Allan and the other to return, leading them down to a secret entrance in the bottom of the tower that let out onto the river.

"We call it Traitor's Gate," Allan had told us. "But seeing as thieves don't have much say about it, I doubt that name will stick."

David and Rob took as much time as they could. We had seven boys hidden in chests, and they made quick work of secreting the ransom away to the water gate and Kate's rowboats. It were a short trip down the river to where her ship were docked.

One by one, the chests disappeared, and the sky didn't fall upon our heads.

Rob and David dropped a chest to the floor of the treasury, and Rob kissed me, sweat heavy on his brow. "We have one more chest," he said. "Get them ready."

There were only two left in the treasury.

I nodded. Allan returned with three boys. Two took the chests that sat there, and one waited anxious for Rob and David's footsteps.

I held my breath.

Long moments passed before Rob and David appeared, hefting the chest down the stairs.

The boy took it, turning under the stairs as a set of metaled boots appeared at the height of the stairs.

I pulled the door shut. "Can someone lock this?" I called.

The knight ducked so he could see us, and came downstairs, replacing the lock and inserting the key. He stood by the door.

We nodded, and started up the stairs.

The night were thick and warm, one of the first that didn't get cooler without the sun. Summer were close, hovering, waiting to make her mark on us. To push us through another year.

I stood at the top of the stairs, and Rob's arm came round me. He were bright and shining with sweat. David glanced at us and turned his head, trotting down the stairs.

Rob kissed me, and I tasted salt on his lips. "I love you, Scar."

"I love you too," I told him. "Let's get back before anyone misses us."

He leaned forward and touched my lips to his. It were quick and brief. A kiss that were meant to be a beginning, a start, the first of a thousand.

We hadn't made it to the bottom of the staircase when the gate began to open.

I looked at Rob, and David.

We hadn't asked them to open the gate yet. It were too early.

We made for the carriage. I had knives in my dress, but Rob didn't have his sword. David didn't either.

The knights stopped us, blocking us off. David, Rob, and I stood close together. I didn't see Allan.

Prince John stood outside the gate, mounted on his horse, with a legion of men holding torches around him, beside him, behind him.

He rode in slow, looking at us with a smug smile on his face, and my heart slammed against my chest.

"Lady Huntingdon," he said. "Earl Huntingdon. Now, tell me this. Why would my mother come to London, escorted by two noblemen and a legion of knights, and then send her precious ransom off with her granddaughter? Hm?"

I didn't open my mouth.

"It's strange, isn't it? Meanwhile, my nattering wife says she has friends, friends that will stop me. There aren't many people foolish enough to cross me. Except you two. So it could all be a rather strange coincidence, or perhaps it isn't."

Rob took my half hand in his.

"Jacques," Prince John called, snapping his fingers. The knight who had taken our accounting stepped forward. "What did they do while they were here?"

"They dropped off the silver, my lord," he said.

"Did you watch them do it? Pick it up, put it down, you watched every chest?"

He paused. "Yes," he said. But he hadn't.

"And you went through each chest? Matched the amounts, verified their contents?"

He paused longer. I tugged Rob's hand to sit on the small of my back over the hilt of my knife, and his eyes met mine for one brief look.

"Go check the silver," Prince John snapped.

He went. We only had moments.

Prince John dismounted. The knights parted for him, and he came into the circle with us with a wide grin. "Anything you want to confess, Marian?"

"Don't speak to her," Rob snapped. "You want to accuse her of something, speak to me."

"Confess," he said, stepping close to me. "And I'll make up a good lie about how you died."

"I'll confess," I whispered.

He stepped a tiny bit closer. "A little louder, Marian."

"You used to be afraid to get so close to me," I told him, and he met my eyes. "That was a good instinct."

I slammed my knee into his crotch, drawing my knife as Rob pulled the other knife from my back. Prince John grabbed my hand with the knife, but I pushed back on his hold, forcing the knights to break the circle as he fell back.

Quick, I grabbed Prince John while he were off balance. I kicked at his knees and stepped fast to the side, grabbing his hair and jerking his head back as I moved behind him.

Two knights came for me, and I pressed the knife to his throat. "Stop!" I yelled.

I saw Rob and David fighting, and they looked at me. A knight hit David across the face, and he fell, and a knight wrapped his arm around Rob's throat.

Rob stabbed his knife into the knight's arm, and the knight dropped him. Another knight held out his sword to Rob, while the other knights were backing up, looking at me.

"Move away from him. Now," I told the knight.

"Kill him," Prince John grunted.

"I will slit his throat," I told the knight.

"No, she won't!" Prince John said. "Kill him! Now!"

The knight were looking at me, not Prince John. "Do it and he dies," I warned.

"You're under orders," John told him. The knight met his gaze. "Kill him! *Tuez-le maintenant!*"

The knight drew his arm back, and I pushed Prince John aside, leaping over him to grab the knight's arm and prevent it from moving forward. I buried my knife in his side.

Another knight pulled me off. He slammed his fist into my stomach, and I lost my breath at the burst of pain.

A hand closed on my wrist with the knife, and someone else hit me across the face. Then I were in the grass, on my back, and people held my wrists and feet; someone even had a boot on my stomach.

"Get her up," Prince John said.

They dragged me to my knees. Rob and David were on their knees too now, and they pushed us into a line.

Our revolt had lasted roughly a minute.

With three against thirty, two knives between us, we'd never had much hope. Except for delaying long enough to let Kate get away.

"Do you men even know what you do?" David shouted. "You strike the daughter of the King of England! A princess!"

"A bastard," Prince John dismissed. "Jacques?" he asked.

I looked at Rob. His mouth were drooling blood, and a cut on his eye were bleeding too.

"My-my lord," he stammered. "*Mon seigneur, il est vide.*"

I didn't speak French, but I knew what that room contained well enough.

Prince John picked up one of my knives from the ground. He came close to us and looked at Rob for a long while. Then he looked at me. "So. I need to know where my money has gone, and I need one of you two to tell me."

We didn't say anything.

"These things—information, and the ways we request it—they're very simple. It's a transaction, you see. For a fine woolen coat I would pay a certain sum. For boots, a different sum. So the question is, what sum will you pay to conceal the information I need? And what sum is too high a price to ask?"

I were trembling.

"Marian, my dear niece, you know very well how I play this game, don't you? You see, I understand that there must be certain negotiations, and well, I like to start the game off right."

He took two long steps from me, past Rob, and he plunged the knife into David's throat.

CHAPTER THIRTY-TWO

I screamed. Blood bubbled fast up David's throat, and his eyes were wide like he didn't know what had happened. Like he were frozen and couldn't move or stop his death from flying swift in. Just like John.

And then Prince John pulled the knife out, and David's body collapsed like someone pulled out whatever made him upright.

Prince John stepped in front of Rob, and I weren't sure if I were screaming or crying or all at once. Men had their hands on me to keep me still, and Rob's hand grabbed for mine, the only thing that calmed me. Rob were very still, looking at Prince John, not breaking his gaze.

"Tell me where the money is," Prince John said. "Tell me how you got it out and where it's gone."

"We won't tell you that," Rob said. "Because you'll use it to kill Richard."

"Yes, I will," Prince John said. "This is my country, and whether it's today or sometime in the next year, when you have fat little children, when you think you're safe, I'll see you dead. I'll see you both dead."

I drew a shaking breath, tears streaking down my face. "Not tonight. You need us to tell you where the money is. And if you harm one, the other won't tell."

"Hm," he said. "Or maybe, like your little outlaw said, you won't tell me anyway. Because your faith in my brother's right is so strong, is that it?"

"I've never met my father," I told him. "I only know that *you* should never be allowed to be king."

"Well," he said. "You may be right. But nobody cares what a stupid, bastard girl thinks. So let's make this interesting, shall we? I'll give you until dawn to tell me where the money is. And then I'll kill him. I'll hang him from that tree," he said, pointing. "So you can watch. So you can remember every detail and take it to your grave. And then I'll kill you too," he promised.

I shivered.

"And do you know why I'll hang him?" Prince John said, coming close to my ear. "Because you're the weak one. You will break, like you sacrificed me for him moments ago. You will tell me rather than have his death on your soul, won't you?"

My eyes flicked up to his. "If you kill him, I won't say a word. And if you kill me, Richard will be safe, and he will return, and he will flay the skin from your bones."

His eyes narrowed. "Let's find out, shall we?"

—∾—

They brought us up in the tower. It had once been a royal residence, but my father had long been rebuilding it to be the strongest prison in the land. The rooms bore the rich signs of their royal past, but also the locks of their future.

They didn't touch me. They left me in a room all night long, alone, and listening to sounds that could have only been Rob. Grunts, short, clipped yells, and then silence. Every so often a man would come to my door and ask where the money were. I never answered, and then the sounds from Rob would start over again.

Once, my eyelids slipped closed, and I saw David behind my eyes, lying dead on the grass. Then the grass changed to snow, and the body changed to John. My eyes snapped open, and for a moment, I gasped for breath, and the vision still burned in my eyes, but it were Rob's body lying crumpled on the ground.

My hands shook, but I folded them in prayer, asking God to protect David like I couldn't in life, to keep John out of trouble, and to protect Rob. It were damned little, but it were all I could do.

—∾—

The sky had begun to turn blue, the first herald of dawn, and I hadn't heard anything from Rob in a long while.

My heart were drumming in my chest, steady and hard, and it made my whole body shake.

The door opened, and Prince John came in. He grabbed my arm, hauling me up. "Tell me—" He stopped, cocking his head. "Actually, I rather hope you won't tell me. I'm very much looking forward to killing you both."

"Where is he?" I demanded.

He pushed me out the open door, and I saw another door hanging open down the hall. A knight tied my hands, and Prince John led me down the stairs to stand in the open doorway. Rob were on a horse, being led to the tree, and the rope tied round his neck were thrown over a thick branch. He were bruised and bloody, and water pushed into my eyes and my heart ached.

I looked toward the gate. The pounding weren't my heart now; it were the gates.

"Yes," he said. "We have visitors. Which means we need to make this very quick, Marian. Tell me where the money is, right now, or I will hang him. Hangings kill people in one of two ways, did you know that?"

He looked at me for some response, but I just stared at Rob.

"The first is the more humane, of course. Often times the fall is so long and sharp that the jerk of the rope pulling tight just snaps the neck." He snapped his fingers, and I flinched. "Dead. Just like that. The other is more horrible. They fall, and instead of instantly dying, their windpipe is crushed. They can't breathe. Blood can't drain out of the head, and it's the worst, most awful headache you've ever had." He leaned close to my ear. "It feels like your head is about to burst open."

A tear fell out of my eye.

"He's only a few feet off the ground," he observed. "Just enough to keep his toes from the grass. I don't think it will be enough to snap his neck, do you?"

My eyes closed, and more water rushed out. "Your mother is right outside," I told him. "You do this, and she will never forgive you. England will never forgive you."

"I am her *son!*" he screamed at me. "She will side with me, she will protect me, she will start the cheer to proclaim me as king once she hears her precious Richard is dead!"

I glanced at the gate, at the guards, at Rob. "Prove it," I challenged him. "If she comes in and sides with you, I'll tell you where the money is."

He sneered. "You think I won't murder you in cold blood with an audience?" he growled. "I'm willing to make it public. My people need to learn the same lesson you do. They need to learn to obey me, and they need to see how high the price will be if they fail."

Prince John nodded to a knight. "Surround the gate, and open it. Guard the prisoner," he ordered.

The knights all snapped to attention, a small group surrounding the tree and the rest forming a double wall in a half circle around the gate, their swords drawn. Once the gate were opened, the people there could only come in so far. If they started to push, like rioters were wont to do, they would fall on swords.

The portcullis were raised, and the gate opened.

People started to rush in, but they halted when they saw the swords.

"Make way!" someone yelled, and I saw a carriage pushing up the way. It halted, and people pushed aside for Eleanor to come.

But not just Eleanor.

Suffolk.

Essex.

Leicester.

Norfolk.

Hereford.

Albemarle.

Hertford.

Pembroke.

"Your Graces," the prince snarled. "What business brings you here?"

"You will stop this immediately, John," Eleanor said as the men spread out to flank her.

He laughed. "No, Mother. I will not play favorites for you; I will not excuse treason for you. Your ill-begotten granddaughter's *first* treason was pardoned, and look where that led? I let one traitor go and another grew up beside her. This time I will cut him down and let him stand as a warning to those who would dare oppose my brother."

"Treason?" she demanded.

"They have stolen the ransom for King Richard's safe return!" He looked at me. "Tell them what you've done! Tell them, and our bargain will stand."

"They can't steal it," Essex shouted. "He's an earl of the realm! They raised that money like we all did. It is their own money."

"Then why take it from the White Tower?" Prince John demanded. "Only a traitor—"

"I know what she did," Eleanor said, raising her chin. "How do you think she got the money away? I helped her do it."

"You *helped* her defy me!" Prince John screamed. "How could you?"

"Because she said if you didn't trust her to hold the ransom—to move the ransom—as is her right as a noble, it proved your wrongdoing. It proved that you were scheming against your own brother to steal the throne." Eleanor drew a breath and shook her head. "I am very disappointed, John."

"She's setting me up!" he yelled. "She's lying! And you, you ungrateful, coldhearted woman, you'd choose her over your own son? You're supposed to love me, but all you ever gave me were the remains of your love for Richard. And now you see the face of your favorite in his bastard, and you choose her over me!"

"You promised to let me go," I told him. "You said—"

He grabbed my hair, pulling me close. "You tricked me, you little bitch! And you will watch your outlaw husband die."

My blood froze, staring into Prince John's wild, stricken eyes.

"My lord Prince," Suffolk called, scowling.

Prince John let me go, pushing me back against the wooden rail. I looked down the twenty or more feet to the ground, but guards clapped their hands on me, holding me still.

"Yes, Suffolk," Prince John said.

"It seems to me this situation has been a grave misunderstanding. Huntingdon is one of us; he has fought in the Crusades and he has acted time and time again in the best interest of this country. Forgive this misunderstanding and let Huntingdon go," Suffolk ordered. "Such aggression against him would be an affront to the peerage, and one my honor—and that of my fellows here assembled—could not withstand."

"Not withstand?" Prince John roared. "Essex! You stand here? You agree with him?"

"Yes," Essex snapped back. "Indeed, it was your *wife* that inspired such passion for his plight," Essex growled, his face a snarl.

Prince John drew a deep, angry breath and blew it out in a way that made him look like a bull waiting to unleash his rage.

"Fine," he said. "A misunderstanding. Lady Huntingdon," he said, turning to me. "If you are no traitor, if your husband is not either, tell me where the money that you stole from the treasury is. Tell me where Richard's ransom is, and I will let you go."

"It's safe," I said.

"It is not!" he cried. "You tricked my knights!"

"If your knights could be tricked, perhaps the ransom wasn't safe," Essex said. "And Lady Huntingdon would never endanger her own father."

"But I would endanger my brother?!" Prince John screamed. "Tell me where it is or I will kill Huntingdon!"

"I will tell the queen mother," I said. "And only her. She's the one gathering the ransom. She can decide how to protect it."

"That's reasonable, my prince!" Suffolk called. This were echoed by several others.

Prince John's jaw tightened and bunched with muscle. "Very well. You want my forgiveness, Marian? Tell me what you have learned from this episode. Tell me what your treasonous ways have taught you. Tell me why I should forgive you."

I looked out over the nobles and common folk, and I looked at Rob. I understood what he wanted. He were humiliated, standing here, forced to surrender to his peers. He wanted me to bend my knee to his pride.

I looked to Rob. Our eyes met across the castle yard, and even in such distance it felt like a punch to my stomach.

My pride weren't nothing compared to Rob. Compared to life, and the love we would have together.

"I've learned how generous you are, my prince," I told him, loud and clear, bowing my head like a proper supplicant. "I've learned of your power and patriotism. I've learned you will do anything to protect your family and England."

The nobles nodded to this, satisfied.

Prince John nodded too. He stepped closer, taking my chin and looking into my eyes. I strained and twisted against my bonds, but guards just held me still.

"No," he said. "No. The lesson that you were meant to learn is that you are a lowly, bastard thief. You're trash. I am a prince. I am next to *God*, and like Him, I can grant life, and I can take it away."

"John!" Eleanor yelled.

I saw metal flash as the earls drew their swords.

My blood ran still as Prince John turned his head to the tree.

Helpless, I followed his gaze, staring at Rob.

"Execute him," Prince John ordered.

"Rob!" I screamed.

The guard closest to the horse drew his sword and hit it against the rump of the horse.

The horse started, and Rob's face paled and turned away from me.

The horse took two steps, breaking into a run, and I heard a sharp snap of the rope pulling taut as Rob's body flew off and fell straight for the ground.

I leapt.

CHAPTER THIRTY-THREE

I hit the rail of the stair and it made me twist, spinning fast and hard to the ground, my arms still lashed behind me. I met the ground hard, and I felt pain crack through me like a whip.

People had broken through the knights. They were fighting, everywhere, and my vision were still spinning as I tried to stand and fell.

Someone touched my arm and I cried out.

"Hush," Essex said. "Be still."

I felt the pain in my wrists ease as the rope slid off.

"My lady, you broke your arm—" Essex tried, but I just stood and ran.

Everything around me were moving, writhing, flashing, and twisting, but I knew nothing of it. With one arm, I shoved and twisted, doing whatever I had to so I could push past them. It weren't a hundred paces to where Rob were, and it took hours to get there. Days. A year, at least.

Someone's elbow caught me in my face, and I stumbled back.

My feet slipped once beneath me but I pushed up, driving forward harder, with more purpose.

Fighting. Fighting to get to him.

The crowd of knights and fighting broke, and walking into the open space felt like falling off a cliff. My heart were falling free, and I ran toward the dark shade of the tree.

Someone had cut Rob's body down and laid him on the ground, a pocket of men protecting him from everyone else. I could see his boots from between their bodies, not moving.

"Robin!" I wailed. "Robin! Robin!"

They opened and let me through, and I fell to my knees beside him. My hands on his chest, his face, shaking to touch the red mark where the rope had been a moment ago.

He heaved a great cough, opening his eyes to me. "Scar," he groaned, coughing hard.

I gasped and fell back.

He sat up slow, grabbing me and crushing me in his arms. He were shaking, hard, the kind of shaking that feels like your bones are fighting you. He lifted his shirt, and I saw another length of rope tied there to pull his weight off his neck. To save him.

"Who? How?" I begged. Tears were pouring hard down my face.

"That would be me," Allan said, chucking off a French knight's helmet and tunic. "I better get out of this kit before someone gets the wrong idea, eh?" he said.

I grabbed Rob harder, my heart beating so hard and fierce that I couldn't even feel the pain in my arm yet. "I love you," I told him, kissing his face, his eyes, his hair. "I love you."

He kissed my mouth. "Christ, Scarlet, I love you. Now get this rope off me," he said.

I tried to laugh but it came out a sob, and Allan leaned down to cut it from his middle.

Rob dropped the rope and stood with me, taking my hand. "Your arm," he said.

I nodded. "I'll live."

"No!" we heard. Prince John came rushing toward us, crashing into one of his guards to do so. "No!" he roared. "You're dead! You have to be dead!"

Rob put his arm around me. "Very much alive, my lord Prince," he said, his voice hoarse and rough.

"You!" he screamed, hurling his finger at me as men kept us apart. "What did you do? You little bitch, what did you do?"

I stepped forward from Robin, going forward to see the mad look of Prince John's eyes, the flecks of spittle on his mouth. "Me?" I asked. "I'm just a thief. I stole your nobles—they will never put their trust in you again, even if Richard never comes home. I stole your power, because without them, you are just a spoiled child with very few lands. And I stole your mother, because she just likes me better than you. I told you when you took my fingers that you would regret this, John. Everything I have taken, you let me steal."

I shook my head, stepping back from him as he sputtered.

"Maybe you should worry," I said. "Because maybe you were right, that night in the dungeon. Maybe the people and history will forget me." I smiled at him. "But you won't, will you? You will remember me, and this day, *forever*."

He screamed. It were a bloodcurdling thing, a cross between a battle cry and a wailing child, and he heaved one of the men holding him off, and slashed at another one's face. I stepped back, but he lunged forward, grabbing me.

His hand swung toward my middle, and I saw the bright flash of his knife. With one good hand, I caught his wrist, twisting it backward so he dropped the knife. I stepped forward and drove my knee into his nether bits.

He wailed, falling to his knees before me. Rob touched my side, always beside me, together and strong.

"A *knife*?" I yelled at Prince John. "A *knife*? You come at me with a knife?"

I let him go completely, and he cradled his sore parts as I snatched up the knife, reclaiming his attention as I held it to his throat. "I will never be the schemer you are. I will never use words as well as you. But there are two things that make me powerful. There are two things that make me stronger than you." I straightened my shoulders. "My heart holds my love, my hope, and my faith. My heart is unyielding, my heart is stalwart, and my heart is true. It will never be broken by the likes of you. But do you know what else makes me strong, you royal fool?" I asked him.

He just cursed at me.

I pushed the knife against his skin, hard enough to press, but not to cut. He swallowed hard. "I could kill you. You killed

David. You killed John. You have hurt so many." My mouth twisted, and I pressed harder. "You *deserve* it for what you've done."

I let him go and pulled the knife away, stepping closer to Rob.

"But I won't," I told him. "Because now it's you who should worry. It's you who will look over his shoulder forever. Because you will scheme again, and I will be here, standing between you and the people of England." I leaned closer. "I may be a bastard, a princess, a thief, and a royal. But do you know what the other thing is that makes me more powerful than you?" I said.

He curled his lip at me.

I held up the knife. "With a knife in my hand, I'm *unbeatable.*"

For the longest time, no one really knew about me. I were Rob's secret, his informant, his shadow in dark places. They didn't see me, and I didn't mind that they didn't see.

But now I'm Rob's wife, and our story isn't a secret. It's a song, a legend, a story people tell to their children at night.

There's a funny thing about light and darkness—like hope, you can never blot out either one completely. They always exist, side by side, bright light making shadows darker, darkness making the light more beautiful, a tempting siren call.

I can't hate the darkest parts of myself. They are the things that showed me how special and rare the bright flames of trust, loyalty, friendship, and love were. My darkness showed me how to love Rob.

But now I choose light and fire and love.

Now I choose freedom.

AUTHOR'S NOTE

In ending this trilogy, one of the things I would really like to address is the history.

First—how cool? Writing this trilogy has been a dream come true for me because I've always seen Scarlet's character, and her nature in general, as being part of the larger story of England. Many people say she's anachronistic, but that's not entirely true either. We see examples like the utterly legendary Eleanor of Aquitaine who rode into battle during the Second Crusade, fought with her husband, and made almost every man in England and France fall at her feet while she was still raising lions as she went along. She's incredible, and she's such an inspiration to write about and to research.

More than that, though, is this idea of the person that Scarlet represents. King Richard did come home, the ransom paid. He never had a legitimate child though. Roughly a decade after the close of this novel, after Prince John Lackland becomes King John, his nobles gathered together and forced him to sign the Magna Carta, subverting many of his divine rights as king—signed by all of the earls mentioned in the final chapter, in addition to several more lords and castle-holders, and clergymen to bear witness.

The common man also (though less publicized) forced him to sign the Charter of the Forest, a similar document for the rights of the people (and, in particular, revolutionizing how the royal forests, like Sherwood, were used). The Magna Carta, though almost immediately trounced and made ineffective in British law, became one of the inspirational documents when America was forming its Constitution and Bill of Rights. What an incredible effect!

I've always thought that this mindset didn't spring up out of the blue. It was created by a society that had grown intolerant, and Scarlet was always meant to be the epitome of that. What if—what if there was a girl spurring all of this change? What if there was a girl at the heart of Robin Hood's legend? What if history forgot all about her, because it's somehow easier to believe a man was capable of such great things and a girl like Scarlet would simply be anachronistic?

I love that. I hope that she—and the long-reaching effect that she could have had—might stir up questions in your mind. I hope Scarlet will challenge your idea of what kind of power lay people, nobles, and women had in this era.

But I also want to come clean. I've always laid a benchmark for myself of this whole trilogy unfolding roughly between autumn and spring of 1191–1192. In some ways this is pretty accurate—it fits fairly well with Prince John's problems (he did come back from France in October of 1191, had a political falling-out with an archbishop, and tried to gather support in England, only to lose to the archbishop and find himself in desperate need of political favor. It's totally reasonable to think that at this point he would have visited his holdings, including Nottingham). So *Lady Thief* is pretty sound. However, *Lion Heart* takes a lot of liberties with Richard's timeline. He didn't leave the Holy Land until late 1192, and he shipwrecked and was essentially walking home for four months before he was captured—during which time he would have been virtually impossible to find. After that, it took months to even call for the ransom (which Eleanor did raise, and John did try to thwart) and more than a year to orchestrate.

Forgive me, I sped things up.

Oh, and just so you know exactly what Eleanor and Scarlet were facing, 65,000 pounds of silver roughly amounts to 2 billion British pounds now. Which, by some exceptionally rough and unqualified math, is about 3.5 billion US dollars.

However, as far as happy endings go, there are a lot of *accurate* pieces of history in here. Winchester does marry Margaret. Isabel and Prince John annul their marriage so that he can marry Isabelle of Angouleme, and Isabel of Gloucester marries Essex. Maud—who has the tiniest of cameos—marries Hugh Bigod, another minor role in the book. Yay, weddings!

I played with history a little; my hope, however, is that you will begin to see that almost all history is a written narrative, and that, like me, *someone* had the authorial hand. The greatest legacy Scarlet could have is to leave you questioning when history may not have gotten it right—and who might be left out.

Thank you for taking this journey with me, and with Scarlet!

ACKNOWLEDGMENTS

Guys—how on earth do I begin to thank people after ending a trilogy? And more importantly, *this* book? *Lion Heart*'s title was actually decided pretty late in the game, and it really took a minute for it to settle in and for me to realize how much it needed to be called *Lion Heart*—because in writing this, I managed to find my courage, my strength, and my perseverance. In many ways, I found my own lion heart.

But this was never something I did, survived, or created on my own. So let's get down to the people who really deserve to be acknowledged!

First, to my agent, Minju—you are wonderful and amazing, and you have always been a fantastic resource to me. You got me through freak-outs and plot twists of both the fictional and real-life varieties. You told me it was totally okay when I needed more time to figure out how to write this book. For these and so many more things—thank you.

To my editor, Mary Kate Castellani—you are amazing. You did an incredible job taking my jumble of words and pushing me to make them better and stronger and, you know, Scarleter. Thank you for everything you've done for all three books—we've been in the trenches together for a long time in a lot of changing roles, and I really love working with you. Of course, I can't mention editing without also thanking Emily

Easton—*Scarlet* wouldn't be here if it weren't for you, and I definitely would never have gotten to *Lion Heart*. Thank you. I'm sorry we couldn't finish the journey together.

To everyone at Bloomsbury, never, ever limited to but definitely including Lizzy Mason, Erica Barmash, Emily Ritter, Beth Eller, Caroline Osborn, Linda Minton, and all the people who contribute to my books that I haven't had a chance to meet—you're all AWESOME.

Honestly, you guys need so much more space than I have to give . . . but the fans. The FANS! Your letters and your kindness and your love kept me going on a really hard book and during a really hard year. To the bloggers who have been so amazing to me, you create a world for authors like me to inhabit. It's essential, and I'm so grateful. For all the fan art, the stories, the squees and the love, thank you all so, so much!

Funny story—I wrote this book while in grad school. Ha! Which means that, whether they really knew it or not, there were some amazing people hauling me through that year with love and cookies and the occasional Burdick's hot chocolate. Caitlin, Tyme, Holly, Leigh—I wouldn't have made it without you. To the entire AIE cohort—thank you for the support, the love, and the unabashed inspiration to keep making quality arts a reality in education (and, you know, the inspiration to just be awesome . . .). To Steve Seidel, it has been such an honor working with you.

To Team Writing Group (which I'm new to and honored to be in)—Tara Sullivan, Annie Cardi, Katie Slivensky, Lauren

Barrett, and Julia Maranan—well, okay, you guys never actually saw *Lion Heart* at all. But I think the fact that I'm still writing has everything to do with you. Thank you!

Team Author Friends—Hilary Weisman Graham, Diana Renn, Zoraida Cordova, Gina Damico, Dawn Metcalf, the whole entire Class of 2k12 with intense love, the Apocalypsies—I love you ALL. I have to give a special shout-out to Tiffany Schmidt, who I am surprised still takes my phone calls after all the crazy conversations we have had. It's really rare to find someone who gets you as a writer and gets you as a friend, and I am so, so honored and delighted that you're in my life.

And then there are people like Totsie, Karen, Jonathan, Susan, Ellie, Grammy, and Ann H., who have known me forever and are such big supporters—thank you. It means everything. To everyone at South Shore and GGLH who put up with my very proud parents, thank you! To my remaining W family: Meghan, Andrew, Matt, Amy, Paul—<3.

BUT, WAIT, THERE'S MORE! Team GLOW—we talk a lot about teaching girls and women to believe in themselves, but at the end of the day, being part of this organization has forced me to believe in myself, in my friends, and in what women are really capable of doing. Leah, Emily, Jenna, Meghan, Crystal, Sam, and Tashia, you inspire me daily. And Sam—thank you for talking me through *Lion Heart* when I was stuck! Fluff festival for the win.

To my sisters—Nacie and Renee, you two are my life and my loves. Maybe we weren't technically born from the same mom, but if our moms all like each other, it's kind of the same thing, right? I love you, and I can't do much of anything without you. To Ashley, Jacqui, Alex—CAN YOU ALL PLEASE MOVE TO BOSTON? I'M SICK OF THIS DISTANCE STUFF.

Thanking my family is idiotic. It just doesn't cover it when they come to every signing, every speaking engagement, when they tell me I'm being dumb for doubting myself, and laughing at me when—well, like, all the time. Hey, it's family, that's how it goes. Mom, I'll love you forever and like you for always. Papa, I love you to the moon and back.

Alisa, you're new to the acknowledgments page, but I can't believe how supportive you have been in such a short time. You're really incredible! Kev, you have earned SO MUCH MORE than your own book, and you're the best big brother ever. Mike, I am so proud of your accomplishments and for making me the only sibling who can't be addressed as "Doctor"—thank you for always loving me, hugging me, and constantly making fun of my hair.